Traces

ALEXANDER JALO

Translation by Jennifer Saalinki

First published in Finland in 2016 by Annealed Stories

DESIGN BY MARKE KAIKKONEN

ISBN-13: 978-952-68582-0-3

DEDICATION

This book is dedicated to my loving wife Leena, who convinced me to go with this idea for a novel after we spotted an angel in disguise at "Shakespeare and Company".

CONTENTS

ACKNOWLEDGMENTS

I would like to express my gratitude to three of my dear friends, Sari, Kari and Ari, for reading my book, offering comments and providing support. I didn't choose you because of your names but because you all know me so well and I trust you.

Most novels have a long list of professionals in their acknowledgments, but I have only two.

Thank you so much, Jennifer, for your excellent translation and for bringing an added female touch to certain parts of the story. I also wish to thank Marke. I was really surprised by how well you were able to internalize my story idea and bring it to life in the book cover. Thank you for taking the time to help me! Although I don't have any famous names among those I wish to thank, perhaps you both, my friends, will be considered famous in the future.

My final thanks goes to my Higher Self; the wisdom you have imparted upon me has been a great gift, and I suppose the rocky road was necessary and the pains were simply temporary. I want to express my deepest gratitude for believing in me.

PREFACE

'When travelling by road, one is a prisoner of the road. It is only by choosing to traverse the unbeaten snow that one is truly free.

-Aaro Hellaakoski

I found traces of myself from 30 years ago. When I wrote them, they were simply random thoughts on scraps of paper. Now, I revisit these same themes and thoughts which, 30 years ago, were only an inkling of what was to come. They were symbolic descriptions, the meaning of which has only now become clear to me.

Writing can be a mystical experience. In my own experience, the events themselves seemed to drive the story forward. When I encountered problems that seemed unsolvable, I often found myself waking at 4 a.m. in the morning with the solution; never at 3:59 or 4:01, always at exactly 4:00. Once, I didn't even understand my nocturnal solution until I checked the facts from the Internet and diagramed the solution on paper in order to grasp its logic.

Sometimes, it feels as if books have a mind of their own. While on business trips around the world, I spent a great deal of time in bookstores, and in 25 years of travel, I managed to purchase thousands of books. Most of them ended up forgotten on my bookshelves, even though something about them had originally sparked my interest. Later, when I undertook to become a writer, each and every one of these books played an important role in inspiring me. Most often, the background information I was seeking was not provided by individual works found on my shelves, but rather by groups of books that supported one another. These groupings only became clear to me in retrospect, since the books, when purchased, where often done so on a whim. Most of the time, I can't even remember why I purchased particular books.

This book is looking to leave its own unique trace, even though it primarily follows well-beaten paths. I endeavored, however, to avoid certain paths and occasionally chose some that were already thick with moss, at the risk that it wouldn't be easy going. Having said this, I would like to add that my book pays homage to all books and their authors. The title "Traces" does not refer to the traces left by this book, however, but to those that, hopefully, are yet to come in the future.

Part One

Most writers regard the truth as their most valuable possession, and therefore are most economical in its use.

- Mark Twain

1 THE AGE OF INNOCENCE
Edith Wharton 1920

As I looked around at the tightly-packed bookshelves, I was filled with my normal sense of enthusiasm and curiosity. Amazingly, I'd never ceased to become enchanted by the atmosphere in bookstores, even though I had visited nearly all the best bookstores worldwide. This particular bookstore had already managed to become like a second living room for me. There was nothing particularly special about it; indeed all bookstores share the same unwritten rule that customers can utilize their space freely for an unlimited period of time. You can read books to your heart's content, and therefore, many of the bookstores, private ones in particular, are even furnished with comfortable armchairs for this purpose. Are there any other stores where customers are welcome to utilize and enjoy the products being sold without any obligation to buy? It's hardly the case for electronics stores. You surely wouldn't be permitted to sit for hours watching your favorite TV programs from a comfy lounge chair while eating your own snacks or, even better, snacks offered by the store itself. At Shakespeare and Company bookstore, however, this was commonplace for its customers.

The shelves of the bookstores provided access to an entire world, in the form of poetry and stories about the human mind, books containing facts and truths, noteworthy volumes, and books that seemed to lack all sense of logic. The Internet may well already provide access to more information than all of these volumes put together, but books leave traces, concrete traces of us for the future, while digital information will, sooner or later, be wiped away or become indecipherable.

"Daniel, do you like ballet?" Lisa, the saleswoman with whom I had already become friendly, asked from behind my back.

"My two daughters danced ballet when they were young, so I suppose I have some connection to it," I answered.

"Look at this book, where it explains the technique behind a pirouette," she said and placed the book in front of me.

I looked at the image of the young woman balanced on the tip of one pointe shoe and wondered what exactly Lisa was trying to get at.

"Do you have some theory for this too?" she asked, teasingly, as was her normal approach.

"I don't have any theory prepared, but I can quickly come up with one if that's what you're looking for." I smirked at her and leaned in to study the image of the pirouette more closely.

"Okay, so we are essentially dealing with a top. In order for it to spin uninterrupted around its axis, the top has to be symmetrical. Similarly, the dancer must also keep her axis, or body in this case, completely straight and vertical in relation to the ground, as well as keeping her center of gravity at the center of the axis. Once she manages to do that, she then has to initiate the spinning motion without disrupting her center of gravity. The rest is simply a matter of angular momentum that keeps the axis in place, like when you ride a bike. Then, if she pulls her arms in against her body, the spinning motion picks up, because there is less rotational inertia. The angular momentum remains stable," I explained, half-jokingly.

"You and your engineering theories! There's no use for that in real life. Look, it says right here that 'in order to accomplish the pirouette, the dancer must hold her head in place with her eyes focused on a specific point until her neck can rotate no further, and then she snaps her head around, in a fraction of a second, to refocus on the same point.' You see, it's all about focus. So, if you ever find yourself caught in a whirlwind, you just need to keep your focus. No inertia momentum is going to help you then," she explained, playfully mocking my explanation.

"Sure it would; one can still always open his or her arms to increase the rotational inertia and slow the spinning," I responded pretending to be insulted.

"Touché," she said as she dashed off.

I put on my overcoat, all the while eyeing the new releases set up on the table beside me. I was starting to be in a hurry, so I just glanced over the table without really noticing any particular book. My right hand grabbed up the first book it came into contact with, and that one seemingly insignificant moment set into motion a whirlwind that would eventually suck me into its core. The next five days would prove Lisa right; I simply needed to retain focus and not rely on being able to spread my arms and shrug my shoulders like the Frenchmen so often have a habit of doing.

I opened the cover of the book, but the content made no sense to me. At that moment, my subconscious registered a growing uneasiness in the bookstore. People seemed to be moving faster than normal and the door opened and closed at a more feverish rate. The people standing close to me suddenly all disappeared, as if by an unspoken agreement, but they were quickly replaced by a stream of new customers. Although I was absorbed in the book, I knew without even lifting my eyes from the page that it had begun to pour outside. The book continued to hold me captive. What followed next may just be one of a number of coincidences, but in that case, the content of the book was a coincidence as well.

Shakespeare and Company is located exactly 150 meters, as the crow flies, from the Point Zero marker set in the cobblestones in front of the Notre Dame in Paris, but if one walks there over the nearest bridge, it adds an extra 100 meters. That, if anything, signifies a central location. The bookstore in question is Anglo-American and, therefore, a peculiarity in the heart of France, but it isn't just any old bookstore. During its 90-year history, Shakespeare and Company has served as a place of pilgrimage for countless world-famous authors and, as a budding writer, I felt myself drawing strength and inspiration from its history. As a literary enthusiast, I had also decided to go one further and strip Ernest Hemingway of his title as the store's 'best customer', a title he had, indeed, bestowed on himself in honor of his excessive book acquisitions and daily visits. Later, during the war, he was involved in the liberation of Paris, or at least the cellar of the Ritz, but taking that credit from him might be considerably more difficult.

Café Panis is situated in a slightly more central location than Shakespeare and Company. To be precise, the distance from Point Zero in Paris to the front door of Café Panis is 135 meters, and one can travel that distance, without deviation, straight over the Pont au Double bridge. Due to its ideal location, it isn't the cheapest cup of coffee in town, but not the most expensive either, nor did it feel like your average tourist trap. It may be that I have a bit of a blind spot when it comes to the café, since it became the backdrop for one of the turning points of my life. The events of the turning point came full circle there, because it was where everything began and ended. In that way, Café Panis would come to be a slightly more significant place even than Shakespeare and Company.

The early spring had been exceptionally chilly and gray. I had brought my umbrella with me, but as I stepped out of Shakespeare and Company, I began to doubt its efficacy. The wind had suddenly picked up and dark clouds seemed to be closing in over the towers of Notre Dame. The weather was strange, since storms like this generally only sprang up in the middle of hot summer days. I considered returning to the warmth of the bookstore, but something drove me on. With my umbrella ready to battle the deluge and my book purchase under my arm, I headed through the Square René Viviani-Montebello toward my apartment on the island of Île St-Louis. When I reached the fountain in the square, the sky opened up and a wall of rain emerged to block all visibility. The water bounced up from the ground, nearly to knee height, and immediately soaked my shoes and the hem of my pants. The wind blew the rain at a near horizontal angle and my umbrella, which was on the verge of collapse, just barely managed to keep my head dry. As the wind was blowing in the opposite direction I was headed, I pointed my umbrella toward my destination and began to push against the wind. I knew that Café Panis was quite close ahead of me, even though I couldn't see anything. I had walked past it nearly every day without ever going inside. By the time I finally made it safely through the door of the café, I was soaked to the bone and my umbrella hung in tatters.

I immediately took in the decor of the café with its modern, Old World approach, complete with wood paneling. I noted two small, round tables accompanied by four dark leather chairs. They struck me as odd, since all four chairs were arranged so as to face the street, looking out toward the Square René Viviani. They appeared to have been placed specifically for clients looking to pass their time with a good book, and I wondered whether they had been set like that with Shakespeare and Company's clientele in mind. It was then that I caught sight of the bookshelf in the back corner of the café, a fact that confirmed my theory. As luck would have it, all four seats were unoccupied and, encouraged by the waiter, I claimed one of the tables for myself, my wet coat and the bag from the bookstore.

The waiters were dressed traditionally in white shirts and black vests with bow ties embellishing their collars. My own waiter, who was on the tall side, was quite young and spoke English fairly well. I was relieved, since my French skills were a bit rudimentary. Even the simple task of ordering a pint of beer had been unsuccessful time and again. I had tried using any means of expression I could muster: une grande bière, une pression, even gesturing, but, invariably, I always ended up with the same piddling glass of beer. This time, however, I ordered coffee and Armagnac, since it had become somewhat of a ritual when I was keeping company with a book in a café. When I first moved to Paris, I missed Finnish coffee, but it only took a few days before I began to prefer the flavor of the French coffee, which was darker but not at all bitter. For practical reasons, I had switched from ordering Cognac to Armagnac, because it rarely led to any inquisition by the waiter. With Cognac, one first had to inquire after specific brands, and the answer was inevitably always negative. Then, once one managed to sort out a suitable brand, there was still the matter of deciding between VS, VSOP and XO, until finally, one generally gave up and ordered the Cognac recommended by the waiter, which, coincidentally, was also the most expensive.

I dug into my paper bag and brought out Martin Heidegger's 'Basic Writings' book, which I had only just purchased on the basis of one chapter entitled 'On the Essence of Truth'. I was completely lost in the book, when I suddenly was brought back to the room by the sound of high heels clicking into the café. I turned, quite by instinct, to look in the direction of the sound and was met with the dark brown eyes of a woman searching for an available seat. Her options were to walk behind me to some seat toward the back of the café or across in front of me where, to my great satisfaction, she selected one of the window seats. Her umbrella had clearly not given her sufficient protection, since the rain splattering off the pavement had dotted her knee-high boots with water and dirt, while sparing her shiny, black nylons. Her short, black dress provided minimal coverage considering the weather, even teamed with the bright reddish-orange poplin jacket over her forearm. She had managed to remain dry enough that I suspected she had been dropped off in front of the café by a taxi. Something about her presence was especially attractive. The color red is scientifically proven to awaken the interest of men, which may explain my spontaneous reaction to her, particularly since the shade of red in her jacket was unusually bright and flirty. The folds on the upper portion of her dress hid the shape of her body, disguising all the details, but I could still tell that she had a slim and shapely feminine figure.

I found it impossible to go back to my reading, but I knew I couldn't stare directly at her either. I chose to simply look up from my book from time to time as if I were contemplating some complex idea while gazing out the window. At the same time, I allowed myself to steal short, imperceptible glimpses of her, and I studied her more closely in the reflection of the window. She appeared to be an intelligent and educated woman, but perhaps quite serious in disposition. There was something soft and soulful about her face. She also projected a sense of authority, which made me feel compelled to try and guess her profession. I surmised that she could be in a managerial position, a public figure or, perhaps, a teacher. All her features were appealing, but at the same time, they were quite common and familiar. She had black, slightly curly, shoulder-length hair and dark brown eyes, but I couldn't manage a more detailed description than that, even when I was looking right at her. Her facial features and the shape of her face were unexceptional, but somehow also completely flawless. The curves of her body complimented her overall slender appearance. She seemed like a woman who was comfortable in her own skin, a fact that accentuated her beauty in a way I was unable to explain.

She took a book from her handbag and began to read it without as much as a glance in my direction. Her indifference only served to intrigue me further. A young waiter approached her table in a manner that revealed he might be interested in more than just taking her order. He stopped right beside her table and leaned his knee, as if by accident, against her thigh, at the exposed point between the hem of her skirt and the top of her boots. I watched the display with interest and expected to see the woman get irritated or, at the very least, pull her thigh away. Instead, she did nothing, said nothing, and revealed nothing of her reaction in her expression or her eyes. Since she did nothing to rebuff his advance, the waiter left his knee where it was. They both seemed secretly to be enjoying the unspoken communication between them and, each in their own way, the forbidden but innocent intimacy of the situation. I thought they seemed to be talking longer than would have been necessary to place an order, but without knowing enough of the language, I wasn't able to follow their conversation. I found the situation amusing, and obviously wasn't able to hide it, because the woman glanced at me and I noticed her blush lightly. The waiter also became aware of being detected and pulled his knee away surreptitiously. The magic of the moment had dissipated. Instead of remaining embarrassed by the situation, the woman looked uninhibitedly into my eyes and smiled warmly. Suddenly, nothing about her face seemed common anymore. I now saw the glimmer in her eyes and the hint of teeth, and even the tiny gap between her front teeth, which acted like a beauty mark amid her soft face.

The woman looked down and continued with her reading as if nothing had transpired. I considered my options for approaching her, even though she hadn't encouraged me in any way. It was likely she wasn't interested in making casual acquaintances, or perhaps she wasn't able to speak English and had already guessed that I was a foreigner. I noticed that the book she was reading had an English title, and it wasn't just any book. Douglas R. Hofstadter's 'Gödel, Escher, Bach' is not just a book, but a journey into the unknown; a book that tells as much about the reader as the title tells about a mathematician, an artist and a composer; then again, it doesn't really tell about them either. It is a book that even the book's author cannot explain, and yet, it manages to be an extremely lucid work. If I thought I'd been curious and interested in the woman up to that point, I was unable, from that point on, to get her out of my mind. There was no way I could leave the café and just remember her fondly as a bright spot on an otherwise dreary, rainy day in Paris. I needed to talk with her and find out more about her. A voice inside me cried out to seize the moment. My innocent curiosity had grown into an unbearable compulsion!

The waiter brought the woman a glass of champagne and a steaming mug of hot chocolate. I chose that moment to ask for the check in a voice loud enough for the woman to hear, because I wanted to see how she would react. I figured that if she was even the slightest bit interested in me, this would be her last chance to show it. Her eyes, however, stayed focused on her book. There was no way I just could walk up and ask if I could join her, since it would have been impolite and put her on the spot. If I hadn't yet managed to peak her interest, I was afraid that taking that type of premature approach would potentially end my game. I quickly formed a plan. I paid my bill and stood up, but instead of putting on my coat, I placed it over my arm and walked straight up to her.

"Excuse me, I assume you understand English, since you are reading a book in English," I stated cautiously.

"And I assume you don't speak French, since you asked an English question from a French woman," she shot back sarcastically, although I did note a twinkle in her eye.

I was afraid for a moment that this was just her way of politely turning me down, but I continued undeterred.

"I was pleasantly surprised to see that you were reading GEB."

In that moment, I knew I'd grabbed her attention, because she looked at me slightly puzzled and paused for what felt like an eternity.

"Only people who are very familiar with this book use that acronym for it." There was an edge of curiosity in her voice. "Can you explain to me what it's about?"

I had, indeed, read numerous theories about the content of GEB, but in that moment, I heard myself simply say, "Intuition."

An even longer period of silence followed, and so I felt the need to break it.

"Could I ask you to do me a favor?"

"Of course."

"Would you mind guarding my things for a moment while I visit the men's room before I head out?"

"Just put them on that empty chair," she said, seeming relieved that I hadn't asked for anything more difficult or inappropriate.

I wasn't accustomed to the social game, but apparently one has to proceed this way with French women. In France, everything must be complicated, if there is any possible way to avoid simplicity. Now, since the game was proceeding according to my plan, I felt quite comfortable with the French approach. My time in the men's room gave the woman a chance to consider whether she missed my company or not and how she could alter her course without losing face. When I got back to the table, I noticed she had moved my coat, umbrella and shopping bag onto another chair in order to free up the seat directly opposite her. She seemed amused.

"Your umbrella appears to be completely useless."

I saw that the rain was still coming down hard outside and so my story about heading out soon with my broken umbrella must have seemed quite irrational.

"Please, sit down and join me for a moment," she proposed, gesturing toward the chair opposite her.

"It seems I was so taken in by you that I didn't even notice it was still raining! But if my tattered umbrella spurred an invitation to join you, then I don't mind if it keeps raining." My comment further revealed my otherwise clear intentions.

"Did you mean that GEB tells about intuition or it is, itself, an intuition?" she inquired, referring back to our earlier conversation.

"I'm actually not quite sure, since I think my response was also based on intuition, but if pressed, I would say that the book is the intuition of the writer as well as being somehow about intuition on some fundamental level." I sounded confident, but I was basically thinking aloud.

"That's interesting, I've never heard that explanation before," she stated, as much in her thoughts as I was.

A moment of silence followed her statement, but it didn't seem to feel awkward to either of us. Suddenly, she perked up, as if she had just remembered that I was still there.

"You were also reading a book. What was it?" she asked,

genuinely interested.

"Basic Writings, the complete writings of the modern philosopher Heidegger, which I actually only bought because of one chapter." I was pleased she had made note of the fact that I'd been reading as well.

"What about that particular chapter interested you?"

"Its title is: On the Essence of Truth. I suppose that was also a matter of intuition, since the concept of truth speaks to me for some reason," I responded.

"What kind of truth are you looking for?" she asked.

"I don't know. Maybe I'm only searching for an explanation for truth; something comforting and forgiving, instead of morals or facts." I stared deep into the woman's eyes as if I were searching for the answer from within them.

She appeared to be deep in her own thoughts. Her face was serious and somehow hesitant, even fearful. Suddenly, her eyes lit up and her whole expression changed.

"If I've read this situation correctly, it seems you'd like to get to know me better," she said with a smile.

I felt as if I had just lost an internal battle to her, but it was a battle I didn't mind losing. I was taken in by her charm and struggled feverishly to think of a response to her statement that would give me the upper hand in the situation. She didn't wait for my response.

"I'll agree to meet you again, if you agree to my terms."

"Okay," I responded, without thinking.

"First, we agree that we won't tell each other anything about ourselves, not even our names. I won't compromise on that, but I also won't explain why," she stated resolutely.

"Isn't that a bit of a paradox, since you agreed to us getting to know one another?" I felt genuinely disappointed, since my curiosity about her had been my greatest incentive.

"I am simply giving you a lesson in truth. You'll be able to form an image of me as you, yourself, experience and understand it." Her response was quite cryptic. "Second, we won't have any more philosophical discussions. For me, it's enough that I know you're capable of such discussions. And that leads to my third term: we will meet just once, and I want you to make our time together so enjoyable that I will only be left with fond memories. There is no room in that for philosophical deliberation, which otherwise fills my life." She managed to lay out her terms in a purposeful manner, but kept her tone very friendly.

"That's all fine with me," I stated, all the while my curiosity increasing.

"Finally, in the name of honesty, I have to tell you that I won't consent to any type of intimacy." She said this with the softest voice, as if it were meant to console me.

I tried, once again, to come up with a sensible reply. I was still frustrated that I wouldn't be able to get any answers to my questions about her background. I hadn't even had time to consider sex, but the attraction was undeniable and I was afraid my desire would continue to increase if I spent any more time with her. There was something irresistibly engaging about her.

I silently accepted her final term and decided to add one of my own.

"Could I make one selfish request for our meeting?"

"Absolutely." She raised her eyebrows as an indication of her own curiosity.

"I'm not suggesting we make this a big part of our program for the day, but I've had some difficulty finding suitable blazers, shirts and pants here. The local models are all too small and the bigger sizes don't sit well on me. The fact that I can't speak French isn't helpful either. Perhaps you could help me by acting as my interpreter and fashion expert, and maybe you could show me the shops where I might find better fitting German or American styles," I explained, suddenly feeling slightly awkward about my proposal.

"That's a great idea!" she stated enthusiastically. "We'll set you up with a new style and then you can return the favor by playing fashion judge for me while I shop."

"Which day is good for you? I'd really like to spend the whole day together." I had hoped she would suggest the following day.

"A fun day requires lovely weather. Is it okay if we agree to meet on the next sunny day at 11 a.m. in Square René Viviani?" She suggested this without a thought for the fact that I might be working or otherwise busy on weekdays.

"Let's agree that it will be a day when there are no dark clouds in the sky or any threat of rain. Even a beautiful day can have small cumulus clouds," I specified further.

"Agreed. Speaking of rain, it seems to have stopped. I believe you'd be free to go on your way now."

I recognized that this was her playful way of asking me to leave her for now. As I was leaving, I extended my hand toward her, but instead of shaking it, she took it between her own hands. That's when I noticed that she wasn't wearing a ring. Oddly, I hadn't even thought to look for one before that.

2 WATCHMEN

Alan Moore & Dave Gibbons 1986

Darkness had already descended on Paris when I headed out from the café along the bank of the Seine toward Île St-Louis. Paris is not referred to as the city of light in vain, and I never tired of admiring the tastefully-illuminated historical buildings. I turned left at the Pont de l'Archevêché bridge, where a young couple stood kissing under the streetlamp. Before my encounter in the café, I probably wouldn't have even noticed them, but I was now clearly more romantically attuned. The rain had scattered the performers at the base of Pont St. Louis bridge, directly to the right after crossing Pont de l'Archevêché. There was generally always someone performing for money there late into the night. After Pont St. Louis bridge, I made a sharp left along the riverbank to catch a view of the lights on the Hôtel de Ville.

The Quai de Bourbon curved sharply to the right and I took a shortcut across the intersection intending to continue down the sidewalk that hugged the buildings on the opposite side. When I turned the corner, I was confronted by three, ominous men dressed in knee-length leather jackets. They appeared to be out of breath as if they had just been running. Something seemed off. I felt a heightened state of alarm and the hair stood up on the back of my neck. The men blocked the entire sidewalk and so I was forced to instinctively step to the left around them into the street, where there was more room to maneuver. The smallest man continued walking past me, but then he slowed his pace considerably. The biggest guy approached me with a cigarette in the corner of his mouth, while the third guy stopped next to me as if to observe the situation.

"Pardon, monsieur. Vous avez du feu?" The one in front of me asked roughly, as he cut off my path.

Although I understood his question immediately, because of the situation, I also knew exactly what was really going on. In an attempt to dispel my fear, I tried to make the situation humorous. In my best New England accent, I responded with,

"No, but I got a wicked good grindah fah ya."

The guy in front of me wasn't dissuaded by my attempt at humor and began spouting aggressively at me in French. This time, I didn't catch a word. The man next to me said something that sounded like a command. I could still sense the third guy standing behind me. Suddenly, a knife appeared in the hand of the guy in front of me, and that was enough to set my reflexes in motion. As had always been the case when I found myself in a dangerous situation, the events would later come back to me like a slow motion film, right down to the tiniest details. The knife was gripped in his hand with the blade facing down, ready to slice open my radial artery if a scuffle ensued. With my left hand, I grabbed the back of the hand holding the knife. I pressed his hand inward toward his arm rapidly and with as much force as I could muster. He cried out in pain and the knife fell onto the street. With both hands, I then grabbed the guy by the chest and lifted him slightly off his feet. In that instant, I was taken back to my days on the American football field, where, as a linebacker, I had defeated blocks and knocked colossal linemen off their feet. I could tell that this guy, however, was completely out of his element as a lineman, because he held his legs straight. I bent my knees slightly and leaned my shoulders forward in order to push him off balance with full force. He rose into the air and literally flew backward. He was completely taken by surprise and his inexperience showed, since he was incapable of focusing on anything other than the impact he made when he hit the ground. His buddy, who'd been standing next to me, was also in shock and by the time he finally sprang into action and grabbed onto my coat, I was already bounding over the guy who I had laid out. His grasp on my coat slipped away, but the momentum of the effort to hang on forced him to trip over the guy at his feet. I didn't catch any glimpse of the guy behind me anymore, but as I started to run, I kicked my legs forward to prevent anyone from grabbing onto my ankles. Once I had managed to free myself from the situation, I was pretty certain they wouldn't be able to catch me anymore. I had raced about 10 meters when I heard a shot from a small caliber gun and I saw the bullet ricochet off the sidewalk in front of me. Fortunately, there was only another 10 meters to the next intersection. There was a short pause and I heard another shot ring out before I reached the intersection and turned right onto Rue Jean du Bellay and out of the line of fire. It was 50 meters to the next intersection, so I dashed down the center of the road like a player on an open field after an interception. I prepared to hear another shot behind me, but it never came. At the intersection of Rue St Louis en I'lle, I finally turned to look behind me and saw the smallest guy standing in the middle of Bourbon's intersection, gun in hand. I was afraid that the two other guys may be circling around to cut me off if I attempted to head back over the bridge. I picked up speed again as I headed toward the center of the island down the Rue St Louis en I'lle's narrow lane. I congratulated myself for continuing to train hard all those years after my sports career ended; I had made it quite far before I felt the lactic acid begin to build up in my thighs and my knees became stiff and heavy. One hundred meters ahead on the right I spotted the Aux Anysetiers du Roy bistro, where I had become a regular while living on the island. I had been planning to turn left toward my apartment, but, at the last minute, I began to doubt the rationale behind that decision. I figured that waiting in the restaurant might be a wiser choice since I didn't want to risk exposing where I lived. There was also the chance that I might come face-to-face with my pursuers again, since it would mean returning to Quai de Bourbon in order to reach my gate. I turned right onto Rue Le Regrattier first, so I could pause and make sure there were no footsteps following me. No one seemed to be in pursuit and, due to the heavy rain from earlier in the day, the roads were still quite deserted. I looked for a considerable amount of time in the direction I was headed as well to make sure the coast was clear before stepping into the restaurant. As soon as I hit the warmth inside the restaurant, my whole body began to shake. My friend Maurice, who was the proprietor of the restaurant, immediately spotted me at the door and made note of my strange entrance. He rushed to my side and reached out to support me.

"Daniel, my friend, are you ill?"

I tried to answer him, but I couldn't manage to utter a single coherent word through my chattering jaws.

Aux Anysetiers du Roy was located less than two hundred meters from my apartment and it was the place where I ended up spending my first evening after moving to Paris. I had been looking for somewhere to eat and had wandered in. Maurice had been there that night and had welcomed me. Even though I knew people would notice my large size and American accent, it still surprised me when he asked whether I happened to ever play American football. Turned out that, when he was young, he had won the French championship for American football on a team called the Spartacus de Paris, and he obviously wanted to talk about those treasured moments of his youth. We had never met on the field, of course, since most of my career was spent on college football fields in the United States, but it didn't deter two veterans from reliving the old days together. Even after the restaurant had closed that night, we sat together reminiscing over his best bottles of wine, and we had been the best of friends ever since.

Maurice helped me into a back room of the restaurant and settled me on one of the chairs. Once I had recovered from the effects of the adrenaline rush, I began to recount the events of the evening. Maurice asked whether I was injured and told me to take off my coat. That's when he noticed a small hole in the back of the coat, underneath the armpit and another matching hole in the front of the coat.

"If that didn't hit you, then it was damn close." His face didn't mask his concern.

My shirt also had holes in the same places and I noticed

then that my side was bleeding slightly. As I removed my shirt, Maurice pulled out a package of tissues and began to search for some suitable alcohol to clean whatever wound I revealed.

"What grade shall we try?" he asked, now grinning.

Despite the fact that my side had begun to sting, I joined him in his game.

"Remy Martin XO of course," I said in an authoritative voice.

Maurice moistened the paper with the alcohol and pressed it gently against my bloodied side.

"It looks like you only managed to get a flesh wound. The gash doesn't seem to go any deeper than the fatty tissue just below the surface of your skin. Apparently the bullet grazed your skin but didn't manage to pierce it. You still might need stitches, but it looks like there wasn't any significant damage," he said, clearly relieved.

"Shall I call the police?"

"Definitely not the police!" I hissed almost angrily.

"Yeah, that would only lead to an interrogation, and maybe it's better if they don't catch the guys who did this. Then they'd know exactly who you are and you might find yourself the target for revenge."

"I can't go to a hospital either, because I'd have to explain how I got hurt. It's enough if you have some gauze or bandages here," I said impatiently as the pain in my side began to throb.

"I'll call a doctor I know and we'll just say you got hurt somehow here in the restaurant. I'll also make sure she understands that this needs to be kept quiet. She's an ex-lover of mine and she knows better than to ask too many questions. She'll just be happy that she gets to admire your muscular body. I happen to know she's attracted to exactly your type."

"Well, we'd better rip the shirt so the holes won't be obvious; that would surely make her curious to ask more about how I got hurt." I was relieved by Maurice's suggestion and my voice softened as I relaxed.

The doctor was a young, slim blonde, who I thought looked like she was fresh out of college. Her eyebrows wrinkled slightly, so I could tell that she thought there was something unusual about how I came to be injured. Despite that, she never asked how it happened.

"Since this is a dirty wound, I can only use loose stitches. If I stitched it too tightly, an abscess might develop in the wound. I assume this happened recently, as in less than 6 hours ago?"

"Yeah, not even an hour ago."

She finished up by placing a paraffin gauze dressing on the wound, covered by an absorbent secondary dressing.

"You should shower the wound daily, and here's a ten-day course of antibiotics you'll need to take." She handed me the medicine and after hesitating briefly, she handed me yet another box.

"This is Ibuprofen for the pain."

"How can I thank you for your help?"

She acknowledged my question by placing her hands briefly on my shoulders and then she turned to pick up her jacket.

"I got to admire some very defined muscles," she said with a smile and extended her hand in a parting gesture.

Once the doctor left, Maurice came back into the room.

"I closed the restaurant, since it was dead in here tonight anyhow." He sighed heavily and I wondered if his decision had been based on poor sales or the events of the evening.

"I got Ibuprofen for the pain, but I'm sure I could still

manage a drink or two. Why don't we throw back a few to ease our nerves?" I suggested, trying to lighten the atmosphere.

Maurice took out two whiskey glasses and poured each of us some of my favorite Jameson whiskey.

He was deep in thought. "I was thinking about what happened," he said. "I'm no expert on muggers, but something just doesn't add up here. It sounds like those guys were waiting for you specifically. Why would they do that?"

There was a short pause, and so I simply raised my glass and said, "Whatever the reason - a toast to friendship!"

Maurice didn't want to let it go.

"If I were you, I'd move somewhere else for a little while. If you stay in this area and someone wants to find you, it won't be too difficult. You always travel over the Pont St. Louis bridge and if I were out to get you, that's exactly where I'd set up a watch to keep an eye out for you. Anyone out there could easily track you to your apartment."

Maurice sounded so convincing that I started to take his theory quite seriously.

"But why would anyone be after me?"

"I might be completely wrong here, but just to be safe, you should probably avoid this area, for a while at least, and stick to the central or eastern bridges." He tried to make his suggestion without sounding paranoid.

"I'll try to be a bit more attentive to things around me, but once you give in to that kind of fear, it just feeds itself," I stated, annoyed that I had allowed myself to be taken in by his fears for even a moment.

"Well, think about it anyway. For now, let's get back to toasting to our friendship!" He said the last part in a celebratory tone, as if by changing the mood, he might dismiss his own paranoid thoughts.

On that particular evening, we didn't drink very much. After one more round, Maurice began to close up and we ventured out together into the Parisian night. In response to our discussion, all my senses were heightened and I felt relieved when he chose to accompany me as I walked home. We both laughed aloud when Maurice jokingly asked if he could hold my hand. Maybe it was just an attempt to diffuse the tension, since we continued to joke the entire way back to my apartment building. The last anecdote I shared with him was about how, as a young boy, I got escorted home once by a strange man, namely a police officer.

When I finally passed through the locked door to the inner yard, then through the grated steel door on the locked gate to the stairs and, finally, locked the door of the apartment behind me, our whole theory began to seem quite humorous. I turned on the TV and was watching the weather report when I suddenly was reminded of my encounter with the woman in the café. The five-day forecast called for the weather to gradually improve, and if I understood correctly, it seemed that the third day might already be sunny and quite hot. Since it was Thursday night, that meant we could meet on Sunday. The image of the woman filled my mind. The thought of seeing her was titillating and, somehow, the horrific events of the evening had sparked passions in me. I realized that I was already completely captivated by her. My desire to know more, or even just something, about her was driving me crazy. Simply knowing someone's first name couldn't possibly ruin anything! She forced her way into my thoughts and I spent time imagining different theories for her odd demands.

My conscience nagged at me. Sanna and I had allowed our relationship to become rusty, and once the kids had flown the coop, we had been living in a vacuum. We never really fought and, although we still felt a sense of cohesion, we also felt the need for change. We had had our children when we were relatively young, so we were suddenly faced with a whole new life that was calling out for us to do something with it. I was also tired of my job, and didn't want that to be my only legacy. Ever since I was young, I had dreamed of being a writer and this seemed like the ideal moment in life to start. Sanna had also wanted a change, but she had wanted to embark on the life I was looking to escape. She had undertaken to become an entrepreneur and me, a writer. I had decided to relocate to Paris for one year, while she opted to stay in Finland.

I was restless all night. In my sleep, I tried to undress my mystery woman, but she got dressed again at the same rate so I was never able to see her fully unclothed. Then, I was in the Rose Bowl Game, where I intercepted the pass of the opposing quarterback and began to run toward the goal line when the opposing linemen dropped into shooting position and started firing at me with rifles. Sometimes I also awoke to real noises in the stairwell of the building and half expected someone to push through my door. I was exhausted when I finally awoke to the sounds of my neighbors leaving for work.

My cell phone rang at 10:18 a.m. I didn't recognize the number.

"This is Lisa from Shakespeare and Company. Do you remember me?" asked the delicate but determined woman's voice on the line.

"Lisa, Lisa...," I rambled half asleep, trying to make sense of things.

"Don't insult me now! The Lisa who always finds the books you're looking for and suggests other suitable books you haven't thought of yet… You gave me your number so that I could call you whenever I find something important or interesting," she blurted out.

"Have you found something for me?" I was still feeling quite confused.

"No, listen! This is something serious and I don't really have time to explain. Don't ask any questions, just trust me and do exactly as I say!" Her message was firm, but she also tried to sound calm since she realized what state I was in.

"I ordered a cab to pick you up from the center of the island, since I don't know exactly where you live. At the intersection of St Louis en I'lle and des Deux Ponts; just take the absolute essentials and get yourself there! Don't go back to your apartment for a while," she continued.

"But I…," was all I managed to get out.

"You don't have a choice, and I mean now, right away! Call this number when you reach the cab. And keep your head low, so no one will see you," she was nearly yelling now as she became more anxious.

3 THE COMFORT OF STRANGERS
Ian McEwan 1981

Marie felt confused. She had already decided that she wouldn't get drawn in by the attentions of men any more, even though she received propositions on a daily basis. Any dates she had actually made during the past year had ended in disappointment, since none of them had ever turned up. She figured they must have changed their minds or, perhaps, it had just been enough for them to gain her interest. She thought that this was probably the case now too, even though the man from the café seemed to be surprisingly genuine. His athletic build had initially given her the impression that he was quite a macho guy, and she had always hated alpha males. All of the men in her life had been primarily sensitive and intelligent, with one exception.

Marie considered his background. He likely worked for some university, which wouldn't be very exciting, since she, herself, was a professor and researcher. Judging by his accent, the man was clearly American. She guessed his age to be around 40 or then he was just very well preserved. None of this mattered in the end, since she was sure that he wouldn't even show up at Square René Viviani and she would be left to fantasize freely about his background. As an activity, it was quite therapeutic, since it offered relief from her work, which had her steeped in facts day in and day out. Essentially, though, she did not believe that science would advance strictly on an intellectual basis and that's why she was so intrigued by the GEB book, which was now also her link to the mystery man.

Marie was just about to ask the waiter for the check when her cell phone rang.

"Hi Raymond," she answered the phone, her voice devoid of feeling.

"Hello there, mystery of my life! I hope I'm not interrupting anything. Where are you?" Raymond asked.

The subtle discord in his voice made it sound like he wasn't amused.

"Why?" Marie's response was a reaction to his tone.

There was a brief pause and then Raymond continued.

"I just heard some noise in the background and wanted to make sure I wasn't interrupting anything."

"You always hear noise in the background if I'm in a café when you call." Marie found Raymond's consideration to be out of character.

"Have you missed me?"

"We've been apart for so long that you should understand I'm not thinking about you anymore," Marie answered coldly.

"Don't you need my warm, safe embrace anymore, like you always said you did when we were together?" Raymond asked, but he sounded almost as if he were begging.

* * *

Marie had once been the victim of a rape attempt in the park of the Palais de l'Élysée. Even though she had managed to get away from the rapist unharmed, she had been left with deep-rooted fears. The dismissive attitude of the police had only aggravated the situation. It was at precisely that moment when Marie first met Raymond, who happened to be dealing with his own matter at the police station. When Raymond got involved in her discussion with the police, their attitude had done a complete turnaround. She was even more impressed with his influence, since it ensured that more effort was put into her case and, in the end, the perpetrator was actually apprehended. Marie knew all too well that this must have required exceptional measures, since it had been a random encounter and they had had nothing to go on except a rough description of the guy. Although it was quite juvenile, logically speaking, the knowledge that the perpetrator was in prison slightly alleviated her fear. Raymond's immense stature had also made her feel safer and she had clung to him like a child to its teddy bear.

* * *

Marie knew that Raymond had a short temper and she didn't want to get him riled up.

"Raymond, I have repeatedly thanked you for being there for me when I needed it, but you know yourself that we just weren't right for each other. You just wanted to own me and you couldn't handle not getting what you wanted," Marie explained in a friendly tone, because she had truly appreciated the support she had gotten from Raymond.

"But I still love you!" Raymond exclaimed, charged by Marie's rationalization.

"A relationship requires two parties, and if you really love me and want me to be happy, you'll just let me go."

"I'm not a quitter and I know you'll come back in the end," Raymond stated confidently, ignoring Marie's comments.

Their discussions always seemed to lead to an argument, but Raymond had a habit of cutting off the call whenever the conversation reached a high note.

"Adieu, my love!" he said in a voice laced with machismo and arrogance.

* * *

The roots of Raymond's family were linked to banking and extended back farther in history than anyone would have suspected. World War II had split the family, however, sending many members fleeing to the United States. Raymond's father's father had worked as a political liaison between England and France prior to the French occupation, but he was transferred as far away from France as possible in order, he was told, to protect him from the invading Germans. The truth was that they just wanted to be rid of him.

His grandfather had been a difficult person with an enormous thirst for power and a complete lack of emotional intelligence. He had divorced his wife when Raymond's father was just a little boy, and had never, afterward, made any attempts to see his son. He also wasn't concerned about the fate of his ex-wife and son in the face of the war. Raymond's grandmother, the tenacious Annie Durand, had, however, taken things into her own hands and driven her son to safety in

Switzerland, where they had hidden out until the end of the war, safeguarded by her family's financial backing.

Raymond's father had inherited one million dollars from his grandfather on Annie's side, and with it, he began to build his own empire. His own father, on the other hand, had left him nothing – not even guidance on banking and financial matters, despite the fact that his father had been an influential force within Europe. Raymond's father had had to learn everything on his own and had been guided in that task by one essential family tradition, namely, the teachings in The Prince by Machiavelli. Having been abandoned by his own father and part of his family, Raymond's father was determined to succeed far better than anyone in his family before him.

Machiavelli taught that a prince should seek to avoid the contempt and hatred of the people. Raymond's father had taken this one step further and decided to remain entirely elusive, hidden in the background. When any scandals had come to light, this had enabled him to avoid the public contempt that was directed at politicians, who were, in fact, largely under his control. His invisible reach had extended to numerous figures in the business world as well; people whom he had led into a trap by feeding their greed and deceit.

* * *

Hidden power lies in one's acceptance or refusal to finance different endeavors. No one engages in direct bribes. Rather, the funding is provided in the form of grants, bonuses and other benefits from various different institutions. They are generally quite minor to begin with, but they increase gradually and disproportionately in relation to the reciprocal service provided. Finally, those on the receiving end grow accustomed to the disproportionate amounts and begin to view themselves as being entitled to and deserving of such benefits. They become completely dependent on the benefits, since the money covers the majority of the expenses accrued by their extravagant lifestyles. Their addiction cannot be purely explained by their fear of a diminished standard of living, but rather by the fear of shame that looms behind everything. For many, the fear of shame is greater even than the fear of death. They begin to view the financier as a god-like persona, whose every wish should be fulfilled, even if no direct demands, as such, are ever issued. Greed is often enough to encourage people to act voluntarily in a particular way.

If someone happens to be strong enough to resist the temptation, the same method is applied, but indirectly. The most honest of them get appointed to important positions in which they end up playing puppet to bosses who are busy taking full advantage of undeserved benefits. From the perspective of the financier, the best results are achieved by these good and righteous individuals, who passionately drive specific issues without any knowledge of the actual agenda behind them.

The most demanding objectives call for the most extreme methods. Figuratively speaking, the victims are left with an open cookie jar, so even though it seems that there is no danger of getting caught, the one who set the trap knows everything. As the stakes slowly increase, the victims find it easier to take it one step farther since they have already given in to the initial temptation. In the end, the victims realize just how deeply they are involved and how serious their crimes have become. If, for some reason, they don't realize this on their own, they can be discreetly reminded. The worst crimes of all are committed when the victims feel the need to try to cover their tracks. That's the point at which extortion works best.

The most diabolic aspect of the system is the fact that the abuser never needs to reveal himself, much less his face, in order to get the victim eating out of his hand. The insatiable greed inherent to human nature and the fear of shame makes people act, spontaneously, in precisely the desired manner. These basic characteristics of human nature serve as an endless resource. They continue to be effective from one generation to the next.

The person behind the money and extortion is never revealed, even by the advantages achieved through his actions. Often, he appears to be among the victims themselves and seems to suffer significant financial losses. As in the game of chess, one often sacrifices his own chess piece in order to achieve a greater aim. Even the queen is not above sacrifice if the play is followed by a series of forced moves that eventually lead to checkmate. Very few have the ability to see the final objective, much less to identify, on its basis, the true guilty party.

* * *

Raymond's father had come into money quickly, since all of his investments were based on information about future events, many of which he had a hand in implementing. In the end, even money had lost its meaning, since he literally had been able to make it as he needed it. He had begun to construct a public image of himself as a mysterious benefactor who donated large sums of money to projects and interests that were socially popular. Even larger sums from company profits were used as pay-offs masked as different forms of remuneration. Despite the outflow of cash, his fortunes continued to grow.

Raymond's father chose a modest and inconspicuous lifestyle. This was in keeping with the teachings of Machiavelli, since they called for the prince to appear as a miser. His role model, however, had been Charlemagne, or Charles the Great, who lived a life of simplicity and temperance. His idealization of Charlemagne grew to such proportions that he gradually had begun to believe that he was a descendant. As a symbol of his assumed family's power, he acquired a sword that he believed was Charlemagne's actual holy sword, 'Joyeuse'. He had even acquired the Enchiridion of Pope Leo, which, according to legend, Charlemagne always carried with him. It was a collection of spells that were supposed to protect its carrier from poisons, fire, storms, and wild beasts. Charlemagne had united Europe at the turn of the 700s and 800s, and legend stated that he would return to do it again. The prospect of uniting Europe became one of Raymond's father's most crucial objectives and it would come to destroy the family connection.

His father had married a woman who did not live up to general expectations; she was a nude dancer who grew up in the slums of Paris. In their marriage, it was the wife, however, who had ended up fostering the family traditions and, in the end, had united the old branches of the family into a functional network.

Raymond had been the couple's first child, and he had received a Machiavellian upbringing in line with the traditions of both sides of the family. Raymond had inherited his mother's nearly white hair and smoldering blue eyes. He had grown nearly a head taller than his peers and, amazingly, had begun to resemble the historical descriptions of Charlemagne. Around this time, Raymond's father was already apprised of the coming unification of Europe and he started to believe that his son would be the future European President. He began to groom his son for the position by teaching him everything he knew, as his own father had never done.

* * *

The sins of the father have a way of being handed down from one generation to the next, since a child who doesn't receive unselfish love from both parents will develop into an adult who is incapable of expressing love. On its own, a mother's love is not enough for the child, but she can sometimes use her love to stop sins from being passed on to her children by affecting changes in her spouse. Parents always leave traces of themselves in their child, and the traces of sin are only wiped away once the child unconditionally forgives the parents for the wrongs he or she has experienced. This is not an easy task.

* * *

The children in Raymond's family received money and power, as well as the related responsibility to carry on the family's traditions. Raymond's father hadn't gotten these from his own father, but he had created his own success on the security provided by his maternal grandfather's fortunes. He had wanted to give his own children many times over that which he had been denied himself. It was a generous thought, but his motives were completely misplaced. Raymond's father had held himself in great esteem and had wanted his own children to be his crowning achievement.

Raymond had not, however, been very enthusiastic about

his father's ideas, and his father had used his fists to express his disappointment. His father had hoped, however, that Raymond would change and he enrolled him in a prestigious private school. It wasn't exactly what Raymond wanted, since he was only interested in martial arts and these, primarily, only as a form of protection against his own father. His father spent most of his time travelling for work and his mother had been accompanying his father or busy establishing family connections, so it allowed Raymond to slack off completely when it came to his schoolwork. In the end, his father was forced to threaten Raymond that he would be left without his inheritance. Raymond, who had already been schooled in the teachings of Machiavelli, despised those who resorted outright to blackmail, so he hadn't been taken in by his father's threats. As payback for his father's threats, Raymond had gotten sterilized, even though he had secretly already otherwise decided not to continue the family line.

After years of feuding, father and son finally saw eye to eye. His father had organized a place for Raymond in the French intelligence, because it was a world that he knew interested Raymond as well. Intelligence services and international banking have always been closely interconnected. Machiavelli stated that a strong army was imperative and the intelligence agencies had been Raymond's father's army of choice. The world of intelligence is at the core of everything and yet secretive, which was a great match for the family's method of operations. Raymond became a channel to sources of top-secret information.

His father had died of a heart attack shortly after their reconciliation. That's when it was announced that Raymond was to receive his share of the financial assets of the family, but that the decision-making power over their father's empire had been left to Raymond's little brother. His brother and mother had known about the will from the start, but Raymond's father had demanded that this information be kept from Raymond until the end. Raymond realized that he was only getting the scraps while his brother was being handed the key to the empire. It had been the last straw for him and he decided to cut his last ties to the family and change his name to Durand after his grandmother Annie.

Through his profession, Raymond discovered that the real reason for his father's death had been assassination. After the surprise of the will, this didn't shock him, but it made him fear for his own life. From that moment on, he had begun systematically to use his position to acquire his own security guarantees and develop his future.

* * *

The waiter came toward the table and although Marie had been planning to head out, she suddenly decided to order a cup of hot chocolate instead. She couldn't get Raymond out of her mind and needed time to think.

Raymond's influential power gave her an idea. Currently, she was in the process of being smoked out of her job. All of the grounds were fabricated, but she lacked the means to prove it. She didn't even know who was behind it and why. One possible explanation was the popular book she had written about the illusion of time, which had caused a minor commotion within the science community. It was, however, scientifically accurate and she had purposefully written it from a personal angle to avoid her ideas from being connected to any of her colleagues. The point of the book had not been to offend anyone or jeopardize her position, at least not officially.

It would have been nice to call on Raymond's connections to solve her problem, but the reality of it gnawed at her conscience. Raymond would be able to pull the right strings and play the same dirty game. She supposed it wouldn't really be wrong to defend herself against injustice, even if it meant using devious methods to refute the fabricated evidence, as long as it hurt no one. She got caught up in the thought and grabbed her phone.

"Hey Raymond! First I need to say this flat out; I want to take advantage of your position and ask for help without you thinking that it's going to bring us back together. Could you, perhaps, think of helping me anyway?" Marie asked, but she already felt she might regret this call.

"I'll be right there and you can fill me in on the details," Raymond blurted out quickly and hung up.

Marie sat staring at her phone in wonder. It had been too easy. Then she realized that Raymond had never asked where to meet her. She was just about to press the call button when Raymond called back. After she told that she was at Café Panis, Raymond hung up as quickly as he had earlier, as if he were afraid she might change her mind. While Marie waited, she had time to think about what exactly she would tell Raymond. She was afraid that this might set into motion a series of events, the consequences of which would haunt her for the rest of her life. There would be no comfort in ignorance, nor in the fact that her cause was justified. She resolved to ask Raymond to use more intellect than force. It called for a solution that could stand up to scrutiny and wouldn't backfire at a later point. She ordered a second glass of champagne.

Raymond arrived quickly and Marie interpreted this as

Raymond's way to show his concern. It turned out that Raymond had come there by motorcycle, and knowing Raymond, she knew it meant that, on his way, he had broken all the traffic rules he considered to be unnecessary. To calm her nerves, she ordered a third glass of champagne along with Raymond's order. A moment later, she realized that she was already feeling the effects of the alcohol and it bothered her, because she sensed that she needed to be especially clearheaded at that moment. Raymond listened attentively to her concerns and assured her that he would take care of her problem at work as if it were just a part of his normal daily routine. Raymond even claimed to know already what should be done and stated that it would all be handled within the week. Knowing Raymond's history, this didn't sound at all impossible, but Marie demanded that Raymond avoid disciplining anyone, even those who were potentially guilty.

Marie began to relax in the familiar and safe company of the Raymond she once knew and it filled her with conflicting feelings. She told herself that it was exactly these types of conflicting feelings that had driven them apart. Raymond had a lot of good qualities and was very attractive, but his dark side was too much for her to bear. Raymond also seemed to sense her softening to him and he took the opportunity to suggest having dinner for old times' sake. She was just about to accept when Raymond's phone rang.

* * *

Raymond checked first who was calling and then he answered, irritated about the interruption.

"What?"

"We lost him," said a rough voice, slightly tinged with

embarrassment.

"I'll call you right back," Raymond responded in an authoritative tone.

He apologized to Marie for the interruption and moved toward the bookshelf at the rear of the café to make his phone call. When they had been together, Marie had been forced to grow accustomed to phone calls that he didn't want her to hear. In the end, Marie thought this was good, since any information about possible illegal dealings would have been too much for her conscience. He couldn't control his emotions and as he began to talk, his face grew red with fury. He couldn't believe what he was hearing. How on earth could professionals screw up so badly, when their target had been a regular dolt? As soon as he opened his mouth, he was already seething with rage.

"Damn, I've got fools working for me! I told you to make him disappear and you go and lose him. Don't you idiots understand the difference?" Raymond huffed into the phone. He would like to have been able to strangle the party on the other end of the line.

"This guy must be a professional. At least it seemed he was wearing a bulletproof vest, because my guy shot him in the back at close range. Besides, no amateur could successfully take on three guys in a scuffle," the man explained in an effort to calm Raymond down.

"I ordered you to take care of the matter without being noticed and without leaving any traces. You think that using a gun is inconspicuous?" Raymond was overly frustrated.

"Don't worry. There's no way for him to trace what happened back to us, much less to you, and my guys have already left the area. If the target happens to call the police, it will be viewed as an average mugging and they'll never find the perps."

"You have to take care of him now, not sometime in the near future. I'll handle the police and you acquire the target's address. You can also work on putting together a group who has the skills to break into his apartment undetected and can take out even the best professional without leaving a trace!"

Raymond's long-awaited evening with Marie would have to be postponed, but at that moment, he didn't have the time or energy to focus on his disappointment.

"This could be a more critical matter than you think, so there's absolutely no room for errors," Raymond stressed.

Raymond seriously wondered if the target could be a professional. In that case, it was highly possible that someone was trying to get to him through Marie. He wanted to see the guy face-to-face before his last rites. The guy also happened to be the first of Marie's interests to remind him of himself, unlike all the nerds she had tried to date earlier.

"I'm coming with you. Get the team ready. We'll agree where to meet as soon as we have the target's address and the police have been dealt with."

He felt the same thrill as a hunter who knows when he's narrowing in on rare prey.

* * *

Marie watched from a distance as Raymond made his call and put the phone to his ear. The fact that he was near boiling point shown on his face. At that moment, she began, for the first time, to feel afraid of Raymond. Her moment of concession was over in an instant and she was now surer than ever that she no longer wanted to have anything to do with

Raymond. At the same time, she felt a deep regret at having asked for Raymond's help, since she was convinced he would retaliate against the guilty parties despite her request to leave them untouched. He would have his revenge, even if for no other reason than for his own satisfaction.

The phone call ended and she could tell from his expression that he needed to leave. It was a stroke of luck for her, because it saved her from having to make a decision about dinner. It would've been difficult to refuse, since she had asked for his help. It would also have been useless to try to cancel her request for help; once Raymond had heard her problem, he would take care of it anyway. They said a quick goodbye and Raymond rushed off looking very determined. She thought to herself that she definitely wouldn't want to be any enemy of Raymond's.

Marie walked to St-Michel Metro station, from which she could reach Montparnasse Bienvenüe without having to switch trains. She was tired from all the events of the evening, a state that was further compounded by the champagne. She no longer had the energy to consider right and wrong, she just wanted to sleep. In the morning, she could decide what to do about Raymond.

During the night, Marie was startled awake. Her subconscious had put together a painfully clear picture that she didn't want to see, but that was undeniable logical. Raymond had not initially asked where to meet her on the phone, because he had already known where she was. His hasty call back had only been a feeble attempt to cover his regrettable mistake. That meant he had either followed her or had someone else shadow her, and it also meant that he knew about her meeting with the foreign man at Café Panis.

She thought about all the earlier dates she had set up with other men and the fact that none of them had ever shown up. At the time, she had convinced herself that the reason, among others, was that the men had changed their minds, particularly because she had always wanted to withhold their names, a practice which may have made the men suspicious in retrospect. Her head was spinning from a single thought that kept pushing its way to the surface: had Raymond known about them all and made sure none of them showed up for their dates? Could Raymond be that sick, or was she just being paranoid? How could she verify the truth behind her hunch? She couldn't call any of the men because she didn't know their names. That's what she had been after as well – a fleeting moment without any strings attached. The only possibility was one musician, whom she had happened to see on TV after the fact. First thing in the morning, she planned to call a journalist friend who might be able to help her track down the musician's contact information.

Marie only dozed for short periods that were haunted by confusing nightmares. She had given up hope for a good night's sleep and checked the clock every now and then. She waited until 8 in the morning before she dared to call the journalist, who answered right away.

"Hi Marie, how are you?"

"Hopefully I didn't call too early, but I have a slight emergency. I'll explain sometime later, but right now I just need to find a way to contact a famous jazz musician named Bruno Girard, if I remember the name correctly." Marie was impatient.

"Didn't you hear that they found him drowned in the Seine

awhile back? The police ruled it a suicide."

"Wh-when was that?" Marie stammered in shock.

"You can check the exact date online, but it was sometime just before Christmas."

The case was widely reported, but she rarely followed the news, and so the whole story had gone unnoticed. She began to shiver with fear and disgust. She and the musician had been planning to spend Christmas together, since neither of them had had anyone else to spend the holiday with. No one sets up a date and then commits suicide, she reasoned out. Surely she wasn't that repulsive. Was it possible that Raymond was completely mad? Had she managed to indirectly cause the death of many men by making dates with them? Was the foreign guy from the café yesterday alright? How could she warn him or even find him in time? A whirlwind of panicky questions began to swirl in her head.

4 THE WOMAN IN WHITE
Wilkie Collins 1860

The first time Daniel had stepped into Shakespeare and Company, Lisa had noted his tall and strapping appearance. Daniel's face had exposed his delight as he looked around at the shelves of the store and the glimmer in his eyes revealed that he had more than the average relationship with books. Daniel had greeted both Lisa and the American intern, Sarah, by smiling cordially and looking them both directly in the eyes. Lisa felt that Daniel's gaze had lingered longer than necessary on Sarah, but she was used to the fact that no men seemed to be able to peel their eyes away from her quintessential sex appeal. She, herself, even enjoyed looking at Sarah.

"Can you smell that testosterone?" Lisa whispered to Sarah as Daniel went farther into the store.

Sarah didn't respond, but settled for shooting a disapproving look at Lisa. Lisa had a way of teasing Sarah with her bold, straightforward way of speaking.

"He was clearly interested in you," Lisa continued, knowing all too well that Sarah found the interest of men to be a slight nuisance.

"Yeah, well, seen one, seen 'em all," Sarah said without even bothering to look up at Daniel, who stood only a few meters away.

Lisa knew that Sarah wholeheartedly enjoyed the atmosphere of Paris and the attention she got from admirers, even to the point of irritation.

Lisa had quickly ascertained that the large gentlemen was named Daniel and was currently writing his first book. She hadn't even wanted to know anything more about him, because she believed that she had the ability to determine all the relevant facts about people on her own. Based on his accent, she had determined that Daniel was American, but his modesty revealed a tie to some other background. In the end, she had been forced to ask Daniel about his nationality. Upon hearing that he was Finnish, she had been able to connect some of Daniel's mannerisms to other Finns she knew, but there was still something about his social approach and presence that seemed very American. Daniel's behavior was an odd mix of an inner confidence and extreme modesty. Daniel was very companionable and discussed freely on any topic, asked questions and listened attentively, but unless he was asked directly, he offered nothing about himself. For the first time, Lisa had been completely at a loss in assessing a customer, a hobby she had developed purely to entertain herself.

Lisa did not have a habit of befriending her male

customers, but she viewed Daniel as a challenge that would also bring something new to her own world. She also felt that she was opening up new doors for Daniel, but he didn't always seem to notice that himself. They talked a lot about writing, but Lisa sensed that Daniel's interest continued to be focused on Sarah. Daniel hid his potential interest so well, however, that Sarah actually seemed to be disappointed in her weakened power of attraction. Daniel always looked Sarah straight in the eyes and smiled handsomely, even though her low-cut, revealing top made it nearly irresistible to keep one's gaze from wandering lower. Lisa was amused by Sarah's determination to convince herself that Daniel was too old for her. Daniel correspondingly referred to Sarah as a young woman, but Lisa could smell the pheromones in the air between them. It never made Lisa feel uncomfortable or awkward, because even though she admired Daniel and enjoyed watching Sarah, she would have needed both attributes in the same person for her to develop a true interest. Mostly, she was just annoyed that the game between Daniel and Sarah was interrupting her intellectual and spiritual bonding with Daniel. Sarah was charming as well as being intelligent and educated, but Lisa knew that she was no match for herself when it came to matters related to writing.

Lisa believed that she knew all of her regular customers through and through, but it was doubtful that any of them remembered or would be able to describe her. None of her customers would probably understand how well Lisa knew them simply on the basis of their literary preferences. She liked to chat with the customers and ask them about imperceptibly small but significant things, which then enabled her to suggest suitable books for each one. Without them even noticing, she led them to discover new areas of interest.

Lisa had grown up in a cultural family, where reading and education were paramount. Her parents had wanted her to go to one of the more prestigious universities, but she hadn't seen any sense in that. She could as well read on her own and study all of the information available on any subject. Nothing seemed to be beyond her intelligence and she knew that many of the great thinkers throughout history had formed their own perspectives without any formal education. Lisa believed in holistic learning, where it was better to know something about everything than everything about something. By combining her experiences of different fields, she believed that she had found her own place as a writer who had something meaningful to bring to the world. Shakespeare and Company provided the ideal environment for her and she considered it to be much more than just a job. The bookstore was her substitute for a family and perhaps that's why she had stayed there so long – maybe even too long.

On that Friday, Lisa had shown up at work in a cheerier mood than usual, because she had a free weekend ahead starting with a dinner date in pleasant company that evening at Le Procope. She loved the atmosphere in the place and had often sat there enjoying a cup of coffee while imagining the great names of French history that had sat in that same spot throughout the centuries. She couldn't afford to think about having dinner there on her own wages, but this evening, that wouldn't be necessary.

Lisa opened the bookstore exactly at 10 a.m. There was a very classy woman waiting outside the door. She seemed quite flustered. The woman greeted Lisa in French and rushed inside, clearly with an agenda.

"I don't know how to begin," the woman stated as Lisa established herself behind the counter. Other customers came in and the woman looked at them nervously as if she was unsure if she should continue. One of the customers asked for advice in English and Lisa responded in a highly cultivated British accent. Lisa noticed that the woman was taken aback by her English.

"I am completely French on my mother's side, but my father is English. We could as well continue in French, if you like."

There was a pregnant pause, which Lisa ended.

"We are primarily here to help our customers, so feel free to share your concerns with me. You wouldn't believe all the different ways we've helped customers out in the past."

The woman's urgency was reflected in her eyes and it appeared to be getting worse all the time. Lisa felt herself growing anxious even though she still didn't know why.

"My name is Marie Allègre."

"I'm just Lisa."

"I absolutely must make contact with a certain man as soon as possible and I believe that he is one of your customers. I think he purchased a book from here yesterday afternoon." Marie suspected it was shot in the dark, but the book he had been reading was all she had to go on.

"Ma'am, I would love to help you, but surely you understand that our customer information is confidential."

In her mind, Lisa ran through the different reasons why a woman might search this desperately for a man. Had she met the man of her dreams but failed to get his phone number, and was he even interested in her? Perhaps the man had had an affair with her and he didn't want the woman to expose the relationship?

"Do you remember what book he purchased?" Lisa decided to ask.

"Basic Writings. I remember it well, because the book had seemed very interesting to me as well."

Marie felt her anxiety growing as the clock ticked on and she feared that she may already be too late.

"Was he tall and robust?" Lisa continued.

"So, you do know him?" Marie's voice rose hopefully and then she charged on in a panic. "He is in serious danger and there isn't much time! You have to help me."

"What kind of danger?" Lisa asked, both out of fear and confusion.

"Just trust me, it could end very poorly for him!" Marie shouted in frustration at the passing of critical minutes.

Marie feverishly considered whether she dared to say that the man's very life was in danger, since she suspected that this all might be her own paranoia speaking.

"He could lose his life," she finally managed to blurt out.

From the beginning, Lisa had taken Marie's concern seriously, as well as fearing that, in one way or another, it would also come to involve her. Now that she knew why and that the threat to Daniel was the worst possible, a chilling determination in her took over. She disregarded all the rules. She told Marie to follow her and shouted to Sarah to mind the cash register. On their way upstairs, Marie briefly explained what was going on and mentioned Raymond's name. Lisa had read about Raymond Durand and she found it hard to believe that such an influential man, who was known for his charity, could be involved in something like this.

"I have Daniel's number here somewhere. It isn't usual for us to have phone numbers of customers, but I have a very special relationship with Daniel," Lisa explained as she rifled through the desk drawer.

Lisa noted Marie's questioning look and felt the need to explain further.

"Don't get me wrong! It's purely about books."

Lisa began to lose her nerves and she pulled out the entire drawer and emptied its contents onto the desk.

"It has to be here! I can't call information, since I don't know his last name or address. I only know that he lives somewhere on Île Saint-Louis," Lisa explained.

"Have you possibly called him on your cell phone at some point, or him to you?" Marie asked a bit ashamedly, since she felt that her question might be construed as being stupid. Lisa looked at her questioningly and then she suddenly realized Marie's point.

"He did call me once. I gave him my cell number instead of the store's number because I wanted to make sure that he only dealt with me. His number must be in the log of answered calls."

Lisa remembered the date of the call and began to search her phone's memory. She told Marie to order a cab to wait at the center of Île Saint-Louis, since they had no time to waste. Since they didn't know Daniel's address, the center of the island was the most natural location. It was easy to find and only a short distance from any part of the island. Daniel would have to leave his apartment immediately, so the cab needed to be standing by, ready to go. Lisa figured that she would hide Daniel out and the cab could take him to the right address, which she wrote down for Marie.

"Raymond will find out about the cab later on and so he'll also get your address," Marie said doubtfully.

"Don't worry. I have it under control," Lisa responded with

confidence.

The first number Lisa tried was wrong, but the next number found its mark. Daniel's voice sounded a bit groggy and Lisa had to be very stern to get Daniel to understand that this was a serious situation. The phone call was short and both women could do nothing but wait nervously for Daniel to call once he'd safely reached the cab. They sat there, exhausted from their efforts. They began to feel relieved of their panic, but the fear and concern they still felt gnawed at their minds.

"Thank you for helping me."

"That's fine," Lisa answered, feeling a bit of a blush rise to her cheeks.

There was something special about Marie, a charisma that made a strong impression on Lisa.

Once Lisa finally began to calm down, seeds of doubt entered her mind. She wondered if her own panic had been a reaction to Marie's charisma. Marie's explanations had been especially brief and Lisa began to worry that Marie was just being paranoid.

"Are you absolutely sure about Raymond's involvement in this? He's really influential and involved in many things. It's hard to imagine he would risk his reputation, or even destroy his position over jealousy," Lisa asked cautiously.

"You could be right, of course. Someone tried to rape me two years ago. Thanks to Raymond, they managed to catch the guy and he went to prison. But he's been released already and may be behind this all. He might be trying to get revenge. If he's cunning enough, I suppose he could also make it look like Raymond's behind it," Marie reasoned.

"Can you even be sure that Daniel is in danger?" Lisa asked without stating how embarrassing it would be if this were a false alarm.

"I don't know what to think."

Marie felt helpless. The intuition about the threat to Daniel had been so strong that she hadn't even questioned it. Lisa's rationalizations now seemed to be eating away at her intuition and Marie began to give in to the paranoia theory. She felt an overwhelming need to lean on Lisa for support.

"I'm surprised if Daniel doesn't feel something for you," Marie said while looking admiringly at Lisa.

"Believe it or not, neither one of us is interested in that way," Lisa responded without the shadow of a doubt.

"I was supposed to have a date with him, but right now I feel so guilty and ashamed that I doubt I'll ever be able to face him after this," Marie stated.

"And here we are saving him like he's our shared lover." Lisa joked a bit to lighten the atmosphere.

"You must be wondering why I didn't even know his name."

"I don't know that much about him either. I haven't asked a whole lot and he certainly hasn't told me very much."

"It seems we both have quite a similar relationship with him."

Time seemed to drag and Lisa suggested that she might get them both some tea. Marie didn't usually drink tea, but she thought this was the perfect opportunity to give it a try.

"At least it suits the British theme here," Marie added after accepting Lisa's offer.

"Actually, this is an American bookstore," Lisa corrected.

When Lisa walked back into the room with the steaming cups of tea, Marie was able to look at her unabashedly. She looked at the way Lisa dressed and wondered whether her style was a way of covering herself up. Maybe it was her English side, since a French woman would never do that. Then she noticed Lisa's shoes, which were quite worn.

"You're looking at my shoes, right? I know I should get new ones, but my feet are so big that I can never find anything that fits well. It's pretty depressing and that's why I hate shoe shopping," Lisa said awkwardly.

"I'm sorry if I've offended you. You don't need to lament about your shoes, and I'm sure you could find suitable ones online. Besides, I think you are a beautiful woman," Marie said, feeling embarrassed for staring.

"I'm pretty fat compared to you."

"You are like a model straight out of one of Rubens' paintings, except you're an improved version," Marie said in response to Lisa's self-criticism.

Just then, Marie's phone rang and she rifled through her purse to find it. It seemed to take forever and when she finally laid her hand on it, she just sat staring at the caller's number – for an unusually long time in Lisa's opinion.

"Hello?" Marie answered with a hesitant voice.

The blood drained from Marie's face and Lisa was afraid she would pass out. Lisa prepared herself to hear that something had happened to Daniel, but after a moment of silence she heard Marie tell the cab driver that he must continuing waiting. Lisa also felt weak, even though this news didn't really mean anything definitive yet. Her mind began to race since it seemed that Marie may actually have been right about the threat to Daniel's life. Marie placed the phone in her lap and the women looked at one another with uncertainty.

"I suppose I have to try to call him again." Lisa's voice shook.

Lisa pressed the call button and put the phone to her ear.

Marie felt tensed with horror as she waited for Lisa's expression to tell her something. Daniel's phone rang many times, but no one answered.

5 THE THIRTY-NINE STEPS
John Buchan 1915

I was stunned, to say the least. Lisa had been so agitated, but I simply couldn't understand why. I still had the bitter taste of fear in my mouth from the events of the previous evening, but I didn't think Lisa could possibly have anything to do with that. She had, however, told me to stay low in the cab, which reminded me of Maurice's advice. Something was seriously wrong here. Fortunately, Lisa had been so resolute on the phone that she hadn't left me any choice or time to think. I would go as quickly as possible, just as she demanded.

Knowledge of the sudden departure caused a familiar physical response and I knew I would have to go to the bathroom before I left. My bathroom was large and neatly tiled in white with stylish blue accents. The size of the bathroom was oddly out of proportion with the rest of the apartment, which was, in all practicality, only one room with a small kitchenette. Everything in the bathroom was new, and I especially liked the modern faucets. Even though the bathroom had been renovated well, there was one strange feature. All of the sounds from the stairwell of the building could be heard in an amplified way, and I suspected it was because of the air duct leading to the stairwell. At that moment, however, the building was quiet, since all the residents had already left for work. The only sound I heard was the running of the water in the toilet. At least that's what I thought at first, but then I began to hear a strange metallic sound every now and then. It was like the scraping noise created when a soft metal is rubbed against steel. The sound was quite distant and only came occasionally, so I didn't pay it much notice.

I wondered what I should take with me. A toothbrush was the first thing to come to mind and so I shoved my folding travel toothbrush into the inside breast pocket of my suit jacket. I rejected my electric razor immediately and decided to let my beard grow undisturbed for a few days. My wallet had to come and a passport might also be necessary. And, of course, I realized I should also take the medications I'd been given to treat my wound. Everything else I could easily leave behind, and I figured that I needed to buy new clothes anyway. I decided I had everything I needed.

I opened the front door and thought I heard, just then, the sound of the electric lock on the grated steel door to the stairwell. I was, however, still inside the apartment, so I couldn't be sure. As I stepped over the threshold, I immediately realized that something was wrong. I felt as if my thoughts were mixing with those of someone else and I sensed that this other person was afraid. I considered going back into the apartment, but then I would have been trapped. I remained in the hallway. I was closing the door when I felt a familiar shiver run up my spine. My instincts told me to move as silently as possible. I decided to shut the door by first opening the lock, ensuring that the bolt wouldn't make an audible click when the door closed. I forced my thumb and forefinger into the mouth of the lock and slipped the key in between them to cushion the sound of the key in the lock. I lifted up on the door handle to prevent the door from scraping against the doorframe, since it hung heavily on its hinges. Once the door was shut, I quietly released the lock and pulled the key carefully out from between my fingers.

All of my senses were so heightened that it felt as if they were utilizing the full capacity of my brain. I was sure that if I had a dog, it would have been bearing its teeth and growling down the stairs. I smelled the slightest whiff of cigarette smoke, the kind that lingers on the breath after smoking. My hearing was so sensitive that I could hear the beating of my own heart in my ears. The stairwell was unusually silent, so silent it raised the hair on my neck. Someone was at the bottom of the stairs and didn't want to be discovered. The stairs spiraled so that one couldn't see more than half a floor in either direction. I couldn't risk exposing myself by peering down, but then again, that ensured that no one saw me from below either. Since my apartment was on the third floor, it would take several seconds to reach my floor, even at a running pace. Anyone trying to sneak up would move slower and the merciless creaking of the wooden staircase would reveal the person's movements.

I didn't have time to think about the reasons behind these events. I made a decision to head up the stairs in the hope that whoever it was hadn't heard me leaving my apartment. If he tried the front door and succeeded in opening it, he would assume I had left the building. Then I was sure I would get the opportunity to slip out. I had often heard the creaking of the upper stairs from my bathroom, so I knew that I had to move without placing my full weight on any single step. Luckily, the stairwell had railings on both sides, so I grabbed hold of them and stepped carefully along the decorative edge of the stairs. My first step nearly slid off the edge, so I used the railing to further lighten my weight and succeeded to creep slowly upward. My progress up the stairs took a painfully long time and so I decided to stop at the next floor to listen.

I didn't hear anything, so for a moment, I thought I had imagined the whole thing. My balancing act had released so much adrenaline into my bloodstream that it had almost entirely extinguished my fear. My senses returned to their state of heightened awareness as soon as I stopped exerting myself. For a moment I didn't notice anything out of the ordinary, but suddenly I recognized the strong cigarette smell, even stronger than I had earlier. Whoever it was had gotten closer! I listened with the utmost concentration, but I didn't hear anything. At least that's what I initially thought. As humans, we are not accustomed to complete silence or to hearing sounds that can barely be heard. Suddenly, I understood that I had, in fact, been hearing something, but my brain hadn't been used to processing such soft sounds. Faced with an extremely dangerous situation, the resources of my brain grew to inhuman proportions, enabling me to detect the sounds of cautious movements. Now I could tell that I was listening to the single-minded activities of not one, but several people moving in a tight space. They were at my door only half a floor below, a few meters from where I stood!

I took deep breaths to try and calm myself, but I was still able to smell my own fear. I wondered about my odds if I were to be discovered. The worst case scenario would be that they would detect me, but wouldn't let on that they knew where I was. If that were the case, the only advantage I had, namely the element of surprise, would shift from my hands to theirs. If, on the other hand, I noticed that I had been spotted by one of them, I would have to attack the person in a blind fury before he had time to recover from the split second of astonishment he felt after seeing me. I would try to use him as my shield, since they were likely carrying firearms. After that, my only hope would be to grab one of their guns and arm myself. It would also be very bad luck if one of the upstairs neighbors happened to choose this moment to come down the stairs. I wasn't at all sure I could convince someone not to expose me simply by placing my finger to my lips. That was when I remembered my cell phone. Damn it, I had forgotten to silence the ring tone! My thoughts raced. A significant amount of time had passed and I should already be in the cab, calling to Lisa. That would mean she would be calling any minute now to find out where I was.

* * *

Raymond swore into the phone when he heard from his contact that the target they were looking for was not to be found from the migration register. They only knew the guy's first name and nationality. If he were just there on holiday, it would mean significantly more work for them. They would have to search for him among lists of apartment tenants, which would prove difficult with insufficient personal information. The worst would be if the man were staying in some random apartment unofficially. Unfortunately, they were going to have to turn to the intelligence system for assistance. In that case, however, he could as well go to sleep and hope the information would materialize during the night. He wondered if this guy was truly worth all this trouble, but in the end, trusting his instincts and playing it safe had, to this point, kept him unassailable. Whether or not his instincts had always proven correct was irrelevant. Besides, the fact that this case concerned Marie made it all the more personal.

Raymond slept restlessly waiting for the phone to ring, which it never did. He was already eating breakfast when his contact finally called.

"We got the assumed address just after midnight and placed surveillance on the roof of a building on the opposite side of the Seine, from where we could easily see the locked door to the inner yard. My team of operatives also gathered at around the same time in a van close to the location. In the morning, one of the building residents went in through the door and intelligence was able to gain the access code. We just got confirmation that the address is correct. The target is not American, he's a Finnish national named Daniel Bremer. Now everything is ready for us to go in," the contact explained the progress of the operation as if it were any daily routine.

"Good! Wait until those leaving for work have cleared the building. Then put your best man inside the door and if the target attempts to leave, he should be put out with anesthetic, if possible. Then we'll move him to a better location. If the target is accompanied by any outsiders, just follow him from a distance and request further instructions. It will take me some time to get there, because I have to make absolutely certain that no one can link me to that site later on," Raymond explained.

Raymond had been surprised to hear the man's nationality.

If he were after Raymond, then the Finnish nationality was likely just a cover. There was no way the Finns could know about his dealings with the Russians, a fact that certainly would have annoyed them. Even if they had found out, he doubted that Finns would immediately take action. Americans were another story, and Raymond concluded that the guy must have some American connection anyway.

When Raymond arrived, he sat waiting in his car in the street while three men dressed like maintenance staff armed with backpacks moved beyond the outer wall to join the others already waiting in the inner yard. One of the guys pulled an aluminum zoom pole camera from his backpack and shoved it through the steel grate of the inner gate. The door release was likely located somewhere around the side of the stairs leading up into the building. The guy was able to see the image from the pole's monitor that was transmitted from a small camera mounted on the other end of the pole. When he located the release underneath the spiral staircase, he pressed a button and the head of the pole fixed itself against the wall next to the release. He was able to make a small lever extend out from the side of the pole to press the release. The lock of the inner gate opened nearly as quickly as if the man had actually had the code for the door.

The team leader examined the old wooden stairs. After a moment's consideration, he got on all fours, evenly distributing his weight to maintain his center of gravity as he moved along the edges of the stairs, where the risk of creaking was the least. He slowly moved upward, step by step, with the rest of the group following behind. He checked each step with his hands and signaled if he was unsure about any of them. The men knew the signal meant they should avoid that particular step and they passed the message to those behind them. Using this meticulous method, they proceeded up the staircase, like monitor lizards moving from side to side.

When they finally reached the third floor, the team leader stopped, and when all the men had arrived, he pointed to the door on the right. One of the men began to examine the door, one stood guard over the stairs leading down and a third guy stood watch over the stairs upward. The team leader pulled out his Beretta, outfitted with a silencer, and stood ready in case the door opened from the inside. The guy examining the door also checked the lock and hinges to try to figure out the best way to get in quickly. They needed to completely take the target off guard, since he was presumably dangerous and possibly armed. Picking the lock had a high risk of detection. Breaking the door or lock was totally out of the question, since their objective was not to draw any attention to themselves. They could lure the target out with a suitable noise or smell, and they had brought equipment for that purpose. They could pump, for example, the smell of smoke under his door.

Just then, a cell phone began to ring in the apartment. The whole team turned to stare at the door and the guy who had been examining the door placed his ear against it. This was the optimal moment to strike. The call would distract the target and the sound of his voice would tell the team where in the apartment he was standing. They had a drawing of the apartment with them. The phone continued to ring. The team leader feverishly tried to decide on the right tactic to take. Perhaps the target had become aware of them after all and he was trying to throw them off by not answering the phone. Their arrival had been pulled off so smoothly, however, that it was highly unlikely that they had been detected. If that were the case, however, it would anyway be in vain to try to sneak in silently. The team leader signaled the door expert to begin picking the lock and all the others prepared to storm into the apartment. One of the men pulled out a stun gun and another had his Beretta ready. The phone kept ringing even after the team was already inside.

Raymond arrived quickly after hearing that the apartment was empty. He studied the cell phone, which had fortunately been left unlocked. The call that had come in earlier was registered in the phone memory as SAC. He scrolled through the phone's address book and noted curiously that along with a few foreign numbers, there were only two numbers in France: SAC and Maurice. He ordered the team leader to call the number for Maurice and tell him that he'd found this phone. He didn't want to take a risk that this Maurice person might recognize his voice.

"Hi there, Daniel! Have you recovered from yesterday?" said a cheery voice in English.

"Do you speak French?" Raymond's guy asked in French, trying to sound as friendly as possible.

"Of course! Why are you using Daniel's phone?" Maurice asked quite surprised.

"I found this phone on the street and chose your number from the address book. Perhaps I could bring the phone to you?" the caller suggested.

"Where are you now?" Maurice tried to hide his skepticism.

"In Île Saint Louis – oh, let's see, what street is this...ah, Quai de Bourbon," the caller responded with a slight suspicion that he had made a serious error.

"Unfortunately, I'm on the other side of the city, so I'm afraid I won't be much help to you," Maurice said, as friendly as possible to try to hide the fact that he knew the caller was lying.

There were no background noises on the caller's end, so he was clearly inside, not out on the street. Maurice was sure that the call came from inside Daniel's apartment.

"Would you like Daniel's address?" Maurice asked intuitively.

"Maybe you could suggest a restaurant in the area where I could leave the phone," the caller said trying to skirt the question.

"If it's not too much trouble, you could leave the phone at Le Lutétia, which is on the corner of Quai de Bourbon and Jean du Bellay," Maurice suggested.

"That's no problem. Thank you. Goodbye."

The caller looked over at Raymond, expecting to be met with a fit of rage.

"He began to sound suspicious, so I didn't dare push it any further. At least he doesn't seem to know where the target is," he offered.

"Find out the address for this Maurice. If necessary, we can have him followed. The Finn had only two French numbers in his cell phone, so they must be important," Raymond said, as if thinking aloud. "Try that SAC number still."

* * *

Lisa and Marie's emotions had been on a roller coaster ever since Marie had stepped into Shakespeare and Company. For a moment, everything had seemed like it might just be the product of Marie's imagination, but when Daniel didn't show up at the cab, they both sunk back into a state of fear. The fact that Daniel didn't answer his phone was rapidly transforming their fear into all-out panic. The only rational explanation seemed to be that something had happened to Daniel.

Lisa and Marie tried desperately to figure out what they could do. It wouldn't help to call the police, because they didn't know where to send them. Marie thought it a bad idea anyway, since the police would tell Raymond everything. If he figured out that Marie knew something, it could turn dangerous for her as well. Lisa's involvement would also raise too many questions and hiding Daniel out at Lisa's home would be impossible. They also considered going to Île Saint-Louis, but even though the island was small, the idea of searching for the apartment without an address would have been fruitless.

Lisa's phone rang. She checked the number and it looked familiar.

"Hey! I think this might be Daniel!" Lisa exclaimed excitedly. "He must have made it to the cab."

Lisa pressed the answer button and was just about to say something when she noticed Marie's horrified expression and saw her waving her hands back and forth as a warning. Lisa was speechless for a second and before she had a chance to pull herself together she heard, "Hello?" This was not Daniel's voice, but that of a man she didn't know!

"Shakespeare and Company. How can I help you?" Lisa said in a formal voice.

"I'm simply returning your call," the stranger said in a questioning tone.

"May I ask who's calling?" Lisa asked.

There was silence and then Lisa could hear a small rustling through the phone, as if the caller were covering the phone with his hand. Lisa began to fear that she might have disturbed a beehive.

"Sorry, what did you ask? Oh yeah, this is Daniel Bremer."

"Oh, Mister Bremer, the books you ordered have arrived."

Lisa visualized an old, boring male customer she was used to waiting on so that she was able to keep her voice as natural sounding as possible. The caller hung up and looked to Raymond for the next instruction.

"It was a bookstore. Should we plant someone there on watch as well?"

Lisa looked at Marie with relief and began to explain excitedly, "It was a stranger calling from Daniel's phone. But if he or they had Daniel, then they wouldn't have called, right? Daniel must have gotten away, but forgotten his phone."

"So someone broke into Daniel's apartment. I guess I wasn't just being paranoid," Marie stated terrified.

"But why didn't Daniel reach the cab then?" Lisa wondered.

"Maybe he's in the cab now. Although I would think that he would have borrowed the driver's phone since you specifically asked him to call," Marie said.

"Call the cab driver and ask!" Lisa said and realized that the instructions that the cab driver had received were not enough without Daniel's further instructions.

"If the cab has left without Daniel, I'll ask him to go back immediately, even if it costs extra," stated Marie.

Marie knew that, despite the delay, Daniel would try to reach the agreed location. He would probably be afraid he would be followed if he tried to walk to Shakespeare and Company.

* * *

Raymond and his men thoroughly turned over Daniel's room and belongings. One guy stood watch outside the door and another in the street just in case Daniel happened to return. It was quite likely that he would, since he would realize at some point that he had forgotten his phone at home.

The room contained nothing out of the ordinary. The table had a laptop and a messy pile of handwritten papers. The bookshelf was full of books.

"This guy seems like some kind of writer," one of the leather-clad guys said to Raymond.

Raymond picked up a stack of papers and tossed them one by one back onto the table.

"I think it's just a cover. These papers contain nothing but dashes, followed by random sentences, apparently in Finnish. He could have gotten those out of books without even understanding the language. Take the laptop with you and we'll study it later," Raymond responded.

Raymond's phone rang.

"There's a big group of huge men dressed in American football uniforms heading into the building! They had the door code, so one of them must live here," the street-level watchman stated.

"What the hell?" Raymond asked in astonishment.

He turned to the team leader and told him to meet the group.

"Find out what they are planning. Don't show your weapon or otherwise act threatening. If you have to, just say you're a cop or something," Raymond ordered.

The team leader ran out, but slowed his pace to normal on the stairs. He walked down the center of the stairwell so that the group on their way up would be forced to stop. Just then he heard a loud shout from below that sounded like a command.

"Quick Split – Speed Counter, hut, hut..."

"Who are you guys?" the team leader asked from the first guy, since he appeared to be the captain of the players, who were all dressed in blue uniforms.

"Our old teammate is getting married and so we're going to surprise him with a final game," the player answered jovially.

"Here I thought we only played rugby here in France. Who's the star of the evening?" the team leader asked.

"Jacques Dupont on the fifth floor," one of the players answered. "We're going to dress him in the opposing team's uniform and give him a group thrashing on the field," he added while holding up a yellow jersey and red helmet.

The team pushed politely past the guy blocking the stairs as if he were just a light cardboard cutout.

"Quick Split – Speed Counter, hut, hut...," rang out in the stairwell.

* * *

I felt exhausted from the stress caused by all the tension and concentration. I couldn't do anything, but listen attentively. The ringing phone in my apartment had saved me from sheer panic, but it was only a momentary relief. I had clearly heard the door of my apartment being opened and people rushing in. After that, I heard a conversation in French. For a moment I had been paralyzed with terror when I heard footsteps racing up the stairs, but whoever it was had gone into my apartment. Then the apartment door had closed and the sound of the talking was muffled. There was no way I could sneak down, because I could clearly hear the sound of someone near my door.

Time seemed to crawl at a snail's pace. Suddenly I heard a familiar shout on the stairs, "Quick Split – Speed Counter, hut, hut..."

Maurice! A smile rose to my lips as I considered how corny the situation was. This was the worst possible place and situation for American football. The insanity of the situation erased my fear and I decided to head down the stairs to meet Maurice. It sounded like Maurice was accompanied by a large group and that their plan was to try to save me with force. That would be a poor choice, though, since the opposition was a heavily armed group. But how on earth could Maurice even know about my situation?

Maurice shouted again and now his group was closer! At the same moment I realized that Maurice was using this method to announce his approach as a coded message that he could be quite sure the opposition wouldn't understand. They must find this situation especially corny. Maurice couldn't know, of course, the details of my situation, but his shout alerted me to the fact that my situation was now changing. In my head I began to recall events on the playing field and the last shreds of my fear disappeared. Was the play that Maurice shouted actually meant to be some kind of instruction? In American football, the quarterback usually communicates a rehearsed offensive play when the players are gathered in their huddle, but sometimes, the play can be called out when the players are already in their starting formation. This approach requires the assurance that the defense will not understand the command for the play. This was precisely such a situation, and it must mean that Maurice was trying to tell me the play. It was a familiar play for me; Quick Split meant that the defense would be unable to anticipate the movements of the ball carrier and route of the ball, because the quarterback could pass the ball in nearly any direction. In this situation, the term carried a suitable irony, the type that Maurice loved: quick split = fast retreat. Counter meant a running play in which the running back takes a step in the opposite direction of the play, thereby leading the defense in a different direction than the ball is intended to go. Maurice obviously had a diversion in mind, not a violent rescue operation.

I lifted my finger to my lips to get ready to warn Maurice not to expose me by expressing his joy at seeing me again. I couldn't believe my eyes when a fully-clad football team charged up the stairs in front of me. At first I didn't even recognize Maurice at the front of the group, because the helmet and facemask hid a large portion of his face and the tightness of the helmet and chin strap made his face appear chubby. The players filled the narrow stairwell so that it was impossible to see anything from behind them other than their broad shoulders. I tried to stand up, but my legs had grown too stiff from crouching in fear. Two of the enormous linemen grabbed me under the arms and started to carry me upward with them without saying a word. We didn't stop until the uppermost floor, and then the men lowered me onto my own tingling legs, which fortunately had begun to work again. Maurice motioned to me to remove my clothes, which he then shoved into a large equipment bag. From the same bag he pulled out a whole uniform complete with shoulder pads and protective gear. Maurice didn't say a word, but the rest of the team kept up a jovial ruckus in French. I knew that speaking English would jeopardize the situation, if someone from downstairs happened to hear. I counted ten players, which made me number eleven, so we had a complete offensive line of scrimmage.

Maurice was clearly our quarterback and he once again shouted out a play in a voice loud enough to be heard over all the commotion.

"Quick Split – Speed Counter, hut, hut..."

This was an actual command and we headed down the stairs in a slightly irregular formation. The gigantic linemen went first and, as I watched them descend, I wondered where Maurice had found these guys. Incredibly, at 192 centimeters and 110 kilos, even I was significantly smaller than they were.

Maurice moved in behind them and the smaller-sized wide receivers shifted to each side to create a plow formation. I was left in the middle of the formation as the fullback, and behind me followed a halfback. He wasn't smaller than me, however, even though in true offensive formations, the second running back was generally smaller and faster on his feet. Maurice handed the ball off to him.

We descended the stairwell in a noisy and rapid manner. There was a man standing guard at the door to my apartment and now I was able to see his face for the first time. Luckily, he wasn't one of my attackers from the previous night, since I was afraid that someone would recognize me despite the gear. This man had rugged, dark features, but he cracked a slight smile when he backed out of the way of the players. I started to relax once we passed my door, but then I saw that there were two men standing on the next landing down. One of them was the thug who had asked me for a light the night before! They probably brought him along to identify me, since he had had the opportunity to study my face closely the last time we met. The thug eyed everyone's faces carefully, but I managed to keep hidden behind the bigger guys in front of me. The guy standing next to the thug looked intelligent and well-maintained, so I assumed he was probably the group leader. He surprised me by saying, in English, "So, that's the hero of the hour!"

6 RUN TO DAYLIGHT!
Vince Lombardi 1963

Raymond had an inspiration and started to search again for Daniel's cell phone.

"Where's that cell phone?" he asked, frustrated as always when things didn't work out right away.

"You put it in your pocket," said one of the guys searching the room.

Raymond mumbled something to himself as he reached into his pocket for the phone. He scrolled through the log of answered calls until he found the most recently answered call. Then he double-checked that the date and time on the phone were correct.

"Shit! The Finn answered his phone at 10:18 this morning, but we were already on the move then, so he couldn't possibly have left the building after that. He must still be here in the building!" Raymond hissed in a voice created by the fact that his teeth were clenched together in rage.

The incoming phone call had also come from the same bookstore. Something about the whole scenario bothered him, but he didn't have time just then to think about it any further. He grabbed his own phone and called to the team leader.

"Stop that group of idiots on the stairs and have the guy who saw the target yesterday check the identity of the guy they picked up. Speak English at first, but then switch suddenly to French. The target doesn't speak French, fluently at least, but the guy getting married was supposed to be French, based on his name. If anything seems suspicious, hold them there at gunpoint and call everyone in to help," demanded Raymond.

* * *

Now I started to understand why the halfback behind me had changed into the yellow jersey and red helmet, even though we others were dressed in identical blue uniforms. It was the same reason that he was also my height! It was a trick play! The plow formation opened ahead of me and I cleared to the side instinctively along with them. The guy with the yellow jersey handed the ball off to me and removed his helmet. The thug looked at him for a long time and then said something in French to the man I had assumed was the leader of the group. He asked something else from the guy in yellow and he responded with a long, informal-feeling answer. Everyone burst out laughing, including me, and the thug backed out of our way into the corner, still chuckling at the joke he'd heard, of which I had understood nothing.

"Fullback dive, hut, hut, hut...," Maurice called out once again in a loud voice.

I was holding the ball and the goal line was close. The

message was clear, we should push full steam ahead out into the daylight. We returned to our formation and continued onward, making it out through the outer gate with no additional problems. Maurice took out his phone and called somewhere. He turned to the right toward Pont Marie bridge with me next to him and the rest of the team following behind. When we had walked about 200 meters, we arrived at an intersection and were met by a bus just coming over the bridge. It crossed the intersection and stopped in the bus lane to Rue des Deux Ponts. We boarded the bus and only then did Maurice begin to explain.

"Daniel, say hello to the French national team!"

I turned and was greeted by a bus filled with applauding players.

"Did you think that I planned something this ridiculous just for the heck of it?" Maurice questioned rhetorically and continued.

"This team knocked Finland out of the World Championship in a qualifying game and happens to be at a training camp here in Paris preparing for the upcoming World Championship. And I just happen to be involved in the arrangements for the camp. We were on the verge of leaving from the hotel when I got a call from your cell phone. So it isn't hard to figure out how I came up with the plan once I realized you were in trouble," Maurice explained. He was in his element and kept right on going.

"I told about your playing career in the US and Rose Bowl, and so it wasn't difficult to get the team to help. I know that you were a linebacker, but I'm an offense guy and it anyway suited my plan better."

"Don't worry, the position of fullback is familiar from my year as an exchange student," I said gratefully and shook the hands of the players who had helped me.

"What's next?" asked Maurice as if we were on some type of sightseeing tour.

All of a sudden, I remembered the cab that had been waiting for me at the center of the island. The designated point was just on the corner of this very street and Rue St Louis en I'lle, in other words, just one hundred meters ahead of us!

"You all need to get to training. Don't worry about me anymore; I've got help from other sources as well. Maurice, I'll fill you in on everything sometime later on. I don't have time now since I'm already very late. You can drop me at the next intersection and I can take it from there," I explained.

I quickly changed my clothes while the bus stood waiting. Then the bus continued on and stopped at the traffic lights for the intersection of Rue St Louis en I'lle. At the door of the bus, I turned and placed my hand over my heart while looking each player square in the eyes. They all understood my gesture of appreciation for them and their help.

* * *

Raymond swore heavily when he found out his suspicion had been incorrect. The Finn was, indeed, still somewhere in the building and that meant that they would be forced to search all the apartments. Raymond had personally had enough and so he delegated tasks to the team before he headed out. If they didn't find the target, a guard should be left in the apartment and a lookout outside for the purpose of alerting the guy inside if the Finn, or possibly the police, arrived unexpectedly. All the bridges leading to the island had been watched by guards since the evening, so it was unlikely that the Finn left on foot. Just to be sure, Raymond decided to find out if a cab had driven anyone fitting the description of the Finn off the island. That bookstore needed to be checked out and someone would need to shadow the person who had called from there. Maurice also felt like a promising lead.

* * *

In my mind, I had envisioned the intersection where the cab would be waiting as a large square, but it was just a modest intersection of two narrow streets, and was hardly bigger than a mere 100 square meters. The cab was there, as promised, waiting on the left in front of me, just beyond the crosswalk in a zone that was painted yellow to signal that parking was prohibited. During my time in Paris, I had learned that 'no parking' zones were meant to be violated. The driver apparently noted my arrival, because he got out of the car to show that he recognized me. He opened the back door for me and handed me a cell phone as I climbed in.

"You need to call the number that's on there immediately," he stammered in broken English. I dialed the number.

"Marie," said a soft, concerned voice that sounded vaguely familiar to me.

"This is Daniel," I said, likely sounding confused, as I had expected to hear Lisa answer the phone.

"Finally," Marie said, relieved. "We met yesterday at Café Panis. I know that you probably have no idea how I'm involved in everything that's going on."

It was silent for a moment, because I wasn't sure what to say. Marie interrupted my thought process and continued.

"I don't have time now to explain the reasons behind all this. And unfortunately I have to cancel our date, since it'd be all too dangerous after what's happened. Lisa can explain everything to you later. I'll give the phone to her now," Marie said with what I thought was a slight wistfulness in her voice.

A feeling of sadness ran through me as, in my mind, I caught a glimpse of the two of us walking along together in the park on a sunny morning. At least now I knew her name; Marie, so beautiful and fitting...

"Daniel, are you alright?" Lisa's question snapped me back into the moment.

"Sorry about the minor delay, and yes, I am physically intact at least."

"Good. Listen carefully now!" Lisa commanded in a voice that demanded my full attention.

"You must do exactly as I say so we can be sure to make you disappear without a trace," Lisa said and began immediately to explain her plan.

The cab driver didn't say a word after I returned the phone to him. I had been so focused that I hadn't even noticed that the cab was already in motion. We circled around the Arc de Triomphe, but I had no idea where we were headed. Lisa had stated the address on the phone, but I was unable to place it in my mind. Next thing I knew, we had reached a boulevard that split into two streets heading in opposite directions and separated by a park. I guessed that we would soon be at our destination, since the address Lisa had given was 220 Boulevard Pereire Nord. The cab stopped, just as Lisa had described, in front of two adjacent front doors, one of which was bright blue and the other dark brown. I knew this was the right place and, as Lisa had instructed, I paid the driver with my credit card and gave him a tip of €100 for waiting. Lisa knew I always carried a significant amount of cash, but when I had suggested paying the cab driver in cash for safety reasons,

Lisa had explained that there was a reason she wanted me to use a credit card. She told me to walk straight up to the blue door, as if it were a familiar address, and pretend to punch in the door code. If the cab didn't leave right away, I was supposed to waste time and punch in a code after thinking for a second, as if the first code I had punched had gone wrong. The cab left immediately, however.

According to her plan, Lisa wanted to intentionally lead the trackers to a place where it would be easy for her to make me disappear without a trace. This was a familiar place to her, because she had visited a friend here several times, but the friend had moved away years earlier. She had no current connection to the building, and there would, of course, be no trace of me, but the trackers would waste significant time and energy searching the area. In the end, they would come to realize they'd been misled, thereby also realizing that I was aware of them and their abilities. It would create the familiar situation in which 'I know that you know that I know'.

My next move was to take the Metro, but not from the adjacent Porte Maillot station. The trackers would likely examine the footage from the security cameras in the station. My instructions were to walk northeast along Boulevard Pereire until Place Du Mal Juin, a distance of slightly more than one kilometer. The lush park running down the centre of the entire length of the boulevard looked much more appealing with its green landscaping and sand-covered paths than the boring sidewalk. I began walking toward the nearest park gate, but right before I reached it, I changed my mind. My intuition was telling me to stay on the sidewalk instead, even though I didn't know why. I just had that kind of feeling.

I wasn't in a hurry, since my instructions had been to arrive at Porte de Clichy at four in the afternoon. Despite that, I felt the need to get as far as possible as quickly as I could. I decided to walk past several Metro stations until I reached the Gare St-Lazare station and then get a train to the rendezvous point. As I walked, the tension began slowly to dissipate and, at the same time, I realized I was growing hungry. I had, after all, skipped breakfast. The day was cloudy, but there didn't seem to be any danger of rain and the temperature was quite warm. I figured I could easily eat outside at some restaurant terrace while waiting. Somehow it seemed corny to be thinking about eating after everything that had happened.

* * *

My instructions were to look around the busy traffic hub for an island with a couple trees and lined with meter-high pillars with rounded heads. I had been told that the place would be obvious when I came out of the Metro station. I was a bit nervous about finding the location, but when I came up out of the Porte de Clichy station, I saw it directly to the left in front of me. The traffic hub had several small islands that divided the traffic and formed part of the busy crosswalks, but only the closest one had trees, and the tallest tree stood out clearly among the rest. I marveled at the fact that the intersection had been built in such a disorderly way, but then I remembered the French principle, which asks 'why do things simply if you can make them beautifully complicated'. On the other side of Boulevard Bessières, on the corner of Avenue de Clichy, I happily spotted the Le Select Bessières restaurant, where I would have a chance to get my coffee and Armagnac. It would also give me an opportunity to survey my surroundings and make sure I wasn't being followed.

I walked to the large island in the intersection well in advance of the agreed rendezvous time. Lisa told me to lean against the tallest tree, which I recognized was a Maple. The traffic was busy and people were swarming from one island to the next in all directions across the intersection. I didn't know what kind of person I was waiting for, so my only choice was to search for anyone approaching me or looking at me. Then I heard a woman's voice from behind the tree on which I was leaning.

"Daniel, I presume?"

Lisa's friend was small in stature with dark hair. She looked at me as if I were from Mars, with her head slightly tilted, eyes wide open and mouth slightly ajar. Instead of starting to talk, she began to chew furiously on a piece of gum. At the same time, she measured me up from head to toe. Suddenly, she stopped chewing, pursed her lips and spit out the gum.

"Follow me," she ordered as she turned to walk in the direction of the sign pointing to the city's outlying areas.

The woman dug in her pocket for a nicotine gum packet. She pushed one piece of gum through the foil of the blister pack into her palm and then tossed the gum into the air, expertly catching it in her mouth. She said nothing, but I understood that I was just supposed to follow behind her. We had travelled two hundred meters when we came to an underpass that passed under the highway to Charles de Gaulle airport. After passing under the highway, we came to an intersection which led, on the right, to Boulevard Victor Hugo. We turned, however, to the left and then to the right onto Rue de Paris. In the way that Boulevard Victor Hugo had appeared to be a street dominated by cold office buildings, Rue de Paris was like a small town within Paris with low five-story buildings and local shops. We turned again to the left onto Rue de Cailloux, which wasn't nearly as idyllic, but still seemed to be a quiet residential section. The woman paused suddenly and, once again, spit the gum out of her mouth.

"Do you know where we're headed?" she asked.

"I have no idea," I answered, bewildered by her question and the fact that she had suddenly spoken after such a long stretch of silence.

She didn't comment on my response, just threw a new piece of gum in her mouth and continued on her way. We walked another hundred meters and she stopped at an intersection that led, to the right, onto Avenue Anatole France. It was like a new world: an idyllic, narrow lane, whose trees bent inward over the lane to form a green roof. Fifty meters from the intersection, on the right side, was a glass front door decorated with large wrought-iron V-letters, one inside another. There was a sign on the wall to the right of the door. I got closer and read the text:

"Ici a vécu Henry MILLER romancier américain 1932 – 1934".

I didn't say a word. The woman asked me to move to the side and opened the door.

"You'll be staying here for a while. Hopefully you like Henry Miller. I, myself, prefer Anaïs Nin," she said, almost as if she were presenting any regular bed and breakfast apartment to me.

7 BETWEEN THE ACTS
Virginia Woolf 1941

Raymond wasn't at all surprised that the cab that the Finn had used had been located, but he couldn't for the life of him understand why the Finn had paid with this own credit card. No professional would make that kind of mistake, even out of carelessness. It seemed obvious that he had wanted them to find the place that the cab left him.

"Where did the Finn get out of the cab?" Raymond asked into the phone.

"Near Port Maillot, at a door on the better side of a residential building. The cab driver said the Finn entered the building. We are just now checking through the residents for possible connections to the Finn and we are guarding the front door, but staying out of sight, of course," the contact answered in a way that emphasized the initiative his group was taking.

"Is there a Metro station or large hotel within a short

walking distance from there?" Raymond asked, contemplating the options.

"Porte Maillot Station and Le Méridien Etoile are a few hundred meters from here. We'll check them now too. The security cameras of the Metro station will definitely tell us if the Finn hopped onto the Metro from here," the man explained as if they were his own ideas. He continued by suggesting that the Finn might also have taken another cab.

"The Finn wants us to waste time searching for him. I would bet my fortune that he won't be found anywhere in that vicinity. But I suppose we have to make sure anyway," Raymond said in a tense voice that was on the brink of becoming infuriated. "For now, keep checking all the possibilities. Question the people in the park just in case the Finn happened to walk in that direction. People in the park usually sit in the same place for a long time, so someone would likely have noticed anyone walking through the park, particularly since it's not a busy area. Try to find women to talk to. I have to think about our next move for a bit, so I'll get back to you," Raymond said and ended the conversation nearly mid-sentence.

Raymond sat thinking about the situation. The Finn couldn't know who was after him. He had known, however, that the cab he used would be easily found. This supported his suspicion that the Finn was no usual tourist. He'd survived last night's attack and the close range shots, managed to outwit them despite the morning's carefully planned strike, successfully disappeared right out from under his men and then pulled off this cab diversion – everything pointed to him being a professional. The Finn seemed to understand exactly what he was up against. It also suggested there was a very powerful player behind it all and the Finn was their agent. An agent who was trying to get to Raymond through Marie.

A professional could easily disappear with the help of a forged identity. He might have a rental car and could be staying at any hotel or, perhaps, another leased apartment. It would be in vain to search for anyone named Daniel Bremer, which didn't even sound Finnish. Raymond's intuition told him that the Americans were behind this whole thing and they had naively sent their own agent posing as a Finn, as if being Finnish would be a sufficiently innocent cover. 'Daniel' probably didn't even know Finnish.

Then Raymond remembered that the Finn's contact list had been especially short. Even though his phone log clearly hadn't been erased, the list of outgoing and incoming calls was no more extensive than his nearly nonexistent address book. The Finn had only just met Marie and, based on what had been heard through the phone tap, he hadn't even learned Marie's name when they met at Café Panis. Raymond's suspicions were primarily focused on Maurice, but he also had a hunch that the Finn's connection to the bookstore was about more than just books. Raymond decided to call his contact immediately.

* * *

Marie felt both relieved and sad. Daniel had survived this round and was now Lisa's responsibility. Despite only having known Lisa a short time, she felt that Lisa could be trusted and this gave her a sense of calm. The decision to leave Daniel in Lisa's hands was made easier by knowing that any contact with Daniel would be dangerous for both Daniel and Marie, because they were both obviously being tracked. Having to give up on meeting Daniel ever again, on the other hand, had been a difficult decision, which surprised even Marie herself. Her intention had simply been to enjoy a moment or two in a gentleman's company and, afterwards, to just relish the memories. Why was it so important to her then, she wondered. As a precaution, Lisa had given her a phone number that was safe to call, as long as she was calling from a safe phone herself. So it was still possible to reach Lisa later and it represented the last connection Marie had to Daniel.

Marie had left Shakespeare and Company immediately after Daniel had called from the cab. They had to minimize the risk that she would be connected to Lisa, thereby revealing her connection to Daniel. When she headed for the bookstore earlier, she had done everything to make sure she wasn't being followed. She should, however, have understood to remove the battery from her cell phone so that the movements of her phone couldn't be tracked. She also should have pulled some of her old clothes and an old purse out of storage, in case her normal clothes had tracking devices. Her worst mistake, however, had been calling the cab using her own phone. In the heat of the moment and under pressure from Lisa, she hadn't realized the risk she was taking. There was nothing she could do about it now. She just hoped it wouldn't be the link to reveal her, at least not before she had a chance to do something about it.

She headed along the bank of the Seine toward St-Michel Metro station, but decided to drop in at Gibert Jeune's bookstore first. It would reinforce the idea that she was simply wandering through bookstores. Deep down she knew that her visit to Shakespeare and Company, at precisely the same time as everything with Daniel was going down, would be quite difficult to explain. In Place St-Michel and its surroundings, there were many Gibert Jeune bookstores, all decorated with yellow awnings that specified the subject matter of each particular store. Marie selected the most familiar to her, a bookstore specializing in scientific literature, located on the other side of the square.

While browsing through the physics' books, Marie was reminded of her conversation with Raymond from the evening before. There was something odd about his reaction when she had told him about her problem at work. She could clearly recollect the look on Raymond's face; it had been untroubled and calm. There hadn't even been an inkling of anger in his expression even though he had just been told that someone close to him was begin treated unjustly. Raymond usually erupted over the smallest things and if someone he was close to were being threatened, he normally turned into a raging bull, unless, of course, he had been behind the whole thing to begin with! The whole situation must be some type of plot to get him back into her good graces. It was well-construed, however, because it seemed that there was nothing that could be done about it.

Marie couldn't imagine seeing Raymond anymore. There was no way she could sufficiently hide her fears so that Raymond wouldn't suspect that she knew something. On its own, the help he was providing to save her job would be enough, not to mention all the other information he had revealed to her. She simply knew too much about Raymond and the idea that he might realize that was horrifying. Everything that had happened felt like an overwhelming mess; a mess that would be both impossible and unpleasant to straighten out. She just wanted away from it all. Her work community had betrayed her and there was nothing else holding her here.

She knew that she couldn't just leave Paris without informing anyone, because that would set off a search. Besides, if she disappeared, it would raise Raymond's suspicions, particularly after she had asked for his assistance. She supposed she also needed to find a way to bring about a dignified ending to her career at the university. First, she would buy some time by saying that she had become ill. After a few days, she could then seek a medical certificate stating that she was burned out, which would make sense after all that she was dealing with at work. It would also serve as an unofficial notification that she was giving up the fight for her job. Raymond could then freely decide to do something to help her or drop the issue completely – that was his choice. After a few more days, she would send Raymond a text message saying that she was flying to Australia to check out an interesting job offer. It wasn't far-fetched, since she'd recently received an actual job offer from Macquarie University in Sydney. She had even acquired a visa to go and visit the university. For now, she would need to keep her phone turned off, but she would notify Raymond late in the evening that she was running a high fever.

* * *

Maurice had immediately suspected that he would end up on the thugs' list of targets, since he also knew he was the only person in Daniel's address book, and he understood exactly why these guys had called him. He decided to take a few days off and stay with the national team at the hotel. It was both a practical move and one that made him feel safer, especially since he'd be sharing a room with an enormous bull of a lineman. His cousin, who worked at the bistro, could run the business as long as he needed, as he had often done in the past. Maurice would notify the staff that he would be out of town for the next week just in case anyone came to the restaurant asking about him.

* * *

Raymond huffed with determination as he began to rattle off instructions to his contact.

"Forget the Porte Maillot area! You won't find the Finn there; instead you need to focus on his circle of contacts. First, find out where they all live."

"Who all do you mean?" the contact asked, just to be sure.

"Find out everything you can about that Maurice, at least. You can find out from the bookstore which women were working there today and then follow each of them. And Marie, of course. Where is she now, by the way? I can't seem to reach her by phone." Raymond asked, his tone increasingly frustrated.

"Yesterday you told us to leave her alone for the time being," the contact responded, but in a way as not to expose his own frustration for fear it would send Raymond into a rage.

Raymond remembered taking the tail off Marie, because he'd assumed that they would be meeting up soon and he couldn't stand the idea of being followed.

"Okay, forget Marie for now. I'll be in touch with her soon anyway. But check out all the others carefully. Make sure your tail is absolutely hidden and be prepared that the Finn could also be shadowing these same individuals to make sure they are not being followed – if he intends on contacting any of them," Raymond continued.

"How do you want us to deal with their apartments?"

"When the tails have ensured that their subjects are far enough away, go inside the apartments and check everything. First, however, make sure that there is no one else in the apartment. In any case, go in dressed as maintenance guys," Raymond answered and then hung up abruptly.

* * *

Lisa felt calm after her friend Elena assured her that Daniel had safely reached his destination. Elena had sounded irritated and, in response to Lisa's delicate inquiry, she grumbled that she didn't like macho men. Nothing about Daniel was macho other than his looks, but it wasn't worth getting into any debate. She was in no hurry to see Daniel, since she had already announced a while back that she was going on a date that evening. Elena had filled the refrigerator with enough food and made up the bed. The apartment's library held enough books to keep Daniel occupied, but he would probably go to sleep early anyway after all the trials of the day. She would be tired herself if she weren't cheered by the thought of her upcoming date.

* * *

Raymond waited impatiently to hear a progress report on the search. Finally, around midnight, his phone rang.

"Hope I didn't wake you," said a familiar voice.

"Tell me what you know," Raymond said without bothering to address the contact's comment.

"Maurice seems to be out of town. At least that's what the staff at his restaurant claimed, and judging by our observation of his apartment, there doesn't seem to be anyone there. There were two women and one old man working at the bookstore. For now, we aren't considering the old guy anyone of interest," the contact explained in a calm voice.

"What did you find out about the women?"

"One of them is a young, goddess-like, organic version of Pamela Anderson, and my guys were practically ripping each other apart for the honor of tailing her. She was picked up from the bookstore after closing by a young French man, with whom she is now enjoying the Parisian nightlife. The other woman is plainer looking, maybe just under forty. She left the bookstore and proceeded directly to Le Procope restaurant to have dinner with some wealthy-looking woman," the contact reported.

Raymond was again overcome with annoyance, since it seemed that his guesswork was leading nowhere.

"Where do they each live?" Raymond decided to ask.

"Maurice lives near the Finn's apartment on Île St-Louis, the forty-year-old woman in Clichy and, I was just getting to this, guess where the sex bomb lives?" the contact asked, barely able to contain his enthusiasm.

"Where?"

"In Porte Maillot, pretty close to the address where the cab dropped off the Finn!" the guy answered with measured emphasis as if trying to lend his statement more weight.

There was a long pause, which the contact felt the need to cut off.

"Did you hear me, Porte Maillot!" he said a bit louder.

"It's just a diversion, a new false lead," Raymond answered, lost in his thoughts.

"A beautiful woman is a good suspect, because we would be likely to believe that the Finn would fall for her," Raymond added quietly.

"Don't you get it? All that and she happens to be American!" the guy snapped. He was irritated that his surprising news hadn't drummed up the reaction he was expecting.

Raymond became more alert all of a sudden. Perhaps the American woman was the Finn's CIA contact.

"Nothing is clear yet. Case the apartments of both women now. The Finn wouldn't have gone to Maurice's apartment, since returning to the island would have been too risky. Especially since he knows that Maurice is listed in his phone's address book. Continue to trail the women, and keep surveillance on Maurice's apartment and restaurant."

"What should we do if we locate the Finn?" the guy asked, since there had been no instructions for that scenario.

"...WHEN you locate the Finn, cut off his balls! That should be enough of a warning for the Americans. Even though they can't seek revenge on me, I don't want to provoke them too much by killing their agent. If the Americans do make contact after that, I can always claim to be getting even with Marie's stalker without them knowing that I know the Finn is their agent or whoever's agent he is," Raymond said, detailing the plan he had already devised.

Once he hung up the phone, Raymond began to feel his self-confidence returning. His intuition told him that the Finn would be found very soon. Cutting off his balls would guarantee, even after recovery, that the Finn wouldn't be any threat with regard to Marie. Speaking of Marie, why wasn't she answering her phone or text messages? He wanted to go and see her, but he knew the search operation might require rapid action and he didn't want to be running the operation from her place. At any rate, he planned to stop by and see her in the morning or to send someone to look for her.

Part Two

I went for years not finishing anything. Because, of course, when you finish something you can be judged.
- Erica Jong

8 SENSE AND SENSIBILITY
Jane Austen 1811

The entire building had been renovated since Henry Miller's time and I suspected that nothing was left from his time other than memories. Lisa's apartment was a loft apartment and, on a Parisian scale, unusually spacious. The apartment was more than 100 square meters, and comprised a living room equipped with a large kitchen bar, two bedrooms, a library, a study, a half bath and a separate bathroom with a bathtub. Lisa's friend had made up a bed for me in one of the bedrooms, which had a wide loft bed with a sofa suite beneath it. She showed me the food she had stocked in the refrigerator and left quickly without saying very much. I had smiled and thanked her genuinely for all her help, but got no response or reaction. In the end, I felt relieved when she finally left and shut the door behind her.

First, I decided to follow doctor's orders and shower my

wound. There was surprisingly little pain in the area of the wound and so I decided to stop taking the Ibuprofen. I was glad that there were no signs of any infection. After the shower, I wrapped a towel around my waist and opened a bottle of red wine, Romanée-Conti 2000, that I found in the kitchen. The wine tasted exquisite and the selection of cheeses that I found in the refrigerator calmed the pang in my stomach nicely. After everything I'd experienced, I was finally starting to relax and exhaustion began to take over my body. My eyelids fell shut of their own accord and I was transported, in my sleep, back to my apartment. I was startled awake when the men I had encountered in the morning forced their way into the apartment. I was just about to shout out, but the shout caught in my throat when I looked around me and realized that I was not in my apartment but in Lisa's empty living room.

I got up off the sofa to stay awake, since even a short doze had proven to be especially unpleasant and I was in no hurry to return to that world. I walked around the apartment looking for signs of Lisa's life, but I didn't see a single photograph or object that would have told me something about their owner. I had imagined Lisa's apartment to be much more modest, and I couldn't figure out how she could afford this kind of luxury. From what I understood, her parents were quite wealthy, but she had given an indication that her relationship with her father was not particularly close.

I turned on the TV and found the CNN channel. I couldn't remember the last time I had watched a program that I could understand entirely. The weather forecast for Europe got me thinking about Marie again and I shut off the TV, because I didn't want to be reminded. I sat down on the sofa again to enjoy the last of the wine and my mind drifted immediately into a state between sleep and awake. I was still only covered by the towel around my hips, but I was too tired to search for anything to wear. I pulled the blanket off the back of the sofa, covered myself with it and promptly fell asleep.

* * *

Lisa was not especially sad, even though the evening at Le Procope hadn't met her expectations. She did, after all, get to dine in a historical landmark that she could never have afforded on her own salary. The last train had already gone, so the only option left was to hail a cab. She kept looking behind the cab the whole ride home for signs of anyone following her, but she didn't see anything, even when the traffic thinned out as they neared Clichy. At the gate to her building, she glanced around for any suspicious people or cars, but didn't notice anything out of the ordinary. The steel fence and gate with its electric lock suddenly seemed useful, and the metal clang of the gate closing behind her was music to her ears. At the front door of the building, she decided to do a final check, and she waited for a moment just inside the dark entryway. From her vantage point behind the glass doors, she could see the entire inner yard and the area around the gate without anyone being able to see her in the shadows. After waiting and watching for five minutes, she felt satisfied that she wasn't being followed.

She opened the door to her apartment carefully, but stopped right inside the door. Something wasn't right. She felt she should turn and leave immediately or get someone's help, but curiosity and anger forced her forward. This was her apartment and she wasn't going to be made to fear being in her own home. She threw on all the lights and waited for a moment. The apartment was empty, but she could tell right away that someone had paid her a visit.

* * *

I dreamed I was playing American football on the French national team. I was playing fullback once again and Maurice was the quarterback. We were in a Double Wing offense formation – so tight that the linemen's little toes were touching. The entire team was in line: two tight ends and, instead of receivers, two wingbacks at each end of the line. As fullback, I was positioned in a three-point stance directly behind Maurice and out of sight of the defense. The whole formation resembled a plow, just like on the stairs the previous morning. Maurice called a trap play in which the intention was to hand the ball off to me after a slight delay.

Through my sleeping state, I heard sounds coming from the stairwell of the building, but my mind reassured me and sleep held me steadfast in her grip. The sounds mixed with my dreams and screwed with our game. Suddenly, I noticed that the opponent's defensemen were wearing long, black leather jackets. I tried to warn Maurice, but he couldn't hear me over his own starting command.

"Down – set – hut – hut..."

The wingback was in motion and Maurice made it look as if he were going to hand off the ball to him, but then he turned and imperceptibly gave the ball to me. I began to follow the blocking guard that appeared in front of me as he blocked the defense from impeding my progress. Suddenly, the entire field was open in front of me and I took off like a shot. I saw the men in black pull out their weapons and I managed to hear the first shot.

* * *

I squirmed on the sofa and a shooting pain in my wound woke me. The room was dark and silent, but I sensed that someone was nearby. I felt the hair on my skin rise and I was suddenly as awake as anyone can be. I didn't tense up, however. I actually felt surprisingly relaxed and calm. I considered pretending to be asleep in order to buy myself time to think of my options and possibilities. I prepared to spring from the sofa once I was able to visualize the threat facing me. Adrenaline pumped through my veins and I shivered. Instead of fear, my head filled with fight and determination. I didn't feel any rage, however; I felt as if I were in the calm eye of a whirlwind of emotions. I was composed and ready for battle.

"Daniel," a woman's voice whispered.

I was completely confused and filled with mixed emotions. Suddenly Lisa appeared out of nowhere in front of me.

"Is something wrong? You look odd and frightened," she said in a soft and soothing tone.

I couldn't get out a single word.

* * *

Raymond waited impatiently for news on the search for the Finn. His anxiety had been assuaged by a text message from Marie, which stated that she had come down with a high fever and had slept the whole day with the ring tone on her phone switched off. Marie said she was going to the doctor the next day, so their date would have to wait. Raymond was, in the end, grateful for the delay, since the search for the Finn called for his full attention.

Raymond awoke to his phone ringing in the middle of the

night.

"Yeah?" he answered half asleep.

"Unfortunately, we haven't been able to find anything. Casing the apartments of those women was a waste of time. The American woman stayed overnight at the French guy's place and there was nothing of use in her apartment. We managed to piece together the identity of the French guy too, and we checked out his apartment while he was partying with the woman. There was no one in the other woman's apartment. She came home from Le Procope alone in a cab. There was no activity in Maurice's apartment either."

"Ok. It appears we're following the wrong leads. Tell your guys to get some rest, but be on stand-by. I need some time to think of how to proceed," Raymond stated, hiding his disappointment.

He knew there was a chance that the whole episode was just a diversion tactic meant to draw attention to the wrong things. Whoever was tracking him may be using this time to plan something completely different. Maybe the Finn, himself, was part of a set-up meant only to lead Raymond to the Finn's apartment. If that were the case, then the information he got from the phone was likely false and the phone had been left behind on purpose. It seemed probable that the Finn had never actually been in the building, which would explain his mysterious disappearing act. It would be best to forget the whole guy and just lay low for awhile. He just had to think about everything that had happened and wait for the true adversary to reveal himself.

* * *

I didn't even have time to get up before Lisa was rushing

forward to hug me. She didn't say anything else, just hugged me tightly. After nearly a minute of silence she drew back and looked me in the eyes.

"I'm so glad you're safe! I should also probably tell you that your towel has fallen open."

I looked down and noticed that, for all intents and purposes, I was naked.

"Sorry about that," I said embarrassedly.

She didn't dwell on the issue and changed the subject.

"Someone broke into my apartment!"

"I don't understand. Someone broke in here?"

"No, silly, this isn't my apartment! Did you think I could afford a place like this?" she laughed and then continued to explain further. "This is the holiday home of my father's American friend. I just serve as the caretaker of the place."

"So you figured your own apartment would be too dangerous for me?" I asked, amazed that I hadn't thought of the danger myself.

"Yeah, but I think I finally managed to get taken off the list of suspects, so this place is also safer now", she said proudly.

"Are you sure you weren't followed?" I asked with concern.

"Don't worry. I waited in my apartment for a long time before I came here. I drove my scooter without the lights on and took a longer spin before I drove here. I also took a route that cars can't take, stopping every now and then just to make sure no one was following. I parked the scooter at the other end of this street and left my phone at home to prevent anyone from being able to track my movements." Both her plan and explanation were thorough.

"Where do you live then?" I was curious to know.

"You would have seen my building when you came here. It's the ugly apartment building about two hundred meters in that direction. I drove nearly two kilometers to come here now though," she added.

There was something different about Lisa that I hadn't noticed earlier. She was a lot more confident in this setting than she was as a salesperson at Shakespeare and Company. At the bookstore, she had always been dressed in modest clothes that hid her figure, but now I found myself staring in amazement at the beautiful flow of her tunic-like dress. The material looked like suede, but was a lot thinner and hugged her figure in all the right places. The tassels and earth-tone beads that hung from the hem of the dress made me think of the American Indian princess, Pocahontas. Most of all, however, I was mesmerized by her strong sense of presence. Her normal lack of presence was the reason I had paid so much more attention to Sarah, even though Lisa had undeniably provided me with the best customer service.

She sat down on the other end of the sofa with her bare ankles crossed gracefully. Her body leaned slightly toward me and she had pulled up the hem of her tunic just enough to enable her knees to settle into a more comfortable and natural position. She placed her right arm on the back of the sofa while her left hand rested lightly on the edge, palm open with her bare wrist facing me. As she talked, she used her hands expressively and freely, and she tilted her head back whenever she laughed. Her green eyes seemed to sparkle and the pupils dilated clearly when she got excited. I couldn't take my eyes off hers, because I was amazed that along with a playful glimmer, they also contained such compassion and deep intellect.

"You look stunning," I heard myself say.

"Thanks!" she said with a warm, wide smile.

Lisa asked me to recount the events of the day and listened closely, interrupting only briefly to ask questions. When she heard Maurice's plan, she burst into laughter, but then she became serious once again. When I was done telling what had happened, she told her side of the story and about Marie's integral involvement. I thought I detected a certain warmth in Lisa's voice when she mentioned Marie.

"Seems like Marie is quite fond of you," she stated all of a sudden.

Ambivalent feelings coursed through me, since it was exactly what I wanted to hear, but at the same time, the knowledge that our paths wouldn't cross again made me feel melancholy. Lisa read my mind.

"There should be some champagne chilling here. How about we crack a bottle of Bollinger?" she asked cheerily.

"That's a great idea! I should confess though that I drank a great bottle of Bordeaux when I first arrived. I'll replace it, but I think it might have been quite an expensive bottle," I said, regretting my careless selection.

"Don't worry about it, pet. I have permission to partake of the bounty in this apartment as long as I am entertaining good male company. My father's friend is worried about my social life," she explained as she bounced off to the kitchen with the beads of her tunic swinging.

A moment later, I heard the joyful pop of the bottle being opened and she returned with a champagne cooler, the bottle and two champagne glasses. The way she walked with her bare feet was particularly sexy. There was something slightly boyish and confident about her gait, but also intentionally flirtatious.

We sat on the sofa sipping our champagne and telling

things about ourselves that we never would have uttered in the sanctity of the bookstore. Our discussion resembled a dance, but instead of either of us leading, we were guided together by a common thread of thought. If one of us tilted our head or leaned forward, the other followed suit a moment later. When the conversation picked up momentum, it did so for both of us. We were like soul mates seeking safety and warmth, each from the other. I began to feel the need for another kind of warmth, even though the room wasn't particularly cold.

"I think I need to put on a shirt," I stated, again aware that I was still just wearing a towel.

"Let me have a look at your wound first," she said as the blanket fell away from my side.

She drank a sip of her champagne and leaned across the sofa toward me, resting on her left hand, whereby her upper arms squeezed her chest up and outward. It also accentuated the otherwise open neckline of the tunic. She stroked my side, being careful not to touch the wound itself, by gently running her forefinger and middle finger along either side of the wound, from one end to the other. The soft, feminine scent of her perfume overwhelmed my sense of smell. My passion had been building up the entire time we sat on the sofa together and now she was completely irresistible to me. A powerful erection struggled to free itself from the towel still around my waist, and it was something she could not ignore. Gentle but determined fingers wrapped around my wrists and pinned them to the sofa as her lips, chilled from the cold champagne, pressed against my lips. She had to move closer on the sofa in order to kiss me properly, but she went one step further and sat astride me, careful, however, not to tighten the towel across my lap. Our lips, softened by tenderness and moistened by champagne, teased one another, caressing and seeking to make contact between every point and nerve-ending. Our kiss lasted a long time, but despite all the tenderness, it wasn't especially passionate. She remained holding my wrists when our lips finally parted.

"I'm not sure quite how to say this. Surely you already know what an amazing body you have, and the guy bulging from beneath that towel would undoubtedly be a welcome sight for most women. You also know how much I value your friendship," she explained slowly.

I wasn't sure how to respond or what was coming, but I did understand now why she had pinned my hands; she didn't want me to do anything but listen.

"I'm a lesbian," she said with complete assurance.

I hadn't seen that coming, but, for some reason, I wasn't taken aback either. My overriding feeling was one of empathy for a friend, and I was sure it showed in my eyes. I remained speechless in place and that encouraged her to continue.

"I wanted you to know before you got too enthusiastic. I think it would be wrong of me to make love to you, since I would only be going through the motions."

"I understand. My arousal was just a spontaneous reaction, but there would be something wrong with me if I hadn't reacted that way to you," I explained.

I was disappointed, of course, but I accepted the situation because I understood the reasoning behind it.

"Maybe I shouldn't have kissed you," she said in an apologetic tone.

"It was wonderful, as was our whole time here on the sofa together. There is no reason to feel any regret," I said.

"I really do love you. Not in the way a woman does a man, but somehow still different from the love one has for a friend. That's why I wanted to kiss you, and I also think it was wonderful." Her voice, at any other time, would have been interpreted as passionate.

Since I didn't respond right away, she continued again.

"Did you know that people are more susceptible to love after they have experienced extreme fear? Many people think that courage is the opposite of fear, but that's actually the opposite of cowardice. Everyone who has the capacity to feel has experienced fear, and the opposite of fear is love."

I still didn't know what to say, because love was a word I never used lightly and any other expression I could have used seemed too tame for the situation. She wasn't waiting for me to respond in any way, however.

"Could you sleep beside me tonight anyway? After all that's happened, I could use some closeness." Her appeal was presented in an innocent way.

9 QUIET DAYS IN CLICHY

Henry Miller 1956

I awoke to Lisa gently stroking my side. I opened my eyes and was greeted by her warm smile directly in front of my face.

"Good morning sweetie," she whispered.

"Morning, my dear friend," I said, half asleep.

For a long time, we just silently gazed into each other's eyes and she continued to stroke up and down the length of my side, from shoulder to pelvis. That's when I realized I was naked. I remembered that it had seemed logical after our discussion the evening before and normal, since I slept in the nude at home as well. Right at that moment, however, I also happened to have a strong morning erection and we were under the same large double duvet. On top of that, I had a pressing need to go to the bathroom.

"I have a slight problem," I said.

"And what might that be?" she asked, with a twinkle in her

eye.

"I need to use the bathroom and I'm naked."

"Go ahead," she encouraged.

"I also seem to have a spontaneous morning hard-on, which has nothing to do with arousal," I continued, feeling slightly awkward.

"Even better! Do you think I don't like looking at naked men just because I'm a lesbian?" she asked and pulled the cover away from my body.

Instead of pulling the cover back over me, covering myself otherwise or charging out of the room, I decided to remain where I was for a moment and see if she was a woman of her word. She read my mind and measured me up with her eyes without even the inkling of a smile on her face.

"Not bad. Didn't you need to use the bathroom?" she reminded me playfully.

When I got back to the bedroom, she was still lying on the bed under the cover.

"Come back and lie down." Her voice took on a slightly commanding tone.

Lisa raised the edge of the cover and I caught a glimpse of her naked body. Apparently my face revealed what I was thinking and it encouraged her to go ahead and completely expose herself to me.

"In the name of equality, I thought it only right that you see me naked too, even though my overweight body isn't much to look at," she said as a means of belittling herself.

I wondered whether Lisa was testing me in the same way I had tested her a minute earlier, and so I decided to remain standing next to the bed calmly admiring her figure. I had thought of myself as being self-confident, but suddenly I was unsure of what I should do with my hands. Letting them hang loosely should be natural, but in that situation, it would have made me look indifferent. Putting them behind my back would have looked foolish, and crossing them over my chest would have been arrogant. Finally, I decided to raise them up behind my neck and my face broke out in a huge smile. I felt even more naked and vulnerable, but I was also showing her that I enjoyed her looking at me. I didn't have to pretend, because my body made my enjoyment obvious.

"You can see for yourself how I feel about your body," I stated, completely enjoying this situation.

I jumped flat on my back onto the bed next to Lisa and the wave it created in the waterbed sent her into the air and directly on top of me. We laughed uninhibitedly at our little mishap and she lingered where she was for a moment. She rose up on my chest, supported by her elbows, and looked at me with such gratefulness in her eyes.

"That was a lovely thing to say. I have always had a complex about my figure, but I'm gradually beginning to accept myself as I am. Even Marie compared me to a painting by Rubens," she said with a satisfied chuckle.

"That's a great comparison, except I think you are an improved version of the women in his paintings."

"Would you eat breakfast in bed, if I get up and make it?" she asked.

"Definitely! And if you happen to find some coffee as well..." I was excited about the idea of a lazy Saturday.

She got out of the bed and I admired the feminine curve of her hips and roundness of her buttocks as she walked away from me.

"Venus in front of the mirror," I said, remembering one Rubens' painting that reflected this vision well. She turned her head and smiled approvingly. It seemed wise, however, not to mention that the female figure in that particular painting was one that I found especially alluring.

* * *

Marie was truly relieved when Raymond had accepted the delay of their date, and hadn't even offered to come and take care of her. It would have been easy to turn down, however, by just saying that she didn't want anyone seeing her in her present state. Such an excuse would have enabled her to be firm without giving Raymond any reason to suspect anything.

The more she thought about her situation, the more assured she was about the urgency to leave Paris. She decided not to care so much about her job. It would be enough to send an e-mail announcing her resignation for health reasons. She could send a medical certificate afterwards, if one was required. She believed her resignation would be nothing short of a relief to the university administration and that they would accept it with little resistance, despite the fact that it wasn't normal protocol. She wrote the message right away without any emotion, but when she pressed the Send button, a flood of relief washed over her. Her next task was to find the first suitable flights to Australia. She chose a KLM flight from Paris to Sydney, leaving at 9:40 a.m. the next morning. That would give her the day to pack what she needed, and what little remained, she could ask a friend to store in her own cellar storage space. The fact that the apartment had been rented, fully furnished, from the university made it even easier to pack up and leave. She also planned to ask a friend if she could stay at her place overnight, just to play it safe. In the morning, she would send a text message to Raymond from the airport stating that she was on her way to a new job in Australia and wasn't coming back. She would say that she didn't mention it earlier, because she hadn't wanted him to try and stop her. Raymond would either believe her explanation or not, but either way, he would likely be furious.

* * *

Lisa had found another bottle of Bollinger, which we savored at the end of our breakfast as we lounged on the bed's large pillows. We luxuriated in a euphorically peaceful state in which there was no need to say anything. After a long while, Lisa finally broke the silence.

"You never told me about your background in sports. Did you really play American football? I'm interested in sports, since I played competitive volleyball when I was younger."

"Well, originally I was into track and field, particularly the discus throw. I even managed to throw the youth record in Finland, even though I was a lot shorter at that time and my arm span was too narrow for a discus thrower. When I threw the small discus, I had great speed, but as the size of the discus increased as I grew older, it screwed up my technique. I tried to compensate with intense weight training, and it did improve my results, but I never felt I was able to get close enough to the results of the top national athletes. Maybe I was just too ambitious, but it caused me to lose my motivation in the end," I explained.

"How did you get into American football then?"

"I was looking for something new and decided to be an exchange student in the United States. I was placed at Everett High School in Massachusetts. Once I got there, I was immediately recruited to the football team, since my speed and strength made me ideal for the sport. During that year, I grew as much as ten centimeters, so that even further ensured that coaches saw me as their dream player. Not many people realize how much physical prowess track and field sports require, but that background enabled me to get results in the team's physical testing that would have qualified me among professionals. That got people's attention, along with the fact that I played both offense and defense, as well as breaking school records for both runs and tackles. It made me sort of a local celebrity. Soon after that, the offers for football scholarships starting pouring in from different universities and I decided to continue my playing career in the US after I completed the matriculation examination in Finland," I explained, not even trying to mask the pride I felt about my accomplishments.

"So you returned to the US to study and play?" she continued, still showing interest.

"American football took hold in Finland just at the time I was returning from my exchange year, and I continued to play in Finland, even though the level of the game was pretty undemanding in the beginning. I trained seriously, though, using the methods I had learned in track and field, since I was ambitious enough to want to play for a big university, as well as being interested in the academic benefits. Eventually, I ended up at UCLA, which plays in the NCAA Division I-A. The UCLA Bruins had been, at times, among the ten best university teams, but when I started there, the team had been on a losing streak for some time. Luckily, the turnaround happened right around that same time," I rattled on, enjoying the fact that I had a captive audience.

"Did you become a college star, too, then?"

"Even though I was physically ready, the speed of the game

came as quite a shock to me. The problem wasn't my running speed, that was fine, but everything on the field happened much faster than I was used to and I felt like my brain was on overload. I did become a legend, but not for my playing skills on the field." I grinned as I played back the memories in my head.

"Oh, do tell," she encouraged, as she noticed my pause as I relived the flood of memories.

"At the team's first weight training session, we were working on the snatch lift. The snatch is an Olympic weightlifting method in which you extend your arms and lift the barbell straight over your head in one fluid motion. I was really familiar with the method, because it's used in track and field and was one of the standard training techniques for discus throwing. I decided that time, however, to play a little joke."

"I love practical jokes!"

"The barbell held 180 pounds, or about 80 kilos, and only the team's strongest were able, despite their poor technique, to accomplish the snatch. I asked the coach if I could give it a try. He didn't know anything about me, but despite his doubts, he gave me the green light to try. I pretended to be completely incapable and fumbled around insecurely, trying to get a grip on the bar. Then I snatched the bar up over my head on straight arms, nearly without any real squat to get me under the bar. But that was just the beginning. I made it seem like the bar was too heavy and was pulling me backward. Everyone started shouting at me to let it go. I didn't let go, however, and when the bar clattered down onto the floor behind me, I was still holding onto it with my body arching backward."

"Did you get hurt?" she asked, concerned.

"Of course not! From that position, I stated in a loud voice, 'Damn it, I am NOT giving up.' Then I did the whole snatch in reverse, lifting the bar straight up from that position. At first, the whole room was silent, but then everyone there broke out in the loudest applause I've ever heard, accompanied, of course, by a lot of laughter. The event was legendary and I hear they are still talking about it today. If I'm honest, I have to admit that I had practiced a similar move with wrestlers and javelin throwers, even with weights, but I had never tried it with weights that big." I finished my story with a boyish sense of pride.

"What happened to your career after that?"

"After a lot of hard work, I managed to keep up with the pace of the game and I ended up playing the position of linebacker in the starting lineup. I started to believe in the possibility of a professional career, which, financially, was quite a tempting option. But that was before the 1983 season, which went unusually poorly for our team. We lost four games, but by some miracle, we managed to make it to number one in our own Pac-10 Conference and into the Rose Bowl. We played against Illinois, which had been ranked fourth in the nation that year. No one really thought we stood a chance." Reliving the final moments of my playing history made me feel a bit melancholy.

"You sound sad. Did you lose the game?" Lisa asked, because she obviously sensed I was describing my last moments on the field.

"It was a Sunday, the second of January 1984. It was sunny and nearly 30 degrees. The stands were filled to the brim with about 103,000 people. You can probably imagine what that might feel like. We actually won the game 45–9, even though half our team was suffering from a stomach virus. So, I ended my career having been part of one of the all-time records, which remains unbroken. During the game, the quarterback for

Illinois threw three interceptions and I succeeded in catching one of them. As I took off with the ball toward the Illinois goal line, my foot got caught between two players who'd been downed. Then one of our players, who was coming to block for me, tripped and rammed into the knee of my trapped leg. I remember that my eyes clouded over, but somehow I remained on my feet. The pain was so intense when I finally limped off toward the sideline that, by accident, I went to the opposing team's bench. They ended up sending me by ambulance to the hospital, where the doctors determined that I had torn my anterior cruciate ligament," I said, wincing as I remembered the pain of that moment.

"So I guess that was what ended your career?"

"It wouldn't have had to end there, if I'd had surgery on my knee and gotten a knee support. But the risks were too high and I knew that my shot as a professional were considerably weakened by the injury. Something else happened during that game, however, that, together with the injury, changed the course of my life," I continued, a smile returning to my lips.

"What was that?"

"In the second half, when the score was 38–3, the stadium's digital scoreboard flashed Caltech 38, M.I.T 3. Those schools represented the high tech elite, and both happened to have especially horrible football teams. The students of Caltech thought it would be a good practical joke, and it got as much attention as the game itself. It wasn't until years later that I understood how their joke had played a key role in inspiring my studies, their application and the foundation of my own company."

"Do you mean optimization programming? Judging by your appearance, it seems that sports stayed a big part of your life anyway," Lisa stated.

"Yeah, programming became my life's work. Sports was just a healthy hobby, since I was never able, due to circumstances or merits, to achieve the level I wanted to. Then again, I also never burned myself out in the hard training that top athletes have to endure. I continued to lift weights, competed in discus throwing for fun and also sparred with wrestlers in a local club."

"My brother was into wrestling. Were you really a wrestler?" she asked surprised.

"Not really, I mean I never competed. My father was a wrestler and he taught me how to wrestle practically from the age I could walk. Of course, that was just playful wrestling; I never could have wrestled with my dad seriously, because of our size difference. It did give me an understanding of movement, however, which ended up helping me in other sports," I said, feeling sad as I thought about my father, who was now deceased.

"My brother always said that wrestling was the sport of intelligent men." I could tell from Lisa's voice that she was proud of her brother.

"Wrestling is a bit like chess. You have to be able to anticipate future moves; each move you make causes your opponent to react in a way that creates a new situation, and so on. Everything happens so quickly, so a good wrestler has to have intuition about where things are leading and whether there is a danger of ending up in a joint lock," I explained.

"What's a joint lock?"

"Joint locks aren't actually allowed in regular competitive wrestling, but their purpose is to manipulate your opponent into a position that causes a specific joint to be pushed to its physical limit. This forces the opponent to surrender, since they obviously wouldn't want any broken limbs," I explained.

"Yuck, that's pretty brutal."

"My father taught me locks from the time I was little so I would be able to avoid them. His one rule was that locks should never be used, even playfully. He was a smart guy and made me repeat this rule to him so that I was sure to internalize it rather than trying to use it as a means of defiance," I added, finally grasping the deeper meaning behind my father's teaching method.

Suddenly, Lisa leapt onto my stomach and with a smirk on her face, said, "Let's wrestle!"

* * *

Raymond's phone rang during his lunch.

"Raymond?" asked a familiar male voice.

"Anything new?" Raymond asked back.

"We found out one new and interesting piece of information!"

"Spit it out!" Raymond demanded.

He felt that a breakthrough was about to occur.

"We went back to that cab that the Finn used and searched the driver's phone. Guess whose phone made the call to order the cab?"

"I don't have time for riddles," Raymond stated impatiently.

"Marie's phone!" the guy nearly shouted with enthusiasm.

"What? What does that mean?" Raymond asked, confused.

The case was taking an unexpected turn and he felt that it was drawing him closer to an unpleasant surprise.

"Well, it means, of course, that Marie is co-operating with the Finn," said the guy on the other end, stating the obvious.

"Fool! I was referring to the overall scheme!" Raymond

blurted out, feeling frustrated that the theory he had already worked out suddenly seemed to be growing more complicated.

"Should we pick her up from her apartment?" the guy asked, but he was feeling defeated by Raymond's lack of gratitude.

"No one touches Marie but me! Are you even sure she is at her apartment? Is her phone being tracked?" Raymond snapped at the guy.

"You said she was sick and told us not to track her," the guy said, increasingly irritated.

"Did I say she was in her apartment? No, just that she's sick. And I never told you to stop tracking her phone, just to stop tailing her!"

The guy on the phone didn't know what to say, and Raymond was too impatient to wait, so he just gave the order to track Marie's phone again and notify him by text message when it had been taken care of. When he got off the phone, he drew a deep breath and exhaled slowly and evenly through tightened lips. He felt his blood pressure lowering and his mind calming, so he picked up his phone and called Marie's number. The phone rang for a long time before a sleepy voice picked up.

"Hello?" Marie said with a questioning tone, since she didn't recognize the caller's number.

"Hey Marie, how are feeling?" Raymond tried to sound friendly.

"Have you changed your number? I don't recognize this one." Marie asked, but then she continued without hearing the answer. "I'm still quite feverish and I'm exhausted."

"I was thinking of stopping by to bring you something to make you feel better. I could also bring anything else you need, so then you don't have to go shopping while you're sick."

Raymond was trying hard to stress the soft tone of his voice.

"Thanks for your concern, but I definitely don't want anyone seeing me when I look like this! Sorry, but I will seriously be angry if you come here," Marie stated.

At that moment, Raymond's phone got a text message.

"Marie, can you wait for just a minute?" Raymond requested and put his phone down.

He quickly logged into the website service and entered Marie's cell phone details. A red dot appeared on the map of Paris that opened in the service and he zoomed in until he could see for sure that Marie's phone was indeed at her home address.

"Sorry, where were we? Oh yeah, so you don't need my help right now. Well, how about if I just check on your situation tomorrow then?" Raymond asked.

"Yeah, that would be better," Marie answered, relieved. "What are your plans for the evening?"

Raymond responded right away. "I will probably just watch TV. Get better and we'll talk tomorrow."

After he hung up, he threw on simple, common-looking riding gear, which he had purchased for just this type of situation. No one would recognize him, at least not on the basis of his appearance. He knew the motorcycle couldn't be connected to him either.

* * *

Lisa rolled me off the pillow so that I lay across the bed. She pinned my hands straight above my head and I didn't resist. She was already so comfortable with our nudity that she didn't quite think about how her wrestling move would end up. Her efforts to pin my hands to the mattress positioned her breasts directly in front of my face, where they brushed lightly against my cheeks. Her skin felt soft like velvet and I could smell the faintest hint of coriander. I didn't know what to think, and she didn't know what to do. The unintentional situation was extremely erotic. She clearly hadn't wanted to seem ashamed and back off, so she remained where she was. We were both silent as we considered our next move. I could feel that she was gripping my wrists even tighter, but the rest of her body signaled that it wasn't because she felt any fear. Finally, I could no longer lie there and allow this situation to pass without taking some advantage of it. I turned my head slightly to the right and took her nipple ever so gently between my lips. She didn't notice right away, which was my intention, since I wasn't ready for her to sense my arousal. Soon, however, her nipple began to swell and I let go to allow my curious eyes to observe the situation.

"I'm not really convinced of your wrestling skills, since you seem to surrender fairly easily," she said while releasing my hands.

"What can I say? Your wrestling holds are unbeatable and you rendered your opponent completely helpless," I answered, smiling at the natural grace of her retreat. Lisa dropped down to my right and supported her head with her left arm while her right hand draped lazily over her stomach. She studied my face and pressed her right palm lightly against the skin of my stomach. I could feel the warmth of her hand and her touch sent a surge through my body. I felt caught in a merciless conflict; there was the humorous competition between a naked man and woman, an ever-growing passion and the temptation of forbidden fruit, and an intensely tender feeling brought on by her gentle touch combined with a burning desire to enter her. My emotions were running high and I tried desperately to quiet myself by breathing more calmly and deeply. The joyful grin disappeared entirely from her face as she leaned close to my ear.

"Don't say anything. Just let me do the talking," she whispered in a soft and soothing voice.

When I said nothing, she continued. "If you don't want me to continue, just stop me gently with your hand."

She pressed her head against my chest and was silent. After a moment, I noticed our breathing had adopted the same calm rhythm. She placed a large pillow behind my neck and back so that I ended up in a half-seated position with my head resting freely on the top edge of the pillow. Then she moved a bit higher than me on the bed so that her chest was at the same height as my head and she gently guided my head to the side to rest against her breasts.

"Let go of your worldly concerns as you rest against my bosom. Close your eyes and try not to think of anything. Listen to the sound of our breathing. Allow your whole body to relax fully." As she spoke, she lowered her voice.

I envisioned myself alone on a sandy beach. The sun warmed my skin and I could feel how a light breeze blew the soft sand unto my stomach. I felt myself sinking and floating over the surface of the sand as if at the bottom of the sea, except that I was able to breathe freely, deeply and slowly.

I'm not sure how long I lay there without moving. Time seemed to have lost all meaning. Lisa's hand caressed all parts of my body, evenly and delicately. I was overcome by a feeling of extreme relaxation and security. The eroticism of the situation had withdrawn to the background, or so I thought.

"You must be strong to resist this, but don't fight against it, because it's a losing battle. No matter how appealing my seductions, you just have to be strong enough to hold your feelings at bay. Listen carefully to what I say and do exactly as I tell you." Her words were like poetry, slow and rhythmic.

"When I tell you to hold back, you will tighten your pelvic floor muscles as if you were trying forcefully to cut off the stream of urine while peeing. At the same time, you will draw your stomach in toward your spine and blow air out through your lips. Don't stop holding back until I give you permission to relax. Try it to see if you understand what I mean," she explained confidently.

It all felt completely natural and it was easy for me to imagine interrupting the flow of urine even without any understanding about pelvic floor muscles.

Lisa bent my legs and spread my knees. Her hands tenderly caressed my torso, working their way down to my lower abdomen. I felt one finger lightly probing the area about two fingers-widths below my naval. She stopped at a specific point and with a bit more pressure began to make a circular motion. It stimulated me in a strange way, as if I were sexually aroused without any direct physical stimulation.

"Just let your muscles relax. Free your mind," she instructed, carefully making note of my reactions.

I felt I was floating in air. Lisa caressed my outer thighs and along my inner thighs slowly, taking her time. I felt myself descending into a blissful dreamlike world, all the while, however, still very much present in the moment. She lifted herself beside me and told me to keep my eyes closed. Her hands found their way to my buttocks and her fingers brushed lightly along the edges of each cheek. Her fingers seemed to be reading my nerve endings like Braille, and it sent cold but pleasant shivers charging through my entire body. I felt myself giving in to this new experience and allowed myself to surrender wholly to her mercy. She read my mind and quietly reassured me. "Don't be afraid. Just try to relax completely."

Lisa's fingers felt heavenly and the only thing I was afraid of was that she would stop. Her fingers paused at my anus and the cold shivers that had passed through me suddenly turned hot. I began to tremble, a little at first, but when her massaging fingers progressed from my perineum toward my testicles, the shaking increased all over and was uncontrollable. Suddenly, the tip of one finger touched a point just under my scrotum and it gave me an immediate and powerful erection. For the first time, she took my shaft in her hand and slid her hand up and down with long, even strokes. All that built up passion that I had been trying to conceal was erupting now in one go. I began to feel the first contractions when she suddenly backed off and stated with emphasis, "Hold back now. Draw your stomach in and blow the air out through your lips."

I felt an insistent need to surrender, but I couldn't give up in front of Lisa. After a few seconds, I felt the orgasm easing off and she encouraged me once again to relax. She pressed her head against my abdomen and we began to breathe at the same even rate.

I didn't even consider the amount of time that had elapsed. I was in such a state of ecstasy that it almost hurt.

"Remember that you mustn't do or say anything, even if your mind says otherwise." Her serious tone was enough to convince me not to even try anything. She got on all fours, turned so that her head was toward my feet and lifted her knee over my chest, so that her spread thighs were positioned squarely over my chest. The scent of a woman entered my nostrils and I felt myself becoming fully excited once again, even though my erection hadn't completely faded from the previous time. She began to caress me with her mouth in slow and carefully orchestrated motions that endeavored to prolong my orgasm. Her vagina was directly in front of my eyes and I saw it open like a butterfly spreading its wings. I heard the quickening of Lisa's breathing and I was sure that she was also aroused. I just couldn't understand why she wouldn't allow me to pleasure her too. But, since she had made it unmistakably clear that she did not want me to do anything, I resolved to close my eyes and focus totally on my own pleasure, just as she had instructed.

I felt the contractions start again and I believed that I was already at the point of no return, when Lisa again stated in a calm but firm voice, "Hold it back. Squeeze, squeeze!"

I was already giving up faith, but her confident encouragement enabled me to hang in there, even when I felt the first drops sneaking through. Again, I was given permission to relax as she licked the drops from the head of my penis.

Lisa got off the bed, grabbed a plastic tube from the closet and squeezed gel from the tube into her left palm. My erection had not yet entirely relaxed, when she swiped her finger through the gel and began to massive the area around my anus. I was nearly driven insane with the pleasure of it all. Suddenly, it felt as if I had sucked her finger inside. She gently probed around my anus and when she located my prostate gland, I felt a sudden overwhelming need to ejaculate. She eased off slightly and my need also retreated. The countless nerve endings in my anus sent tremors of excitement through my body. After what felt like an eternity, she ordered me to open my eyes and we looked deep into each other's gaze. She must have seen the imploring look in my eyes, because she began again to rub her left hand up and down my penis at an accelerated rate. As I felt the first waves of the orgasm approaching, I feared that she would once again command me to hold back, but surprisingly she said, in a deep, sultry voice, "Let it go now."

While continuing to stroke my hard-on, she used the finger of her right hand to milk the prostate gland in my anus. When I finally started to ejaculate, she tightened her grip around my shaft and I felt for a moment that I might explode. As she eased up, I erupted like a megaton volcano.

I lay there for a long time, spent and panting, while Lisa gently stroked my hair. I was incapable, in that moment, of even formulating a thought.

"Do you know that you have made a lasting impression on me and will surely be a meaningful entry in my journal," she whispered.

"How did you learn all that? I didn't think pleasuring men was your specialty," I finally managed to ask.

"That's what books are for," she answered briefly, clearly not wanting to go into any more detail.

"But I'd really like to do the same for you. It's literally painful not to be able to reciprocate when you've been given such an unbelievably amazing experience," I said with growing feelings of guilt.

"You were probably wondering at one point why I was also aroused. Unfortunately, it wasn't because I wanted you specifically. Arousal is infectious and making someone feel good is very arousing," she explained in a way that made my position very clear.

We lay there quietly again. Lisa was tightly wrapped in my

arms with her back to me. I squeezed her tightly against me, since it was the only way I could think of to show my gratitude.

"I gave Marie the cell phone number of the owner of this apartment and the phone is in the kitchen. You can feel free to use it and it'll allow me to get in touch with you if I need to." Her statement took me totally by surprise. "I have a strange feeling Marie will be calling you and that the two of you will meet up yet. So, if you're looking to find a way to reciprocate for what I did for you, then I encourage you to save it for Marie."

10 WARPED PASSAGES
Lisa Randall 2005

Marie knew that Raymond was lying on the phone. The whole time they had been dating, Raymond had never once spent any time watching television, not even to keep her company. He had a continuous need to be doing something and an endless list of plans that needed implementing, so there was no way he could be planning a mindless evening of staring at the TV. The only rational motive for making such a claim had to be that he was covering up his true intentions; in other words, Raymond was actually going to be going out. His lie told her that he intended, indeed, to come by unannounced and unexpectedly. Raymond had also been unusually friendly and understanding on the phone. The fact that he had so easily accepted her rejection of his offer to visit was completely in conflict with who Raymond was as a person; he never took 'no' for an answer. So that must mean that the opposite was now the case and Raymond was livid.

Marie understood that Raymond must have found out that she'd helped Daniel. That also meant that he knew she had information about his role in the whole affair and that he would be afraid she might know much more. Raymond was definitely not coming to yell at her about cheating on him, but rather to find out what she knew and to whom she'd told. She was terrified at the thought of how such an encounter might turn out. She was overwhelmed with panic and felt unable to form a clear thought. She looked around frantically and her eyes locked on the packed suitcase standing ready in the center of the floor. She got an idea, but she needed to hurry.

* * *

Raymond decided to enter Marie's apartment without ringing the doorbell. The guys tailing her had provided him with the code to the electric lock on the outer door and he also had a copy of the key to Marie's front door, which he had made without her knowledge. He was relieved to notice that there was no one in the building lobby or on the stairs. He decided to keep his helmet on, however, just in case someone happened to come along. The stone steps of the building posed no threat of exposure, since they wouldn't creak. Ascending the stairs at a slow rate would be enough to conceal the sounds of his arrival. Marie's door was on the second floor and he paused in front of it to put his ear to the door. He heard no sounds from inside, so Marie wasn't anywhere near the door at least. He had greased the key with Vaseline to minimize any sounds it might make in the lock. He began to ease the key into the lock and when it finally was in place, he carefully turned the key, trying hard not to use any force. He managed to open the lock almost soundlessly. The door seemed new and felt as if it would open without any squeaking of the hinges, but to be safe, he decided to cautiously ease the door open, inch by inch, while also lifting up on the handle to lighten the weight of the door.

The apartment was completely silent and so Raymond could tell that Marie wasn't home. He continued quietly anyway and checked every corner of the entire apartment. No one was there and the only noteworthy thing was a packed suitcase standing in the middle of the floor. Marie was obviously planning on going somewhere. He grabbed his PDA out of his backpack and logged into the cell phone tracking program in the net. According to the program, Marie's phone was still in the building, so he decided to try calling it. It rang for a long time and when no one answered, he tried to hear if it was vibrating somewhere in the apartment. He heard nothing, so he opened the front door to see if it might be ringing somewhere else in the building. He was greeted with total silence. He thought that was strange. Marie must be in the attic or cellar getting something. He figured his only choice was to wait in the apartment for her to return. After all, she had to come back for her suitcase before leaving to go wherever it was she thought she was headed.

Raymond sat on the living room sofa and surveyed the room for some clue of Marie's plans. He spotted her PC in the corner. Its faint hum told him that the computer was on, even though the screen was black. He decided to see what information he could get from it. When he touched the mouse, the screen sprang to life and he smiled when he noted that she hadn't protected the screen with any password. He had urged Marie to protect her computer numerous times and, every time, she had sworn she would do it right away. She also always stated, as an afterthought, that it didn't really matter since she had nothing to hide and, living alone, no one to hide anything from.

He checked her browser and noticed that she had visited the Eurostar train website. If she had ordered her ticket online, it would likely have been sent to her e-mail. Her e-mail program was already open and voilá, the most recent message was a train ticket to London on the last train at 9:13 p.m. So Marie wasn't sick, she was fleeing Paris. Raymond smiled to himself when he realized that Marie's train ride would fit right in with his plans; the trip to London would do well to explain why Marie left Paris, except for the fact that she would never arrive.

* * *

Marie erased her browsing history and then quickly opened several new sites to create a new list, since an emptied history would seem suspicious. Then she went to Eurostar's website and ordered a ticket for the day's last train to London. When the ticket arrived in her e-mail box, she got a better idea. She ordered another ticket for the train departing at 6:13 p.m. When that ticket arrived in her e-mail, she deleted the message immediately. She would also leave her suitcase where it was on the floor as a hint for Raymond.

Marie would need to take the Gerber multi-tool that Raymond had once given her as a gift. She threw on her poplin jacket, grabbed her sweater off the coat rack and walked out the door. She heard no sounds in the hallway and proceeded to climb the stairs. On the top floor, she took out her cell phone and turned down the ring tone as low as possible without shutting it off completely. Then she used the Gerber tool to wrench the vent free from the wall using the pincers. The opening in the wall led to a long ventilation shaft. She shoved her cell phone in as far as she could reach. Then she jammed her sweater in after it and reattached the vent to the wall.

She was just about to start down the stairs when she thought she heard the electric lock of the building's front door. She listened very closely, but heard nothing after that. Even though she figured that she had likely heard wrong, she removed her shoes and began quietly making her way down the stairs. On the third floor landing, she stopped again to listen, because the next floor down was her own. Some intuition told her that Raymond was in the building and, in that case, he was less than ten meters from where she now stood. Just the thought sent cold shivers down her spine.

Marie understood that she was in a stalemate situation. She no longer dared to continue down the stairs without knowing whether or not Raymond was in the building. On the other hand, there was no way to know without making some type of concrete observation. She knew she had to hear or see something and then she could make a decision about her next move. She also knew she couldn't wait too long, because, sooner or later Raymond or his men would begin searching the whole building for her cell phone. The straining to hear something was beginning to make her head ache, but she just had to keep at it. Time was moving threateningly fast and she felt the panic rising within her.

Suddenly she heard a door open on the floor below her and someone stepped out onto the landing. Her heart began to pound and she felt faint. It took only a moment and then the door shut again. She realized that it had been Raymond trying to listen for her phone. She also realized how close she had come to catastrophe. What if he had heard the phone and started up the stairs? Raymond had apparently entered her apartment while she had been on the top floor. And what if she'd taken a bit longer to leave the apartment and had come face to face with Raymond on the landing? This was, however, her last opportunity to get out of the building, even with the risk that Raymond's men were standing watch. She peered carefully around the corner of the stairs and having ascertained that it was clear, she began to make her descent.

* * *

Raymond sat down again on the sofa and nervously drummed the armrest with his fingers. It was taking too long and there was no sign of Marie, even though her phone appeared to still be in the building. He began to get a feeling that something wasn't right. He had no other choice but to call for help.

"Are your guys ready to go?" Raymond asked his contact.

"How many do you need, where and for what?" the contact asked back.

Ten men dressed as maintenance workers arrived in less than 30 minutes and began to search the building, from apartment to apartment. As their cover story, they told everyone that a dangerous, poisonous snake had escaped from its owner; there wasn't a single apartment that objected to their thorough search after that. In each apartment, the men tried conspicuously calling to Marie's phone and then listening for it to ring. Finally, in one of the top floor apartments, they heard the ring tone coming from the neighboring apartment. Once they were inside, they realized that the sound was actually coming from the previous apartment. After spending some time searching back and forth between the two apartments, they decided to recheck the apartments on the floor below as well as in the attic space. After nearly an hour of searching, they located the phone in the hallway ventilation shaft. The group's leader found the stunt humorous, so he had to collect himself before he dared to meet with Raymond.

"Marie managed to deceive us," he stated firmly, but then had to cough at the end of the sentence to cover the smile he felt stirring at the corners of his mouth.

"That means that Marie knew we were coming and left before we even arrived," Raymond said, primarily to himself, and dialed the phone for his contact.

"Put a guy on the train departing for London at 9:13 p.m. I'll send you Marie's ticket by e-mail so you can see where she'll be sitting. She has to be brought back alive, since I want to have a conversation with her first. Tell your guy to drug her or whatever works best in the situation. Make sure it's someone who knows their stuff and call me as soon as you know something."

Raymond sent the search team on its way, but told them first to visit each apartment again to tell everyone that the snake had been found and put down. The panic from a potential snake in the building might have drummed up unwanted attention, if someone decided, say, to call the police. He decided to wait in Marie's apartment for his contact to call. After all, Marie just might come by the apartment at the last minute to retrieve her suitcase or send someone else to pick it up.

Raymond's watch read 9:14, but there was still no phone call. He walked nervously in circles around Marie's apartment, constantly checking the time. At five to ten, the phone rang.

"Don't tell me you failed," Raymond said flat out with a threatening tone.

"Marie never got on the train. My guy searched every corner of the entire train, but there was no sign of her. He is still looking, since he's on the train anyway, but he says he would swear already that Marie is not on that train," explained the contact.

"Merde! That fucking, deceiving whore is still in Paris! Have all the guys you can round up descend on Marie's contacts and find her! I'll send you her e-mail address book by e-mail, and you can start with that. Check all the hotels too, even though I doubt she would dare to stay in any of them. Call me the moment you find out anything," Raymond huffed and hung up the phone before he started to cry with rage.

Nothing could aggravate Raymond more than a woman making a fool of him. He sat down in front of her computer again and opened her e-mail program, while wondering if there was any way to send the entire address register all at once. At that moment, he realized that he hadn't checked anything in the program other than Marie's inbox. He found Marie's letter of resignation to the university in the e-mail's sent folder. It was obvious that Marie had planned on leaving Paris permanently. There was nothing else of interest among the sent mail. Next, he opened the trash folder...

* * *

Marie didn't dare to take a cab, but rather, she walked as far as she could, giving herself some time to consider her next move. It would be too dangerous to stay with a friend overnight, because any of her friends would be too easy to locate. She would just have to pick up her belongings later and mail the key back to the university once she was far from Paris. After walking for a while, she stopped at a café to rest. Many men turned to study her from head to toe. At the rear of the café, she found a suitable corner from which she could observe her surroundings unnoticed. It occurred to her that she could pick up some male company in order to get herself a place to stay for the night, but the thought of that prospect was too displeasing. She suddenly noticed a friendly-looking woman reading a book on the left side of the café, just inside the front window. A woman would surely understand another woman's moment of need.

* * *

Raymond stared at the trashed e-mail, which revealed that Marie had already departed on the 6:13 p.m. train. He smiled at Marie's clever plot, but his smile soon transformed into a grimace. So Marie had left Paris after all! They had been wasting time rattling around this building for hours and waiting for the 9 o'clock train when, all the while, Marie had been seated in the 6 o'clock train on her way to London. Now it was already too late to initiate anything on the London end, since the train would have arrived ages ago. He would never have believed that Marie could pull off such diversions, and if her stunts hadn't embarrassed him so completely, he might even have admired them. He had no choice but to call his contact, even though he felt ashamed of his own stupidity.

"Call off the whole operation. Marie is already in London. She has been surprisingly slick, but she has no idea what I'm capable of. I'll get back to you if I need to," Raymond said, cutting the call short.

He made another call and got a number in London. MI5 owed him a favor and his task required pressure from higher up. The call received a surprisingly warm reception, since the person who answered at the other end was well-versed in the value of the services Raymond provided. Raymond was told that the search for Marie would be easy using methods developed for the war against terrorism, and the Englishman even went so far as to dare Raymond to time the search process. He stated that it would be good practice.

Raymond felt his self-confidence returning and he left Marie's apartment in good spirits. No one steps on his toes without paying for it and Marie would definitely pay dearly for her betrayal. He felt quite weary by the time he reached home, so he headed straight to bed. He was awakened again a bit after 2 a.m. by the phone.

"The woman you're looking for wasn't on the train," a male voice stated curtly.

"I know she wasn't on the train that departed around 9, because she took the train that left three hours earlier," Raymond responded, frustrated.

"I was, in fact, talking about the train that left at 6, but we also checked all the other trains that departed this evening," the man responded calmly.

"What? You're telling me that Marie isn't even in London?"

"I don't know about that, but I do know that if she is, she didn't come by train. Are any further measures required?" the Englishman asked.

"No, that's fine. Thanks," Raymond answered and hung up the phone. He was completely astonished.

He was about to throw his phone against the wall, but he

controlled himself. It would take too much time to acquire a new secured and unregistered phone, and he had no time to lose. He needed to call his contact again. This continual shilly-shallying was beginning to be humiliating.

* * *

Marie arrived by cab at Charles de Gaulle airport. She had slept unusually well, because it had felt safe to be in the apartment of a complete and random stranger, and she had been exhausted after everything she had been through. She travelled exceptionally lightly; only taking her ticket, passport and the prepaid cell phone she got from the woman she met. The suitcase she had planned to take with her had had to be left behind in her apartment.

Marie checked in and proceeded to the waiting area. She wondered if she dared to send a message to Raymond yet, but decided to leave it for the last possible moment. Once she was seated on the plane, she typed him a text message: "I'm on my way to Australia and I'm not coming back. All my deceptions were necessary, because otherwise you wouldn't have let me leave. Try to forget about me, even though I know you're angry. Marie."

She looked out the window of the plane. The sun had come out for the first time after a long stretch of rain and she felt free and ready for an adventure. What she had decided to do was, perhaps, rash and a bit stupid even, but her love was greater than her fear.

11 THE TIME MACHINE
H.G. Wells 1895

Raymond was overcome by exhaustion. He had hardly gotten any sleep the whole night, and the two previous nights had been cut short because of the Finn. Over the last few days, he had experienced more losses than in his whole life put together and it was eating him alive. There was a battle between fury and self-pity waging within him, and he tried to feed his fury to reinforce his self-confidence, but exhaustion endeavored to devour the last of his fury as well.

The beeping signal of an arriving text message roused him from dozing fully dressed in his armchair. He snapped awake and glanced at his watch, which showed quarter after nine in the morning. There was no message on the unregistered cell phone he had stashed in his breast pocket, so it had to be on his official phone. After searching a while for the phone, he finally found it in the kitchen. The message was presumably from Marie and he prepared for the worst. Subconsciously he wished he could just give up for a moment, so that he could finally get some rest.

Raymond read the message and had clarity for the first time in a long time. Now he knew where Marie was and where she was headed, but he still couldn't get over the fact that she had managed to completely pull the wool over his eyes. The flight to Australia would give him enough time to arrange things so that, upon arrival, Marie would find out the full extent of his reach. He also planned to rest undisturbed for an entire day. But then his unregistered phone rang.

"Yes?" Raymond answered calmly.

A male voice confidently stated, "We've located Marie".

"Yeah, she's on her way to Australia," Raymond said indifferently.

"How do you know that already?"

"Do you really think I was just sitting around waiting for you to find something? Raymond retorted.

"We still have time to grab her off that flight, but we're starting to be in a hurry," the guy suggested.

"Don't be daft! If we did anything that visible now, then whatever happens to her after that would lead them immediately to us," Raymond shot back angrily. "I'll call to Australia and arrange a reception for her. Once there, she could disappear without anyone wondering where she is right away. She can be packaged up and sent back to Paris without anyone being any the wiser. In the end, she will be declared missing in Australia and no one will be able to link it back to me." Raymond felt like he was back in control once again.

"What should we do with the Finn? Should we continue looking?" the man inquired.

"Let your guys rest. It's probably best to hold off on the

Finn and let our adversary reveal himself – whoever he is. The fact that they got Marie to ally against me makes this all quite complicated. I think we'll go with the old saying on this one; 'If you don't know which direction is right, it's better to stay put'."

* * *

Marie sat in her seat on the plane and waited. The aisle was full of people searching for their seats and she hoped that none of them were going to take the seat next to her. Her hopes were dashed a moment later when she noticed a business man in a dark suit placing his newspaper on the seat while he tried to fit his bag into the overhead bin. The bag proved, however, to be slightly too large and it stuck out just enough so that the door couldn't be closed. The man appeared to be really flustered and he pushed at his bag with both hands while fuming with irritation. The bag shifted slightly and he was finally able to close the door on the bin, but it opened on its own the moment the man was seated. With a slew of curse words, the man stood up again and slammed the door shut with both hands and stood back to see if it stayed shut. Nothing happened and the man flopped down triumphantly into the seat beside Marie. Just then, Marie's phone signaled that she had received a text message and the man looked at her disapprovingly.

"Sorry, I forgot to turn off my phone," Marie said kindly.

She read the message anyhow and stiffened. It only took a moment for her whole body to start shaking and the man next to her leaned away from her as if he was afraid she was contagious, but he kept his eyes glued to her phone.

"Is something wrong?" he asked.

Marie couldn't get a word out, but she shoved her phone into the man's hand. He looked at her, perplexed, but then turned to read the message on the phone.

Your husband has been in a car accident. Please call home immediately!

"You should really get off the plane," the man stated, horrified by the idea that he might have to travel the whole way seated next to a hysterical woman.

Marie just stared at the man with glazed eyes, which motivated him to stand up and walk rapidly to the front of the plane to find a flight attendant. They had a heated discussion and then the flight attendant came toward Marie with a purposeful gait.

"Ma'am, I think it's best that you remain in Paris and go to the hospital to see how your husband is doing," the flight attendant said with as calm a voice as she could muster. Marie stared at her without saying a word.

"We'll remove your luggage from the plane and deliver it to your address later," she added.

"I don't have any luggage," Marie stammered as she stood up. "I really do need to get off this plane."

* * *

Lisa laid on her back starring into the darkness. She couldn't sleep, so she just listened enviously as Daniel snored next to her. Saturday had been a frivolously lovely day in Daniel's company. They had lounged around in bed until late in the afternoon followed by hours of food preparation while discussing the fundamental questions of life. Actually, it was Daniel who made the food while she kept him company. Daniel had been almost insulted when she seemed amazed that a Finn was able to cook. He had explained proudly that Finns had a great understanding of the value of foods prepared from ingredients found in their own natural surroundings. He also told her that the nature in Finland created a bounty that was high in nutrients and flavor due to the abundant sunshine of the Finnish summers. The sparse population also meant that fish and game were plentiful. For this meal, however, they were limited to the ingredients that her friend had stocked in the refrigerator. The friend was from Tuscany and they were forever debating about whether Italy or France was the better food and wine country. This evening, Italy won out, since the ingredients found in the refrigerator had led Daniel to make Italian-inspired dishes. For an appetizer, he made a tricolore salad from avocado, tomatoes and mozzarella, flavored with a special dressing that he whipped up effortlessly. He decorated the plates for the main dish with lollo rosso lettuce leaves, placed to resemble butterfly wings, and layered with avocado, toasted pine nuts and parmesan flakes. He then drizzled a mixture of olive oil and balsamic vinegar on top. He used a grill pan to fry two steaks to a golden brown on the outside, while leaving them expertly pink on the inside – in fact, he left his own quite rare. The whole dish was topped off with a creamy mushroom sauce that Daniel said was usually made in Finland from chanterelle or horn of plenty mushrooms instead of button mushrooms. Daniel had claimed that his creations were just pure, basic dishes. The dessert, however, had been Lisa's responsibility and she impressed Daniel with a dark chocolate mousse. The eating process had also stretched out and so, by the time they finished their last glasses of wine, both of them had been more than ready to call it a day. Daniel had fallen asleep as soon as he hit the pillow, but Lisa just laid there waiting for sleep to come.

The phone that Daniel had been given made a beep in the kitchen to signal the arrival of a text message. Lisa looked at Daniel, who wasn't stirred by the sound of the phone, and she got up out of the bed. She tiptoed to the kitchen to read the message.

"Call me as soon as possible. This phone is safe. Marie."

Lisa copied the number from the text message and called back.

"Hey Lisa! I'm sorry I had to send you a message this late," Marie said.

"I just knew you'd get in touch, even though you said you weren't going to," Lisa stated.

"A lot has happened and now Raymond knows I was involved. It's a dangerous situation, so I have to leave town. I do, however, want to meet with Daniel first, so it's tomorrow or never. I know it's dangerous to meet because of Raymond, but I still want to. I think I won't feel completely free until I do," Marie explained.

"Are you sure that's the most reasonable thing to do right at this moment?" Lisa asked, expressing her concern.

"Reasonable? This all has nothing to do with reason. But somehow, meeting with Daniel doesn't frighten me at all," Marie stated confidently.

"Would you like to talk to Daniel? He's sleeping but I can wake him."

"No, don't. I'll call around ten in the morning, if everything goes as planned. If I don't call, don't expect to ever hear from me again. In that case, you can tell Daniel that I am safe anyway. Tell him all this immediately when he wakes up in the morning so that he'll have time to mull it over. Let him know that I'll also understand if he thinks it's too dangerous to meet."

"Hopefully everything will work out," Lisa responded, feeling quite unsure about the whole situation.

"Yeah, let's hope so. Good night."

"Good night," Lisa said and hung up.

Lisa thought about Marie. She had exuded a confidence that spoke for her exceptional intelligence and wealth of experience, but Lisa sensed that underneath this exterior, there was a more fragile side as well. She had initially feared that Daniel's lack of commitment might hurt Marie, and that he was only after a little adventure. While her last day with Daniel had alleviated those fears, she was still worried about the threat that Raymond posed to both Marie and Daniel.

Lisa walked quietly back to the bedroom, where she found Daniel lying awake on the bed.

"Was it Marie?" he asked.

"It was and she wants to meet with you tomorrow. Raymond found out she was involved, so it would be extremely dangerous to meet. I think it's downright foolish. Marie wanted you to know that she understands perfectly well if you think it's too risky."

"How can I get in touch with her?" Daniel asked without commenting on Lisa's concerns.

"She said she'll call tomorrow around ten, if everything goes as planned," Lisa said with a deep sigh.

* * *

I awoke on Sunday morning feeling well rested. The wound on my side didn't ache at all and seemed to be healing at a rapid rate. I was in a great mood and filled with expectation for the day ahead. I noted that the sun was shining brightly against clear skies, so if our original agreement still stood, it meant that I would be meeting Marie at 11 a.m. in Square René Viviani. That wasn't for several hours yet.

Lisa was already in the kitchen making breakfast, but she told me to go ahead and get cleaned up. I showered my wound carefully, in accordance with the doctor's instructions, and covered it again with a new bandage I found in the bathroom's medicine cabinet. I had washed and ironed my clothes the day before, since I only had the one set of clothes with me. When I had originally made plans with Marie to go shopping together, I had no idea how appropriate that plan would turn out to be for my current situation.

Lisa said that I looked refreshed and she liked my smooth, freshly-shaved skin. She stepped in front of me and we kissed one another in the French manner, on both cheeks.

"The only thing you forgot was cologne. I know there's a bottle of Venezia Uomo by Laura Biagiotti in the bathroom," she stated and darted off for the bathroom to retrieve the glass bottle. She drizzled a little of the cologne on her palm, rubbed her hands together and ran her hands along the lower part of either side of my face. She also unbuttoned my shirt a little way and spread what was left on her hands on my chest.

"If nothing else works on Marie, this will certainly do the trick," she said smiling slyly.

Lisa had put together a very unusual breakfast for the French, simply because she knew that I needed food that was high in protein. She had laid the table with bread and croissants, ham, cheese and pâté. In a separate dish, she had put nuts and small squares of dark chocolate. We took our time eating, but we scarcely said a word to each other. Lisa seemed to sense that I was nervous and excited and apparently had guessed that I wasn't in the mood for chatting. She said she could take me by scooter to Porte de Clichy Station, from which I could quickly reach Square René Viviani. A cab might be a risk in this situation, so we decided against that option. My cell phone rang at 9:45 a.m.

* * *

Marie tried to focus on thinking about her husband, who died years earlier, in order to maintain her distraught appearance in the company of the airport agent.

"Is there anything else I can do to help?" the agent asked when they reached the door.

"I'll be fine, but thank you so much for your help and support," Marie answered as if she were trying to hold back her tears.

"I hope everything will turn out okay."

"I'm sure it'll all be fine soon," Marie stated as she walked away.

It took a moment before she had the ability to smile again. The memories she'd been forced to call up had been so vivid. She found it a bit unsettling that she had the ability to relive her memories, especially when they seemed to be even more detailed than her present. This ability or burden, depending on how one wanted to look at it, had appeared after the car accident, which she had survived, but which had taken the life of her spouse. She'd been seated next to him as he drove the car. It had been raining hard and the car had seemed, for a moment, as if it were flying over the surface of the road. At that instant, she began to visualize the events of her life with unbelievable clarity. Suddenly, she realized that she was looking

152

down on the scene from above as their car slammed into a tree. The body of her husband was crushed between the smashed door and the car seat. She could also see herself, sitting, seemingly uninjured, next to her husband. As she examined the damaged car, she had a strong sense of her husband's presence and they exchanged thoughts without saying a word. Her mind had been completely calm and she had felt no emotion – no grief, no sympathy. They came to a mutual understanding that she would return to the world alone, and the next thing she knew, she was sitting again in the car, in a completely conscious state.

The ability to relive those memories held a special significance for her as a physicist, because it concretized her ideas about a dimension of time in which history is simultaneously present along with the future. The airplane episode made her smile and she imagined travelling in time according to Einstein's theory of relativity. In one moment, her thoughts were accelerating from Paris into outer space with incredible speed, while the current time in Paris had nearly come to a halt. At the same time, however, the thought was already headed back toward Paris and the next day flashed by, arriving in the Paris of tomorrow, but younger than those who had actually lived through it. She was ensured that she and Daniel now had a window of one day to spend in peace together without Raymond being able to pursue them.

Marie placed the new prepaid card into her phone. The card she had purchased to send text messages to Raymond would likely be too risky, since Raymond now had that number and could use it to track the use of her phone. The number Lisa had given her was already programmed into the phone. The phone only had time to ring once before it was answered.

"Daniel," a soft baritone voice answered the call.

In that moment, Marie was totally convinced that she had made the right decision. She knew, deep inside, that Daniel had a purpose in her life and that, perhaps, she had a purpose in his life, even though she couldn't explain the feeling with logic. And why should she, she wondered. It was just an intuition about everything that had happened and a feeling about what was coming. Intuition – the word that Daniel had used when they met at Café Panis.

"Are you sure that you dare to meet me and honor our agreement after everything that's happened?" she asked, afraid that Daniel would suddenly begin to think rationally and would decide to put safety first. If he did that, then she would know she had been completely wrong about him and it would be better if they didn't meet after all. In her heart, she hoped this wouldn't be the case. She was still amazed at how many thoughts she could have in-between the spoken words. The intense suspense of the situation seemed to have slowed time.

"Well, the sun is shining," Daniel said and she heard the smile in his tone.

Marie felt her heart fill with relief, even though Daniel hadn't answered her question. Would it be safer not to say out loud where they would be meeting? On the other hand, the phones were such that Raymond shouldn't be able to track them. Besides, Raymond still thought she was on a flight heading for Australia.

"So I guess that means it's Square René Viviani at 11 a.m.?" Marie asked.

"Nothing on earth could prevent me from being there on time," Daniel said, his voice turning more serious.

12 THE LONG GOOD-BYE

Raymond Chandler 1953

I stepped off the train at St-Michel Metro station and walked along the Seine to Square René Viviani. When I reached Shakespeare and Company, I considered dropping in to say hello to Sarah, since I still had 15 minutes before my meeting with Marie, but the thought of Marie was enough to keep me heading straight for the northwest gate to the park. I paused at the gate to search for her in the park, but I didn't see anyone who looked like her. Immediately to my right, behind the dark, wrought-iron fencing, I saw a young man lying on the lawn, shirtless, with his shoes arranged neatly by his side. On the right, there was also a semicircular, low stone wall decorated with cross openings. Behind it, there stood several park benches. Over the benches, the trees had been trimmed so as to form a thick roof of branches that threw shadows over the entire area and prevented me from clearly seeing the faces of anyone seated there. At the southern edge of the park, there was another similar area covered by trees, but I doubted that Marie would be lurking in the shadows waiting for me, unless she had wanted to observe my arrival first, unnoticed. In front of me, in the central section of the park, which measured about 30 meters in diameter, there was a nearly four-meter-high, triangular bronze fountain that looked like it had been blown apart and partially melted. Its edges were decorated with human figures and water droplets, and each side bore the head of a male elk. Water flowed from the mouths of the elk down into the openings at the base of the fountain. The fountain stood on a three-tiered foundation, the base of which rested in an area of ground that was lower than the surrounding park area. This area was in the shape of an octagon with flowers planted along each side. At the top edge of the depression, on four sides of the fountain, a vine-covered trellis created an entryway to the four stone steps leading down into the fountain depression.

The sunny Sunday morning had attracted a large number of people to the park, the majority of which were milling around the fountain area. Marie might assume that our rendezvous point would be the fountain, as it stood precisely in the center of the park. I considered waiting there, but the swarming crowd would have made the wait rather unpleasant for me as well as difficult for Marie to spot me. Stone benches stood around the edges of the central opening, and the one in the middle of the southern side appeared to be unoccupied. It was the perfect vantage point from which to view the whole park and the gates on the Seine side, which is the way I assumed Marie would come.

The sun was already nearing its southern position and it

shone over my right shoulder. The canopy of trees created shade over the entire southern side of the park and may have been the reason why the benches on that side were still available. After the long rainy period in Paris, the residents were desperate to catch whatever rays of warmth the sun was offering. The sunny weather apparently also brought out the romance in people, since there were couples embracing all over the park. I watched the gates to the park closely and noted that the majority of the adults I saw were couples walking hand-in-hand. It would be easy to spot Marie, even at a distance, since she would be walking alone.

From the direction of Café Panis, through the northeast gate, there strolled a woman dressed in a beige dress. Her steps fell with a relaxed rhythm and despite her high heeled shoes, her stride was slightly longer than average. Her hands swung loosely by her sides and she exuded confidence. The way she moved was extremely feminine, but there was the slightest hint of masculinity to her as well. It was almost hypnotic to watch her walking and it took me a moment to realize that this woman was, in fact, Marie. The sun filtered through her dark, wavy hair and danced across her face. I felt a wave of emotion rise up to fill my chest and heart. I stood up and Marie noticed me and turned toward me without slowing her pace. As she approached, I admired the strong swing in her hips. I shifted my gaze upwards to her narrow waistline and from there to the way it emphasized her ample breasts. There was something mature about her well-trained body, a maturity that comes only with age. Suddenly she was right in front of me, smiling sweetly. As we exchanged kisses on both cheeks, she placed her hands on my shoulders and I placed mine on her waist.

She smelled good. She paused almost imperceptibly in front

of my face and I thought that, perhaps, she was reacting to the scent of the cologne Lisa had put on me, but she only wanted to ask, "Is something wrong?"

Just then I understood that I must appear thunderstruck. I was also breathing faster than usual.

"I didn't realize…," was all I got out initially.

It occurred to me that this woman may not want to hear, as the first words out of my mouth, excessive gushing about her good looks, particularly from a man she hardly knew. I smiled and continued my sentence in a slightly moderated manner.

"…that the spring sun could make me feel so dazed. I was beginning to feel quite faint when you entered the park."

Marie shot me a questioning look at first, but then she smiled back, having realized what I was trying to say. I thought that if we had been speaking French, this would have been the moment to drop any formalities we might have had.

"So, are we sticking to our plans to go shopping, even though it's Sunday? The majority of the shops are closed," I said, hoping that her response would be 'yes' nonetheless.

"My plan was to serve as your guide and I've taken that into consideration. Let's start with Rue des Francs Bourgeois in Marais, which is a popular Parisian shopping street on Sundays," Marie responded.

"Could we begin at the Place des Vosges square?" I asked.

"You are familiar with the area?" Marie asked, sounding surprised.

"Place des Vosges is my favorite place in Paris, but I never realized that the street was also a good shopping mall." I wanted my answer to give her the feeling that she was showing me something new.

"How about if we walk there? It's not too far, the sun is shining and we both have a lot to say. The last two and a half days have been intense for both of us, for the same reason, but we don't actually know what each other has experienced," Marie suggested.

It didn't matter what she suggested, it all sounded great to me. I pointed toward the northeast gate of the park and we headed back in the direction she had come. I was affected by all those couples around us and so, gently, I also took her hand in mine. She met my eyes and smiled with approval at my intimate gesture.

* * *

Marie exited the cab in front of Square René Viviani and decided to walk into the park from the end facing Café Panis. It was exactly 11 a.m. and so she walked quickly. There were lots of people in the park and she wondered whether it wouldn't be better to just walk straight through the park and try to spot Daniel. She also figured it would be easier for Daniel to see a moving target. Just then, she saw a large, familiar figure rising from a park bench. Daniel looked handsome in his white shirt with the sleeves rolled up. It accentuated his muscular forearms. She turned toward him and looked him straight in the face.

She was struck with a feeling that something was wrong. Had their meeting been compromised after all? Even though the thought occurred to her, she didn't feel any fear for some reason. She was deeply focused on the moment and although she was walking at a rapid pace, she felt like she was approaching Daniel very slowly. She had a strong desire to feel Daniel's upper arms, so she grabbed onto them as they exchanged light kisses to one another's cheeks. His arms felt astonishingly thick and her palms detected the indentation between his rounded shoulder muscles and the muscles of his upper arms. As Daniel's hands lit on her waist, she could feel their warmth radiating onto her body. She was met with the scent of a wonderfully masculine cologne.

Daniel's chest rose and fell at an unusually rapid rate and Marie thought he seemed nervous about something. Was she right about their meeting being discovered? She paused to see if she could read anything in his bright, blue eyes before she spoke.

She felt an unbelievable sense of security with Daniel, and it wasn't just based on his physical presence. Even though, for a moment, she had feared that her plans to throw Raymond off her trail had fallen through, she didn't fear the consequences at all while in Daniel's company. Daniel had a sort of raw honesty that she had never before encountered. When Daniel uttered his veiled compliment for her, she had become confidently aware of her own beauty and hadn't felt embarrassed or flustered by the attention. It also seemed that Daniel could read her thoughts. At precisely the moment when she was looking with envy at the other couples walking hand-in-hand through the park and wondering whether she might dare to take Daniel's hand, she felt his fingertips slide in next to her own.

* * *

The journey to Marais seemed to Marie and Daniel to have taken minutes, as they were so caught up listening to each other's experiences. They both had the sensation they were reliving the events of the past few days, but through each other's eyes. Marie knew that something intimate had passed between Daniel and Lisa, even though Daniel hadn't said anything to suggest it. Intuitively she just knew, even though she, herself, had no idea how. She respected Daniel's choice not to tell her, because it was a personal matter for Lisa too. It was likely that Lisa would make the same choice and whatever had happened between them would stay between them. She also knew with certainty that Lisa and Daniel were not in love, even though love can also be shared by two friends, and this was clear whenever Daniel spoke of Lisa.

Daniel suggested that they sit for a moment and bask in the sun in Place des Vosges park before continuing on up Rue des Francs Bourgeois. All of the park benches were taken, so they sat on the lawn, cross-legged and facing one another.

"Have you thought about what a coincidence it was that we decided, at Café Panis, to make a date to go shopping for clothes? Then, without any inkling of what was coming, we both ended up being forced to leave all our old clothes behind and buy new ones," Daniel stated, pondering the bizarre chain of events.

"Do you know what I thought? Don't take this too seriously, but I just happen to have a strange interest in time. As a physicist, I know that the past and future both exist at the same time, even though, in the physical reality, we have to resign ourselves to causality. In some extraordinary situations, however, I believe our awareness can shift for a moment or perhaps can get a flash of another time. I suspect that, for example, strong desires derive from the fact that we see something particularly great in the future and it affects our present subconscious," Marie explained.

"So you believe that our shopping date will be something particularly great?" Daniel asked.

"From the moment I met you, I was completely convinced

that our meeting was meant to be and would be good for both of us," Marie said, then added, "Do you think I'm a complete idiot now?"

"Definitely not! I believe that new things can be discovered by turning self-evident truths on their head. Personally, I don't doubt or believe anything straight away either. Time has a way of dissolving all lies and reaffirming truth," Daniel stated.

Daniel told her that he was so much looking forward to their day that not even the magic of Place des Vosges was enough to hold him in place. He stood up and extended his hand to Marie. She took his hand and stood up so fast that, mostly by mistake, she ended up face to face with him. They stared into each other's eyes and seemed to reach an unspoken agreement that this was not the right moment to kiss.

"How about we grab a quick lunch first, so that we don't get hungry while we're shopping?" Daniel suggested.

"Good idea. I know just the place, on the corner of the park, at the beginning of our shopping street. There is a little restaurant called Côté Place. Shall we go there?"

The waiter studied Marie and Daniel for a moment and then led them to a small table for two almost at the rear of the restaurant behind the coat racks, presumably because he figured they would want some privacy.

"Have you noticed that everyone always turns to look at you, both women and men?" Marie asked.

"No, but I've noticed how everyone looks at you."

"Try looking around the next time you walk into a room. It's pretty funny. I know I would look at you, at least, and the men are probably jealous of your physique," Marie speculated.

"I'm not so large that I stand out everywhere I go," Daniel

asserted.

"Raymond is larger than you, but there is something threatening about him, so men don't dare to look at him. You, on the other hand, project physical strength without being intimidating in any way. You also have a certain charisma that fills the room around you," Marie explained.

"That would be true of you too. Personal beauty is comprised of much more than just one's clothes and external appearance."

"Well, thank you," Marie said with a smile.

They both ate lightly and only drank a minimal amount of wine, because they wanted to be as present in the moment as possible. They knew something important was happening and they wanted to be prepared for it. This was not just about lust or passion, although both seemed to be rearing their heads despite their owners' original intentions.

* * *

In France, it's impossible to leave a restaurant without acknowledging the staff. The staff, at least, always makes note of departing customers and bids them farewell in a friendly tone. Marie stopped on our way out to say something to the waiter and I stood waiting for her at the door. As it was hot out, the doors were propped open. The right door was held in place by a wine cask, which also partially blocked passage in or out. The left door was held open by a wedge shoved beneath the frame. I stood sideways in the doorway with my right hand extended out the door as Marie passed, almost as if I were holding the door for her. In her effort to step around the cask, perhaps exaggerated, she found herself face to face with me as she skirted out the door. When we were on the street, I placed my left arm around her shoulders and she responded by wrapping her right arm around my waist. We turned automatically to begin the ascent up Rue des Francs Bourgeois.

I could feel the heat radiating off Marie's hand on my side. We were drawn together like magnets. Her hand around my waist was a signal that I belonged to her and I certainly had no objection. I thought of the old Chinese symbol of Tai Chi Tu, in which yin and yang symmetrically create a circle, a circle that represents dynamics and a focus on the eternal dialogue between two polar opposites. In that moment, I felt the perfect harmony between the two of us – a man and a woman, and yet, it felt different from falling in love. Marie turned her head to look me in the eyes and smiled warmly.

"Did you know it's part of the coat-of-arms belonging to the physicist Niels Bohr?" she asked out of the blue.

I had no idea what she was talking about and my confusion must have shown on my face.

"Yin and yang," she explained.

I couldn't believe we had been thinking exactly the same thing! It seemed to be a rhetorical question for her though, because she had already turned her gaze back in the direction we were headed.

We crossed over Rue de Turenne and strolled on without even a glance at the shops we were passing. I was desperately longing for something. My time with Lisa had been wonderful, but had left an emptiness that needed to be filled. Marie also seemed to be deep in thought, as if she wanted to say something and was just building up the courage. Suddenly, she stopped, turned toward me and placed her right hand tenderly against the side of my face. I raised my own right hand and slipped it around the back of her neck beneath her hair. I leaned toward her and our lips met and were welded tightly together. Her lips were soft and warm. It would only have taken a minute spark to ignite our passion, but we were both more in need of tenderness in that moment. Time seemed to stand still and our kiss to last an eternity, but when we finally began to walk again, the people around us seemed only to have progressed a short distance.

We walked another hundred meters before Marie stopped again. In that short distance, I already felt I had grown up with her, as if we had known one another our whole lives. One can fall in love over less, but still, something inside me blocked the possibility. I could say, however, that I loved her and I was sure that she understood it the same way. Our eyes locked and we couldn't contain our joy.

As we looked at each other, we also looked past one another, her to the right, along our side of the street and I, to the left, toward the other side of the street. I caught a glimpse of a stunningly beautiful dress that seemed to have been made just for Marie. I thought the light, pastel blue of the dress would suit perfectly with the olive tone of her skin. The hem of the dress only reached mid-thigh, but a decorative, transparent cloth had been added over top, which hung lower than the dress itself and allowed glimpses without being too revealing. Similarly, the deep neckline of the dress was covered up to the neck with the same see-through material, but the pattern of the material became increasingly decorative as it flowed outward toward the shoulders, lending the top an even more decorative flair. I got excited just imagining her in the dress. The name on the shop was Etincelle.

"Here is the shop I wanted to take you to – Melchior," Marie said and grabbed my elbow, turning me to the right toward the men's shop across the street from Etincelle.

"These are the types of clothes I'd like to see you in," she said as she gestured to the mannequins in the front window. "Their clothes are stylish, but not over the top. Conservative, but modern."

"But I saw a dress on the other side of this street that you absolutely need to try on," I said, trying to turn her back in that direction.

She was determined, however, and grabbed my upper arm tightly to lead me toward Melchior. "We're doing this first."

The salesperson in Melchior was dressed in the style of the shop. Marie spoke rapidly with him and I didn't understand a word. She said something with a wide grin, whereby the salesman glanced at me and they both laughed pleasantly. I must have looked confused, because Marie placed her hand on my upper arm and whispered in a soft voice, "I was complimenting you, but you don't need to know everything I said."

I shrugged my shoulders slightly, held my hands out with the palms upward, tilted my head and adopted an innocent-looking expression. Then all three of us laughed at my parody of stereotypical French gestures.

The salesperson measured my neck size and disappeared to find something for me.

"I think you would look best in simply-styled shirts that are only one color. I definitely want to see you in a black shirt, even though it may not be very appropriate for this weather. The color black emphasizes masculinity and tones down size a bit, but that's not a problem considering your measurements. For women, it's always more attractive and intriguing to hint at something rather than to accentuate it, if you know what I mean," Marie pointed out.

The salesperson returned with a white shirt and began to explain something to Marie.

"This shirt is just a model so that he can verify your size. If it fits, then we can start to look at other colors," Marie translated.

The salesperson showed me into the fitting room and Marie remained on the showroom floor to wait for me. I knew right away that the shirt was too small. My arms barely fit in the sleeves and it was all too tight across the shoulders. I was afraid the shirt would tear if I stretched my back.

"This isn't even close," I said.

"Show me anyway," Marie insisted.

Rarely had I heard such unreserved laughter as I heard when she caught a glimpse of me in the shirt.

"That is the exact opposite of what I meant about just dropping hints," she managed to say in between her fits of laughter.

She slapped her hand against my chest and tried to stop laughing as the tears rolled down her cheeks.

"So, now what?" I asked once Marie had managed to collect herself.

She talked briefly with the salesperson, who disappeared again into a back room.

"He said that he had been afraid that the shirt would be too small, but he was surprised with how small it ended up being. Now he's getting shirts that have been used on the mannequins. The mannequins are made with exaggerated muscles to give a more manly impression. You will also get to try the black shirt immediately, so I'll get to see it too," she said as a summary of her conversation with the salesperson.

The black shirt fit as if it had been tailored to fit me. As opposed to most large-sized shirts, the stomach region wasn't too cut too large; instead, it tapered in from the chest down. Nothing was too tight and, yet, I could feel the shirt securely against my skin. Marie handed me a pair of black pants through the curtain of the changing room and said that they had been used on the same mannequin. The pants also seemed as if they'd been made for me. The thighs and rear were perfect without the waistline being too loose.

"Can I see?" she asked and pushed the curtain aside once she had my approval.

She eyed me from head-to-toe and back again without saying anything, then placed her hands on my waist and slid them upward along my sides until she reached my arms.

"It fits perfectly! Turn around."

I felt her hand on my buttock and was surprised to note that it felt completely natural. She grabbed onto my shoulders and turned me back around to face her, straightening her arms so that she could get a good look at me again. At that moment, I could swear that I saw a glimmer in her eyes and I knew we were both thinking the same thing. It was hard for me, at least, to hide what I was feeling.

After the initial trial and error, it was easy to make my purchases. The same combination came in a tan color and gray, so I bought them all. I put on the light colored outfit, since it was the most suitable for the weather and it went well with my brown shoes. Marie picked out some black underwear that she thought would be nice on me and I purchased a few pairs of socks. Now I knew that I could survive several days without needing to do any more shopping.

"There is only one problem with these clothes," Marie said with a smile. "They cost a third of the target price, because they've already been worn by a mannequin."

Marie loved the dress in Etincelle's window, but she claimed that the style was too bold for her. After a bit of encouragement, she agreed to try it on and so I stayed behind with the saleswoman, who was stubbornly keeping her distance. I assumed that she was avoiding having to speak English with me, but I did notice her trying to check me out without being noticed. Finally, I turned directly toward her to make eye contact. Her eyes lingered on me for a moment and then she looked down with a smile. I had just decided to push it and test her English skills when Marie stepped out of the fitting room. My heart skipped a beat as my breath caught in my throat. I didn't think I'd ever seen anything so feminine!

"That dress is so beautiful, nearly as beautiful as you, and it looks even better than it did in the window," I stammered in amazement. Marie spun around and smiled broadly.

"Thanks. I've never felt comfortable in revealing clothes, but the transparent sections both reveal and conceal to just the right extent."

"You know, what you said about clothes only needing to give a hint of what's underneath is also applicable to women. I prefer just getting a glimpse, rather than seeing too much; then again, if the clothes cover up too much, it suggests that the person might be reserved and inhibited, which men, or I at least, might interpret as a subconscious rejection. I know you said you aren't too comfortable with revealing clothing, but this is a good opportunity for you to try on things that are outside of your comfort zone. You don't have to buy them, but you could test how they make you feel," I suggested.

I saw the already familiar glimmer come back to Marie's eyes.

"What garments were you thinking of?" she asked playfully.

"Let's try that outfit first," I said and indicated a Marilynstyle ensemble.

I thought the outfit would emphasize all of her feminine features in a sexy way. The whole outfit was pure white except for the sleeveless top, which opened in the front and was decorated with black edging. The skirt was sleek and body-hugging through the hips, but then it fell in folds all the way to the knee. The waistline had a wide, black belt with no buckle that joined the skirt and top to form a dress. The belt also held the top closed, since it didn't have any buttons or zippers.

"But that's completely open in the front!" She exclaimed apprehensively.

"Not it isn't, but that outfit would teach you to appreciate your figure and be proud of your femininity. You can adjust how much you want to show on top, but I think you'd realize that having it pulled too tightly closed would look as ridiculous as leaving it too open. Everything is more beautiful when you reveal it just a little." The depth of my clothing analysis took even me by surprise.

Marie appeared to be gathering her courage and then she gave in. "Ok, let's give it a whirl, if that's what you want."

The saleswoman had followed our conversation with interest and, encouraged by Marie's spirit of adventure, she ventured to exchange a few words in her heavily accented English. When Marie stepped out of the fitting room, both I and the saleswoman were pleased with what we saw. Marie spun around a few times to allow the skirt to rise slightly, and I believed that she was beginning to understand how freeing it was to dress more daringly. She asked the saleswoman something in French and they began to discuss intensively. She glanced over at me with a smile.

"Do you like exposed shoulders?" Marie asked suddenly.

She showed me a white shirt decorated with tiny holes. The

left side of the shirt only came up to the armpit and the right side was held up at the shoulder by four narrow straps around the side, which left the entire shoulder area bare.

"I'm game if you dare to give it a shot," I replied calmly.

She stepped back into the fitting room, but instead of coming out to model the shirt for me, she asked me to come into the fitting room. I figured she was just embarrassed about how revealing the shirt was.

I was curious about Marie's strange expression, until I realized that it was the same expression she had when she had been looking me over in the men's shop. The shirt was quite revealing through the shoulders, but I didn't understand why she should be too embarrassed to come out and show me. It only took a second before my gaze moved downward and I understood that she wasn't wearing anything other than the shirt. The hem of the shirt just barely covered her hips, leaving her well-trained yet feminine thighs entirely exposed.

"Did you notice there isn't anyone else in the shop? The saleswoman said the shop has been empty all day, since people would rather be out on terraces and in the parks enjoying the sun. I shared a bit about our history and asked if it would be okay if we had a moment in private. The saleswoman smiled, so that's a yes," Marie whispered and turned her back to me.

I caressed Marie's long neck and bare shoulders with my eyes. I gently grasped the sides of her shoulders and touched my lips to her neck. She was shaking and drew in a deep breath through her nose as her head tilted back. My lips moved downward from her neck to the back of her right shoulder and my breath quickened so much that I was sure she felt it on her skin. I couldn't get enough of her soft skin, but the gentle kisses were becoming difficult as our breathing intensified and I was forced to open my mouth to get enough air. She turned around and pressed her mouth forcefully against mine. There was nothing tender about our kiss; rather, we grabbed on hungrily to each other with our mouths and let our tongues explore and entangle. Suddenly, she pulled away and crouched down in front of me.

Marie groped me through my pants, which were beginning to be a bit tight around me. She undid my belt, pulled the pants down and continued to stroke me through my underwear. Even though they were quite elastic, I began to feel very uncomfortable. She continued to tease me by grabbing onto my buttocks with both hands while laying kisses on me and nibbling gently with her teeth through my underwear. Finally, she pulled them down as well and her eyes took in the full extent of my throbbing, engorged manhood.

Marie stood up once again and forced me to sit on the stool in the changing room as she straddled my lap facing me.

"Hopefully it doesn't hurt. Just let me control the rhythm, since I'm a little frightened and want to do this slowly," she whispered in my ear and guided me into her before I even had a chance to make a move.

I wondered what she meant when she said she felt frightened, but I knew this was the wrong time to ask her to specify. She moved slowly up and down, as if she were carefully exploring each sensitive area. We studied each other's faces and shared in our mutual pleasure. Her lips were slightly swollen and I wondered if it had been caused by our passionate kissing or by her general arousal. Whatever the cause, it made them look especially appealing. I pressed my face into the crevice between her breasts and grasping them from the sides, pressed them against my cheeks. I wanted to open her shirt, so I began to grasp the zipper between my teeth. She stopped me, however, by pressing her body firmly against me.

"Let's save something for later," she whispered. I consoled myself by cupping her face in my hands and kissing her lust-filled lips. Her expression was a combination of lassitude and torment, which I interpreted as a sign of extreme pleasure.

"It's a lovely obelisk," she said with a light, breathy voice into my ear.

It was too much for me to handle and I felt an emerging constriction of my pelvic muscles. Now, more than ever, I needed Lisa's instructions, because I wanted this feeling to continue as long as possible. I grabbed her hips and halted her movement. I squeezed, held back and tensed my pelvic floor muscles. She thought I was ejaculating and she kissed me to prevent me from making any audible groans. I had to pull out and blow air out slowly from my mouth.

"Fortunately, you were able to stay quiet," she said.

"I didn't cum yet; I stopped it," I responded quietly.

I could see from her eyes that she was overjoyed with this turn of events.

"Then we can continue – as soon as the next suitable situation comes along," she purred as if she were just gaining momentum.

We purchased all the clothes that Marie had tried on and I expressed my desire to pay.

"You don't need to try to impress me. I'd just feel better if I paid for these myself," she explained.

"Just to be on the safe side, it would be better to pay in cash so no one could track us here. I happen to have a lot of cash on me, and this isn't about the money or trying to make impressions."

"I can't help that it makes me feel guilty. I'll thank the shop for our private time by recommending it and I'll come back myself, if I ever dare to step foot in Paris again. This is, after all, the cradle of my memories now. But how will I repay you?" she asked. Her voice had a tone of longing, almost sadness to it. We were both thinking the same thing; it wasn't about the money, it was about the fact that we might never see each other again.

"If you care about me, just forget about the money. Let's not think about tomorrow now," I answered.

The look on the saleswoman's face was very telling and when exited the shop, I said, "I have a feeling I know what she'll be doing this evening".

We continued our journey up Rue des Francs Bourgeois, looking for another suitable shop. Almost immediately on the right, we noticed Boutique-Rayure, whose window displayed the most amazingly stunning white blouse. It was tight around the waistline and the front was held together the entire way with laces, leaving a gap in the middle of about 3 cm wide.

Marie surprised me by saying, "I definitely want to try that on".

"Seems like you're starting to get over your complex," I stated.

We entered the shop and Marie asked to see the shirt in her size before disappearing rapidly into the fitting room. After a moment, she asked me to come and take a look. Behind the curtain stood a confident woman, who seemed to be thoroughly enjoying her newly found freedom. The gap between her breasts ran the entire length of the blouse without, however, exposing too much.

"That illustrates perfectly what I meant," I said, astounded.

She opened several of the laces from the top to reveal half of her breasts.

"Is this better?"

"Right here and now it is, absolutely, but not, perhaps, in public," I said with all honesty.

"So, I understood you correctly. I guess that's all the glimpse you're getting." She pulled the curtain closed in front of me.

We bought the blouse and moved on. While the beginning of our date had been all about getting acquainted, by now we were feeling like two animals in heat. We paused now and again to kiss, all the while searching for the next suitable place for an intimate moment together. We were met with another intersection and noticed the English shop, Ted Baker, on the other side of the street. The shop didn't appeal to me, but once we had crossed over the intersection, my eyes caught sight of a yellow dress in the display window. Yellow would be precisely the ideal color against Marie's skin! A long, yellow scarf hung around the mannequin's neck as if it were part of the outfit, and the waistline was accentuated by a wide, black belt. The flowing hemline fell at different lengths in different places, like a wave. I stood and stared at the window, and it took Marie only a second to realize what I was looking at.

"Shall we see if it suits me?" she asked, knowing full well it was a rhetorical question.

The salesperson in the shop had probably never come across customers as goal-oriented as Marie and I. We requested to see the dress in Marie's size and asked after the location of the fitting room. When the salesperson replied that the fitting room was upstairs, Marie and I shot each other a knowing glance and began ascending the staircase together. The upper level of the shop was a bit smaller and housed the men's section. It also happened to be completely free of customers at that moment. I heard Marie's breathing accelerate as she took in the fact that we were all alone. The fitting rooms were much more spacious than those at Etincelle and were equipped with doors instead of curtains. The rear wall had a built-in seating level covered with a brown leather cushion. The wall, itself, served as a backrest and was also adorned with the same type of brown, leather cushion, which extended nearly to the ceiling. The light radiated from behind white plastic covers located between the edges of the back rest and the side walls. The changing space was magnificent, but for our purposes, it also enhanced the taste of forbidden fruit and further incited our lust. Marie went straight into one of the stalls. After a few minutes, she invited me in too. When I looked at her, I saw a changed woman.

"In that dress, you are, again, like an entirely different woman."

"Isn't it good that you are getting to see me from many perspectives and with many different looks? But you still understand it's all me, right?" she asked. Her question made me wince. I couldn't have been more aware of being with any single person, even though her external appearance was completely different in each outfit she tried on.

"I'm yours! Nothing, ever, with anyone, in any situation, not physically nor spiritually, not in my imagination nor in real life, not even in my wildest dreams has ever felt this good," I heard myself say to this woman, who was so devoted to me in that moment, but would never be mine in the future.

She acknowledged my sentiment and whispered to me to

come inside her slowly and gently. "Your size is fantastic when you're gentle, but it might hurt me if you go too deep. Just go slowly and focus on shallow thrusts; that will ensure it feels like heaven to both of us," she explained in a low voice and then she turned her back toward me and bent over.

I admired her figure from the back. Her slim upper body narrowed further to the waist and then spread out wonderfully to her rounded hips. The yellow dress flattered every rise and fall. I lifted the hem of the dress and noticed that she wasn't wearing any panties. Since she was wearing high-heeled shoes, I only had to spread my legs slightly to find the proper height. My cock rubbed up against her labia as I concentrated on caressing the perfect composition of her back and buttocks. When I could no longer resist, I guided myself in and Marie sighed with ecstasy. I was now armed with a new understanding of what pleasure can be gained by proceeding slowly and holding back. I had time to focus on her arousal and it only served to heighten my own. The dress had a zipper that ran from the neckline all the way to the buttocks and I opened it. She didn't resist. I pulled the straps of the dress over her shoulders and waited for her to tell me to stop. She never did. I cupped my hands around her breasts and felt her nipples harden beneath the material of her bra. She still did nothing to hinder my intentions. My curiosity and passions grew even greater and I removed her bra. She reached around and took my right hand and placed it on her bare breast. She wanted this! She, who had had a complex about her breasts, was now becoming ever more excited as I fondled them. I softly teased her breasts with my hands and gently squeezed the engorged nipples between my fingers. Half of me was practically lying on top of her back and I feared I would accidentally push my cock in too deep in the heat of the moment. It was almost impossible to move. In the end, I stood up straight and grabbed onto her hips with both hands. As if led by her thoughts, I began to accelerate the speed of my movements, while ensuring that the head of my penis went no deeper than the opening of her vagina. Suddenly, I felt her tremble and her vagina tightened powerfully. She let out a muffled sigh and her back arched slightly. At first, her vagina tightened at an irregular rhythm, but then, it clenched every other second for at least twenty contractions. I tried to hold back, but it felt nearly impossible as her vagina pulsated rhythmically. Finally, I just stopped thinking and allowed myself to reach the point of no return.

We bought the yellow dress she'd tried on, or should I say tried out, and continued on our way. We came to an intersection, which led on the right to Rue Elzévir. In front of us was Camilla-Café, and we made the decision to sit at the café's terrace for a bit. Marie asked me to order glasses of champagne for us while she visited the restroom to refresh her make-up, which had suffered a bit from the watering of her eyes. When she returned to the table, we both just sat in silence for a minute. Then, she took hold of my hand.

She said seriously, "I believe I can say this without exaggerating or downplaying the issue. If we were to fall in love, we would eat each other alive with our sexual appetite. We would inevitably enjoy philosophical conversations, of course, but in the end, we would still long to spend all our time having sex. Besides, I think that there's something else in your life that you should be focusing on."

"Is there something else that draws your focus?" I asked instinctively.

"I'm in love with a man who lives in Australia. Our sex life has never worked. He's too sweet and I was too traumatized. I think you've cured my traumas, however, so I believe that I can now make him happy," she stated.

"What did you mean in Etincelle's when you said you were afraid? I felt that you were referring to something other than pain."

"Ever since my husband died, my sex life has been no less than a catastrophe. I lived with John, the guy in Australia, for a brief period, but we split up, largely because our sex life was so dysfunctional. A couple years ago, someone attempted to rape me, and since then, I've clung onto Raymond for emotional support and a sense of security. In the sexual arena, he proved, however, to be quite dominating and what he found pleasurable was pure torture for me. So, over the past year, I've only reached out to form platonic relationships." As she analyzed her life, I didn't detect even a hint of anxiety.

"That orgasm I just had was the first I've experienced since before my husband died. For once, I was able to relax and focus just on the pleasure. For the first time, I was able to let go of my fears." Suddenly, she switched focus. "Do you know what shop that is across the street?" I looked across the street to see which shop she was indicating.

"Aubade. Judging from the display window, it's a women's lingerie shop," I answered.

"This time, you aren't coming with me. Just tell me what kinds of lingerie you like," she asked, with a hint of a smile.

"You already know; promising but not too revealing. Just remember, you can't use your credit card," I said handing her some cash.

"You must be the only man in the world from whom I can take money without feeling guilty. It's really freeing, and besides, this purchase is actually for you." Her face reflected her enthusiasm. I stood up to pull out her chair as she rose.

"There's nothing more attractive than a gentleman."

"If I'm honest, I also got up for a kiss," I retorted lightly and pressed my lips against hers.

Marie returned from Aubade, glowing like a young girl. I stood up once again to pull out her chair, but she stopped me by pressing her palm against my chest and stepping in close to me. She flashed a set of keys at me and smiled mysteriously.

"An old friend of mine works in Aubade. She gave in and agreed to loan us her apartment for the night. I mean, we have to stay somewhere where we can freely model our new purchases for each other. I also need to shower, since our activities have made me quite sweaty. And, now that I'm on a roll, my breasts are aching to be tortured by slow disrobing and ceaseless fondling."

13 CAUSE FOR ALARM
Eric Ambler 1938

Marie laid on her side on the bed listening to Daniel's breathing next to her ear. His breath felt like a warm breeze blowing rhythmically and calmly over her neck. Daniel was spooned against her from behind with his arm over her side and his hand relaxed next to her breasts. She scooted her buttocks closer to his body, but she was careful not to move too much and cause Daniel to turn in his sleep. She wanted to stay awake, prolong this moment in Daniel's arms, and store every detail of their encounter in her memory.

She had felt an unbelievable attraction to Daniel already at Café Panis, even though she had fought it on a conscious level. The feeling had strengthened all the time and now she was faced with a difficult choice. Her instincts said that Daniel did not belong with her and that the establishment of a serious relationship would be damaging for them both in the end. She had repeatedly insisted to Daniel that their affair was temporary and he seemed to be thinking the same way. She also knew that if either of them made a plea for something more permanent, the situation would quickly get out of hand. If she truly loved Daniel, she should let him go. Their affair had left its mark on both of them and it was a mark that would never fade.

Marie wondered whether it were possible to truly love two men at the same time. Other than the physical differences, John was a lot like Daniel, and she wasn't sure if her attraction to Daniel was precisely for that reason. She had known John for a long time and had fallen for him quite soon after the loss of her husband. They had tried desperately to make their relationship work, but without a functional sex life, their love had gradually transformed into a friendship. John had followed her from Australia to Paris, but he eventually moved back to Australia and their relationship had continued through daily e-mails and phone calls. Raymond's jealousy had been the strain that had cut off their contact with one another, but it never diminished her longing for John, and she had occasionally resolved to follow him back to Australia. Each time, however, something happened to change her mind.

Making love to Daniel had awakened a passion in Marie that she believed she could transfer to her relationship with John. Above all, the hours of this night that she had spent with Daniel had reaffirmed her faith, while exhausting all her physical strength. Those hours represented the most impassioned and glorious sexual experience she had ever had in her life. Daniel had devoured her body from head to toe, pausing to focus on certain areas, the eroticism of which had surprised her. Even armpits and fingers had been a source of arousal for them both, and the genuineness of Daniel's arousal was unmistakable even before he had an erection. Having an orgasm had been secondary to their desire to explore their passion. After making love, they had sat together in a bubble bath by candlelight and listened to Rachmaninoff. Then they had taken turns washing each other like this was the last rites. Daniel had feasted on her breasts with his eyes and drank from the stream of shower water cascading off her nipples; a vision, he said, would remain emblazoned in his mind forever. She marveled that it was possible for one to become aroused simply from the caressing of another's eyes.

Marie had no doubts about John's love for her. She had called him immediately once she had understood about Raymond's background, and it had taken all her imagination to find a way to call that ensured that Raymond wouldn't be listening in. The driving need to talk with John had made the risk and inconvenience secondary. Upon hearing her situation, John had announced that he was flying to Paris to help her. He hadn't even been dissuaded when she told him about her feelings and desire for Daniel. John wasn't jealous that she had planned to spend this day with Daniel; rather, he had absolutely supported the idea and reassured her that he knew she was a free woman. John's love for her had been strong enough for him to let her go and now she would have to do the same for Daniel. Anyhow, she really couldn't be sure about the depth of Daniel's love for her, since he was sleeping so soundly despite the fact that their time together was coming to a close. She didn't, however, feel bitter or angry, because she knew that Daniel felt love toward her, he just hadn't fallen in love because of his survival instincts.

The more Marie thought about her decision, the stronger her resolve. Daniel's words came back to mind. He had said that, in time, all lies fade away and the truth gains strength.

Although Daniel wasn't a lie for her, he was the wrong target for her affections and John was the right one. She just couldn't abandon John a second time. Instinctively, she had arranged things so that Daniel would meet John at the moment when they finally parted ways. It would be like discontinuity in physics. Daniel would be able to let her go with no feelings of guilt and John would see that her love had gone to a good man. It would be much easier for Daniel to move on and forget about any longing for her if he saw that he was handing her over to another man. She was sure that Daniel would be mature and strong enough not to feel any jealousy brought on by a desire to possess her and that his love would only wish good things for her.

* * *

We were quiet and reflective throughout breakfast. The night had not even turned to morning quite yet. I just wasn't able to think clearly; it was as if my survival instincts were shielding my eyes.

"When we part, don't think about what we're losing, but rather, what we shared," Marie said as a means of breaking the silence. I felt a sudden surge of emotion rising from my gut and my eyes filled with tears. Marie walked around the table to me, climbed onto my lap, facing me, and wrapped her arms around my neck, pressing me tightly against her chest. She said nothing and I was unable to through my desperate weeping. It felt like I was in a thick fog, until I slowly began to see the light emerging.

Once I had calmed myself, I managed to tell her just how I felt.

"I just had to let it out. I feel more happiness about our

moments together than sadness about our inevitable parting. I don't even feel like I'm losing you, since our time together seems to have been burned into my memory. If only I could give you the gift of happiness and be assured of your safety, everything would be fine."

"I have been thinking about the moment we part. If you want, you can meet John, my love from Australia, before we say goodbye. Then you would at least know that you were placing me safely in the company of another good man."

"How will John react to knowing that I spent the night with you?" I asked a bit confused at her proposal.

"I have already told him all about you and my realized hopes for our time together. I also plan on telling him about everything we experienced, because we don't have any lies between us, not for the good or bad. After being with you, I have hope that my relationship with John will work out, and there will no longer be any need to seek out other relationships."

"And what about your safety in terms of Raymond. Can John protect you?"

"Protect? John is older than we are and not a particularly physical type, but his intelligence is better insurance that any amount of strength. Together, we're unbeatable, so don't worry about us." She chuckled a bit to herself as if my question had been ridiculous.

"John has acquired a car and we are planning on driving to his friend's ski chalet in the Austrian Alps. We'll wait there for the situation to calm down and get reacquainted with one another," she continued, turning serious once again.

"Just remember about surveillance cameras," I reminded her.

"I'm sure we'll be fine."

I looked closely at her face, since I had learned already to read her expressions.

"You look like you still want to say something," I stated.

"I know this is totally the wrong moment for philosophy, but, for some reason, I just have the need to say one thing," she said, almost apologetically.

I encouraged her to go ahead and say it.

"At one point, you spoke about how intrigued you are by the truth. The truth is in all things and even if everything were to be destroyed, the ultimate truth would remain. Everything we've experienced is part of the truth. Even if we forget all about this and the traces of it fade away, the truth of what we have together will never be lost. That's why I wanted John to know about all this and it's why he supported my freedom. In that way, it's also shown me the truth about the love that John and I share." As she spoke, she studied my reaction.

"I don't think I quite understand," I said simply. I felt a bit confused about her interpretation of the truth.

"If you want to embrace the truth, don't try to understand it. Let it come to you. When you someday come face to face with the truth, you'll be forced to consider what's right and wrong. I'm considering now whether I acted wrongly toward John; perhaps, I should have avoided our relationship. I just couldn't and didn't want to. The truth seems to be that I would never have found my way back to John without you. What does that say about right and wrong? John made up for my digressions with his understanding and that's right. There is no wrong without right and each of us is sometimes in the wrong. This is way we have forgiveness, and John has already forgiven me in advance. Do I regret what happened? I regret any possible pain I have caused, but not what I've experienced. The truth is that we have shared exquisite moments together and that can never be taken away. I will always remember both the right and the wrong of our time together, and I know I'll never do anything like it again. I don't even believe that something like this could ever happen again for me. I would say, 'no, thank you' even to you."

We arrived at the Place des Vosges park just as the sun was rising. Other than a lone jogger already circling through the park, there was no one else in sight. Marie looked around, concerned, and sat down on one of the park benches. I felt a bit like an outsider, like her assistant, and so I remained standing next to the bench. She had really thought carefully about how we should part ways! I felt my distress and anxiety evaporate.

From the northwestern gate, a solid-looking guy who was slightly balding and tanned entered the park. For a moment, I made the mistake of wondering what Marie saw in him, but the thought vanished immediately. Marie rushed to meet him, wrapped her arms around his neck and pressed her lips against his. They kissed for what seemed a long time. It looked to me like John was taken aback. Marie took him by the hand and led him over to where I was standing. John and I studied each other closely as they approached. The closer they got, the more sure I was that they belonged together. I also felt an inexplicable respect for him. His face was characterized by a remarkable charisma, with eyes that simultaneously exhibited both confidence and gentleness. We shook hands warmly.

"Thank you for everything, Daniel," John said in a friendly tone.

"Take good care of her," I responded, knowing full well it was an unnecessary request.

John moved aside so that Marie could say her goodbyes to me. She stepped in close to me, took my face lovingly in her hands and kissed me gently.

"Goodbye my love," she said as tears slipped down her cheeks.

Then she turned, took John's hand once again and they walked off in the direction from which John entered the park. I just stood there watching them draw further and further away from me.

I wandered aimlessly around the streets of Paris, but kept being drawn back, as if magnetically, to the Place des Vosges park. I was surprised by my own feelings, which were far from painful, even though the image of Marie was burned into my memory like an image on a screen. Particularly the vision of her in front of me with the shower water tracing the lines of her body was so vivid it seemed I could reach out and touch her.

Talking to Lisa would have helped me get back to reality, but when I checked the time, I realized that she was probably heading for work and I didn't want to bother her. Finally, I got up the nerve to return to Rue des Francs Bourgeois to reminisce about all the moments spent with Marie. I crawled along slowly, stopping in front of each shop that had influenced our story in one way or another. I ended up at the Camilla-Café terrace, at the same table at which we had been seated. I ordered coffee and finally began to see the present world around me once again.

There was a classy woman in her thirties seated near me and she was staring at me shamelessly. At that moment, I couldn't have been less interested in other women and I tried not to pay her any notice. I decided to call Lisa to send a clear message to the woman that someone was already occupying my mind. I figured that Lisa would be at work now and so I took out the cell phone she'd given me. I was just punching in the number when I heard someone speaking Finnish. The woman who'd been staring at me was now speaking directly to me in Finnish!

"Sorry to bother you, but it looks like you have the same cell phone as me and I really need some help with mine. The battery is dead and I need to make an urgent phone call. Would it be possible for me to borrow your cell phone battery?" she asked.

"I could have sworn that you were French," I responded.

"Is that supposed to be a compliment?" she asked in a friendly tone as she grinned playfully.

"Absolutely! I made my assumption based on your sophisticated sense of style. How did you know I'm Finnish?"

"One always recognizes a handsome Finn," she answered without really answering and then immediately asked again if she could borrow my phone battery. She had taken me so off guard that I had already forgotten her request. I shut off my phone and tried to figure out how to remove the battery. After watching me struggle with it for a minute, the woman placed her hand on mine. "Allow me to do it. I am pretty handy with these things."

Her voice took on an almost seductive tone as she took the cell phone from my hand. The situation was odd, since I still was uncertain about the woman's intentions. She removed the battery pack easily, attached it to her own phone and turned the phone on.

"Excuse me," she said briefly as she moved away from me

to make her call in private.

She walked to the other said of the street and I watched her tilt her head as she lifted the phone to her ear. I couldn't quite make out what she was saying, but it seemed that she was speaking fluently in French. When she'd finished her call, she walked back over to me and reconnected the battery to my cell phone. Maybe it was just an innocent request, I thought as I drank my coffee. I allowed myself to get lost in my own thoughts once again.

"Thanks ever so much," she said as she placed my phone back on the table. "It was nice to have met you. So long." She spoke quickly and disappeared around the corner to the left up Rue Elzévir.

I didn't need anyone to comfort me, but I realized that I did need to talk to someone. I had never asked Marie for permission to tell anyone about our time together. How could anyone console me if I couldn't tell anyone? In the end, I decided it was probably better not to mention the whole episode to anyone and try to pull myself together on my own. I gulped down the last drops of coffee and glanced at my phone. I found it suddenly odd that the woman had placed it face down on the table. It occurred to me that the Finnish woman may have been a grifter after all, and so I decided to call Lisa just to check if the phone worked properly. That's when I noticed that the phone was on, even though I hadn't restarted it. It wouldn't even be possible without my PIN code... then I saw that the screen was filled with text...

* * *

Raymond had slept well for the first time since the Finn

came into the picture. The knowledge that Marie was sitting on a long flight calmed his mind, since it gave him plenty of time to arrange a proper reception for her on the other end. There was now a professional with a team waiting for her in Sydney, and they wouldn't fail. Raymond had offered such a high reward to ensure that the team would do whatever it took to get the job done.

For once, he had time to savor the moment and read, at leisure, the morning paper that his assistant had brought in with breakfast. He rarely had time for this kind of luxury. At exactly 12 noon, his phone rang.

"The woman wasn't on the plane," said a gruff male voice without even taking time to introduce himself.

"No way in hell! Fucking incompetents!" Raymond shouted.

"You only hired me to deal with her once she got here, not to escort her onto the plane," the man stated angrily.

"I was talking about my own guys. Do you know whether she stayed behind at her layover in Amsterdam or Kuala Lumpur?" Raymond questioned, already beginning to calm slightly.

The guy explained that she had already deplaned in Paris, and his voice took on a threatening tone as he told Raymond that he still wanted payment in his account by the next day. Then he hung up. Raymond couldn't comprehend how this woman was able to make such a complete fool out of him. This was one battle she wouldn't win, no matter what the price. It was time to call in the big boys, even if it increased the risk to his own life. He got out a carpet cutter and went into the bedroom. Carefully cutting along the seams, he removed the wall panel that concealed his wall safe. He punched in the code to unlock the door. Then he removed the STU-III secure satellite phone and carried it over to his bed.

"Hello," Raymond said into the phone.

"Please identify yourself," an official-sounding voice requested on the other end.

"Nightingale 69. One second," Raymond stated. He removed a cover from the phone's handle, detached a key from its secret compartment and inserted it into the phone.

"Changing to secure mode," Raymond confirmed into the phone. After pressing the 'secure voice' button, the small horizontal panel lit up to indicate the initiation of the encryption sequence. After 15 seconds, the phrase 'TOP SECRET' appeared on the phone's screen.

"I have you TS," the man said.

"I have you TS," Raymond echoed.

"Could you give me your password, please?" the man asked politely.

Raymond used the formula he had been given to quickly calculate the day's password in his head.

"Tango 3-3 Whiskey 4-5-9. ID: Bravo 6-5 Zulu."

"Confirmed. Mike Dawson, senior operational officer. What can I do for you, Nightingale?" the duty officer asked.

"I know it's really early in the morning where you are, but I'm in a hurry. Contact the seventh floor and report that I called using the white code. Tell them to have the DDO call the DCI, request the authorizations and call me back. I'll wait by the phone," Raymond instructed the duty officer.

The entire intelligence organization was reorganized in 2005 and the CIA was placed under the jurisdiction of the Director of National Intelligence, a move that met with fierce resistance within the CIA. As their own form of rebellion, they used the abbreviations for their old job titles instead of their names.

"You do understand what you are asking, don't you?" the

officer asked insecurely.

"Do it," Raymond responded. He turned the key and pulled it out of the phone to wait for the call.

The satellite phone rang after an hour. An unfamiliar voice went through the encryption operations with Raymond and upon confirmation of the connection, he stated, "Now I'll forward the call to the DDO."

"This had better be important," the DDO stated in a sleepy and irritated voice.

"I'm ready to turn over the Perkshere file if you'll locate two people for me. I've been saving the file as collateral and I know that, once you've read it, you will be able to make it harmless for yourselves. Do you know what I'm referring to?" Raymond asked, charged with confidence.

"I don't know what that file contains, but I have received the order to accept your proposal. I presume you are looking for a Finnish man named Daniel Bremer and a French woman by the name of Marie Allègre," the DDO said calmly.

"I have to admire your skills. I didn't think you would be so up to speed on these issues, or are they, in fact, working for you?" Raymond asked sarcastically.

"We received tips about the connections between you and the Finn purely by coincidence already two days ago. The woman entered our radar through the Finn. We know, within the radius of a few feet, where each of them is at any given moment. We'll give you the Finn's current location as proof. Once you've confirmed it, you'll give us the file, after which we'll divulge the woman's whereabouts as well. Do we have an agreement?" the DDO laid out his predetermined terms.

"Agreed!" Raymond stated with enthusiasm at the thought of finally gaining the upper hand.

"You do realize that handing us the file means that you'll already have one foot in the grave," the DDO added.

"I'm saving my best card for last, because I know it will ensure you'll do whatever it takes to keep me alive," Raymond stated, trying to mask his condescension.

14 CONTACT

Carl Sagan 1985

With clouded vision, I stared at the cell phone screen and felt shivers running up and down my spine. I'd come to the realization that I was part of a chain of events that I couldn't even begin to comprehend. The long Finnish text on the screen said:

Don't look around, just try to act completely normal! This phone is not yours, it's a specially encrypted device. Your phone only looked like your phone, but was actually a CIA tracking device. It's now in our possession. With data from that device, you have been tracked over the past two days and you are also currently displayed in the image from the camera in that device. The device has been deactivated, thus giving you a small window of time to evade the CIA. You don't have much time before they notice that their device is not working properly. Get up calmly now and walk at a normal pace in the direction you originally came from.

Make the next right onto Rue Pavée and continue on this street until you reach the St-Paul Metro station. Take any train and change to random trains several times before you resurface again. Try to stay under roofs, and if you are forced to walk through any open spaces, move among crowds. Keep this device safe. We will be contacting you. PS. We are Finnish. You can confirm this by sending a question of your choosing as a text message to the only number stored in the device's address book.

My instinct told me that I'd be wise to follow the instructions. I stood up and, as requested, began back in the direction I'd come. I turned right and noted that it was only about two hundred meters until the Metro station.

* * *

An alarm light at the Information Operations Center (IOC) of the CIA headquarters signaled a problem with the tracking device. The officer on duty was immediately informed and began looking for the source of the problem. The target was still on the monitor, clearly holding the device and reading or writing a message. Signal intelligence did not detect any movement of the device, but since they could still see the target, the device must be functional to some extent. It was, however, just a matter of time until the target disappeared from the screen. The duty officer decided to alert the Operations Director, even though he knew it meant interrupting his meeting with the DDO.

The DDO had called a meeting with the Operations Director as soon as he finished his conversation with Raymond. It was clear from the DDO's expression that the matter was serious.

"The targets became hot this morning, and we can't lose them – no matter what the cost! For now, just give me the Finn's coordinates hourly or as soon as he stops anywhere that's free of bystanders," the DDO explained with such a cold voice that the Operations Director could literally feel the chill.

"The target had already proven to be completely harmless. How can he be hot all of a sudden without any new information from the field?" the Operations Director asked.

"Azael made contact and it seems our hunch about the usefulness of the Finnish and French targets were correct," the DDO explained.

"Azael? Who the hell is that?"

"Forget what I said! I meant Nightingale, which is still his pseudonym for you." The DDO was spooked by his own slip of the tongue, so his response took on a threatening tone.

Just then, the Operations Director's phone rang.

"The Finn's tracking device is showing a disturbance that I've never seen before," the duty officer reported.

"Contact the ghost and make sure that EDT has a visual on the targets, particularly the Finn. Give the coordinates hourly or immediately if the target finds himself somewhere without any bystanders." The Operations Director wasted no time passing on the instructions and then hung up.

There was a moment of silence while he contemplated the call, but then he turned to the DDO and said, "Something's wrong and I fear the worst."

As the reality of the situation set in, he felt the blood leaving his face, since he remembered that he had lowered the priority of this operation only that very morning.

* * *

Bruce "the ghost" Brock was a CIA legend and one of the last dinosaurs from the Cold War era. Brock had saved the president of a foreign nation from assassination, prevented several terrorist attacks, and personally hunted down and apprehended numerous dangerous terrorists. Brock had top ranking, GS-15, within in the CIA. It was the highest level before the SIS level, which was the equivalent of a body of army generals. Many of Brock's colleagues, who'd been at the farm with him, and who hadn't been nearly as successful as Brock in the field, had been promoted to the SIS level, but it would never happen for Brock. He didn't ask permission for decisions he made in the field; rather, he chose to apologize after his failures, which were few and far between. Brock didn't back down or submit to anyone or anything, and he was ready to accept penalties for his errors. He knew well that, in the field, his life was primarily his own responsibility.

Bruce was half Cherokee Indian on his father's side. He was born into poverty during the 1950s in the wooded mountains of northern Georgia. As a young boy, he had learned to ramble, hunt and fish, since they were nearly the only entertainments available for an active boy. From his mother's side, Bruce had inherited a passion for books and often took off on his own into the mountains with his hunting rifle, fishing gear and a book in his rucksack. If his mother asked when he'd be back, he always responded by saying he'd return when he was done reading his book. Sometimes, he spent up to a week in the mountains. Bruce's father had taught him to understand time as the American Indians do: they went fishing when the fish were biting and came home when they had caught enough. Bruce also hunted according to the Indian traditions. When the family needed meat, they prayed together for the Lord to provide. Then they headed out to the woods.

Once, when Bruce was 7 years old, his father fell ill, so Bruce went out alone into the woods and was met on the trail by a bear. Since its vision was poor, it stood up to sniff the scent of human wafting downwind. It slowly turned so that its body was positioned sideways across the trail. The bear was old and ready to die. Bruce aimed carefully for the bear's shoulder and the bullet from his large caliber hunting rifle killed the bear immediately. Afterwards, Bruce was considered a hero, but his father reminded him that the bear had come from upwind and had surely known that Bruce was coming from nearly a mile away. His father had taught him that one should only eat a bear in situations of extreme hunger, but, according to his father, the bear that Bruce shot was meant to be eaten.

Bruce's father had died when Bruce was only nine. His mother sold what little property she owned and bought tickets to Europe for herself and Bruce. Bruce was a curious and studious young boy, so Europe was a paradise for him, even on their tight budget, and they were constantly moving about. Bruce turned out to be exceptionally gifted in languages and he learned all the primary European languages like they were his mother tongue. His mother schooled him as they travelled and Bruce read every book he could get his hands on, but when he reached the age of 15, his mother realized that he was in need of something more communal. Soon after that, they had moved back to Indiana in the US and Bruce entered the Culver Military Academy.

Brock was a natural in the army. He ended up going to the Ranger School for Jumpmaster training. While a sergeant at the end of the Ranger course in 1977, a high-ranking officer came to see him. That same year saw the establishment of the top-secret Delta Force and Brock proved to be ideal for the small elite team. That was the start of the peak of Brock's military career; a career that ended, in all practical terms, in the early morning of 25 April 1980 in Dasht-e-Karir, 450 km to the southeast of Teheran. A mission to rescue hostages from the US Embassy in Iran had just been aborted due to technical problems with the helicopters and Brock was loaded for transport back to base along with the rest of the Delta team in a C-130 carrier intended to transport fuel. The floor of the plane was covered with flattened rubber fuel bladders. Brock laid down and fell asleep immediately, but was awakened again by a burning sensation. The entire plane was on fire and the Delta team was assembling into jump order. He was shocked to notice that no one had a parachute, but the plane was burning and the rubber tanks on the floor below them contained 10,000 kilos of fuel. Brock knew he had to deal with one problem at a time and he was the last one out of the plane, hitting the ground after only half a second of free fall. Afterwards, he realized that the C-130 had still been on the ground when it had been struck by a helicopter trying to make an unsuccessful lift off. The Delta team had been saved by the Staff Sergeant, who, amidst the panic, had ordered the team to act as it would in a short drop zone.

The total failure of that operation had been a turning point in Brock's life. He was not afraid for his life, but he was afraid to give his life based on plans devised by others. The Delta team was disbanded after Teheran and they were assigned to different missions all over the world. Brock ended up working with the CIA. It didn't take long before he understood that he wanted the position of DO officer. His education, language skills and character were all seemingly ideal for the job. He handed in his resignation to the army, went through the DO officer training and soon proved to be the best field officer the agency had ever seen. The nickname 'ghost' was bestowed on Brock in recognition of his amazing ability to appear and disappear like a hologram.

The activities of the CIA had diminished considerably throughout Europe with the fall of the Iron Curtain and the winds of change were especially tangible in Paris. The Americans had difficulty finding intelligence agents that were skilled linguists and knowledgeable in French culture, so the agency's collaboration with French Intelligence suffered. Brock had always worked well with the French and he enjoyed a high level of respect from his French colleagues, but that also created a problem; he was simply too well known. At that moment, Brock worked in the CIA Special Activities Division, and he was only called in to lead rapidly organized special operations forces. Brock felt that tracking the Finnish man and French woman was an odd assignment, because there didn't seem to be anything particularly special about either of the targets, or at least not anything worth putting together an EDT team. He was very familiar with Raymond Durand, since Raymond had once worked as one of his agents, but the elimination of unreliable agents surely didn't require an EDT team. The order had come, however, from higher up the ladder and he had a feeling that even they had been handed down the order from elsewhere.

The size of the team had to be kept small, because it would be hard to conceal a large team from the French. A small team would have difficulty carrying out the assignment, however, so many of the tasks would need to rely on technology. On Monday morning, Brock was faced with a decision, since Daniel and Marie had parted ways. He decided on his own to designate part of the team to follow Marie, who had since left the city, and to turn his personal attentions to Daniel. He was then forced to let the rest of the team to sit this one out.

Brock assumed that his own task would be easy, as Daniel was unaware that he was carrying a tracking device that could hear him and pinpoint his coordinates in real-time. Based on the tracking so far, he knew that the relationship between Daniel and Marie was genuine and that Daniel was not out to harm Raymond. This was confirmed by Daniel's retracing of the route he had travelled the day before with Marie. When Daniel had stopped at the café, Brock had decided to wait for him out of view. The visual connection with the IOC was surely sufficient. The whole assignment started to feel like it was in vain and that there was absolutely no connection to Raymond. This operation could quite easily have been handled by the local agency in Paris, which made him suspect that certain facts had been withheld from him. He had had to reign in his thoughts, since they had a tendency to wander during this type of down moment. He emptied his mind and focused only on the tracking device and letting the time pass calmly by. Suddenly, the coordinates provided by the tracking device disappeared. He immediately headed for the café and saw Daniel standing up from a terrace table and turning toward him.

* * *

I tried to walk as normally as possible, even though my nerves were crying out for me to run. The Metro station was getting closer, but I was constantly on edge, prepared for someone to step in front of me or surprise me from behind. It wasn't until I began to descend the Metro station steps that I felt my nerves relaxing. I had already purchased a book of tickets, so I marched straight through the stamping gate with other passengers hurrying that direction. My initial instinct proved correct and I ended up getting to the platform at the same time as an arriving train.

Upon finding an available seat I began to listen to the flood of thoughts crowding my mind. Was Marie also being followed by the CIA, and was she in danger? The tracking device had been given to me by Lisa, so did that mean that Lisa was working for the CIA and had simply been using me? I didn't want to believe that. Fortunately, I didn't need to suspect Marie's involvement, as that would have brought my world crashing down. How were the mysterious Finns involved in this? The CIA's involvement could be understood on the basis of everything Marie had told me about Raymond, but why would they be interested in me? The Finns seemed to be surprisingly privy to the situation, so perhaps they could provide some answers. First, I just needed to come up with a question that would verify their nationality. This would be a relatively easy task, even though the answer had to be such that it couldn't be easily found by Google Search. I pulled out the cell phone and typed in the following question:

An archer, evolution and a perch?

I checked the time and waited. The response came almost immediately:

Hey guys, listen to this! Listen to what our boy Yrjö has to say! Well, I'll be damned. Now you've really started it. Listen, guys! I guess I'm a perch, 'cause I've got stooped shoulders.

Definitely Finns, no doubt about it!

I changed directions several times. I boarded a train that was nearly full. I was forced to stand in the area between the doors and to hold onto the central pole. Suddenly, I was certain that one of the men holding onto the same pole was following me. I waited for the car to empty and when seats finally became available, I chose one facing the man. I looked him straight in the eyes and he began suddenly to move toward me.

* * *

Brock knew that shadowing someone alone was extremely difficult. The target could turn at any point to look back, so there always had to be a sufficient number of people in between them. On the other hand, as distance grew, the risk of losing the target also increased exponentially. In addition to good observation skills, one needed to have the ability to intuit the target's next move. He suspected that Daniel would be headed to the St-Paul Metro station. At that same moment, his secured phone rang.

"Spook," he snapped, once he saw that the call was coming from the IOC.

"You sound a little on edge," the coordinating officer stated, knowing full well that Brock only used the name 'Spook' when he was highly irritated.

Brock expressed his frustration as he barked back at the guy, "I'm tracking the target alone, so I don't really have time for instructions".

Despite his plea, the coordinating officer handed down the command knowing how Brock would react. "The DDO sent the command to track both targets manually and report their location hourly or immediately when they are somewhere that has no bystanders."

"So the field operation is now being led from behind a desk and we have to report in every hour?!? That is the most ludicrous command I've received in my entire career!" Brock exclaimed in rage.

"There is something wrong with the Finn's tracking device and the visual connection has been cut," the coordinating officer explained calmly.

"Understood. Notify them that both targets are being tracked," Brock said and hung up.

The whole mission had bothered him from the get-go. It had seemed like a trifling task for an agent of his stature. It was obvious that he hadn't been told everything. At the same time, he understood the whole picture. The DDO, and thus the DCI, were clearly ready to hand the targets over to Raymond in order to get something they wanted, and it must be valuable for the operation to be worth all this. It also meant that Raymond possessed something that had secured his own immunity with the CIA and the French despite the severity of his crimes.

Brock had a serious problem. In the course of different operations, he had come in contact with stout, nature-loving Finns, who reminded him a great deal of his own American Indian roots. He had always liked and respected them. In his training for the special forces, he had heard tell about Finnish guerrilla tactics and scouting techniques that made use of nature and were based on an unscrupulous approach. Everything he had heard about the Finns had inspired great respect, but the Finn he was now shadowing had had an even greater impact on him. It was as if he could hear his father's own words through Daniel's and he'd begun to see visions. His father had encouraged him to act according to his heart and do the right thing. He could hear it in his mind, as distinct and clear as his father's own voice.

Brock broke into a sprint to catch up to Daniel, who had disappeared from view into the Metro station. Once he got a visual, he was forced to continue running to make it onto the train that was just pulling into the station. Fortunately, the fact that he was running was completely natural, since he was just one of many who were trying to catch the train. He boarded the same car as Daniel from the opposite end. He observed Daniel from his reflection in the window while also taking advantage of the camouflage of those standing in the aisle. Daniel appeared to be focused on his phone, which was odd since it was supposedly not working properly. At the same moment, Brock felt his own phone vibrating in his pocket. He couldn't believe he was getting new instructions yet again.

"GH," he answered using the cryptonym he had been instructed to use around outsiders.

"The target's gone missing," his EDT team member Abigaile stated, embarrassed.

"Details?" Brock asked, being careful not to expose anything in what he was saying.

"We followed a car over the German border and when they stopped to fuel up, we began to suspect something. The couple in the car was, indeed, on their way to a rental cabin in the Austrian Alps, but they were completely different people, albeit very similar-looking to the targets. They had no idea about anything and they showed us their reservation to the cabin, made weeks ago. I don't understand what happened, but we were badly duped."

"Understood," Brock said. This simple response also served as an order for his team to stand-down and await further instructions.

Brock was suddenly overcome with a feeling of satisfaction. He knew exactly what to do and, even though the coming path of events was still a mystery, his intuition about the final result couldn't be more certain. He decided to notify the IOC that the targets had disappeared and there was no longer any reason to search for them. He had a new plan. Right then and there, he also decided that this would be his last assignment before returning to the land of his ancestors – either to the mountains or the blessed woodlands. He stepped out of the train car and allowed Daniel to travel on alone.

* * *

The man who'd been observing me in the car met my gaze, walked directly toward me and sat in the seat opposite mine.

"You received my answer to your question. Were you satisfied?" the man asked in Finnish.

"Well, you are undoubtedly Finnish, but what are you after and why?"

"I'll fill you in later, but can I ask you something first? How did you figure out that I was following you?"

"There was a woman seated next to the door. All the other men in the car were checking her out. You didn't even give her a glance, but you looked at me one time too many," I answered, noting the sharpness of my own intuitiveness.

"You're learning," he said with a smile.

Part Three

In general…there's no point in writing hopeless novels.
We all know we're going to die; what's important is the kind
of men and women we are in the face of this.
-Anne Lamott

15 THE PLAYER OF GAMES
Iain M.Banks 1988

As he stepped into Shakespeare and Company, Brock immediately made eye contact with Sarah, who was sitting behind the cash register directly opposite the door. She was happy to see him, since he was the one who arranged her internship and apartment in Paris. Brock raised a finger to his lips almost imperceptibly and, without a word, walked past her to the table beyond the cash register where all the newest books were displayed. After a moment, he came back with a book he had chosen. Sarah talked to Brock about the book, just as she did with any customer who selected a book that also piqued her interest. As she was ringing it up, she noticed a piece of paper sticking out from between its pages. For one reason or another, customers sometimes left post-its in books they were browsing through, so Sarah automatically removed it before she put the book into the small, paper shopping bag.

Brock looked her directly in the eyes and then shifted his gaze slowly to the paper. Sarah followed his gaze and saw the name on the paper. Instead of a direct question, she just looked questioningly at Brock as she handed him the bag. Brock thanked her naturally with a smile and left the bookstore.

* * *

We sat in the train like two complete strangers, and strangers we were, although we were both Finnish. He didn't say a word and I didn't feel moved to initiate any conversation. The chances were slim that anyone around us might be Finnish, but I thought it wise not to discuss things in crowds. We changed trains once more and re-emerged to street level at the Gare du Nord station. We came out in Pl. Napoléon III square and walked over to a silver Peugeot 206 with French plates that had been heading along Rue de Dunkerque, but stopped in front of the taxi station. My escort opened the rear door of the car for me and when I stepped in, he slammed the door shut and remained standing on the side of the street. The car immediately sped off, but I saw that my escort had taken out a digital camera and was photographing the traffic behind us. For a split second, I feared I was being kidnapped, until I noticed the Finnish woman from the Camilla-Café sitting beside the driver of the vehicle.

"Hello Mr. Bremer. It's nice to see you again," she said in a friendly manner.

"Why are you being so formal? That's not very Finnish-like," I asked.

She laughed and said, "I'll take that as an invitation to be on a first name basis. I apologize. We've lived in France for so long that I suppose the formalities become a force of habit".

"You both obviously know who I am, but who are you?" I was getting frustrated with being in the dark on everything.

"I'm sorry. I'm Anneli and that man was Pekka. He had to stay behind to make sure that no one was following us. He'll be joining us later." Even though she was talking to me, she also seemed a bit distracted as she checked the rearview mirror to see the traffic behind us.

"Why was he taking pictures of the traffic?"

"We'll pass Pekka several times at agreed locations and he's going to photograph the traffic around us. If any of the same vehicles show up in the photos, we'll know we've been detected," she explained, then added, "Let's just keep quiet now and observe our surroundings. Everything will be explained once we reach our destination."

We drove around randomly, causing me to lose my sense of where we were. I didn't see Pekka anywhere along our route. Finally, after about 30 minutes, Anneli's phone rang and she answered without saying a word. She just listened, hung up and turned toward me. "It's all clear, so now we can go to our destination. First, however, we need to change cars in the parking garage."

* * *

Sarah silently cursed her own naiveté. Brock's message had stated that he worked for the US Government. She had been under the illusion that her internship and the free apartment had been awarded by some foundation that Brock represented. Now she realized that she should have been suspicious about everything being free. And now the homeland was calling on her services.

Conveniently, her lunch hour was just starting, so she

headed through Square René Viviani toward Café Panis. Once there, she turned right onto Rue Lagrange and then took a sharp left onto the narrow Rue de la Bûcherie. Her heart was racing faster than her rapid steps would have required. Brock's appearance at the bookstore obviously had to do with something bigger than a job in a bookstore, and it seemed that whatever was coming was going to be unpleasant, maybe even dangerous. Rue de l'Hôtel Colbert was the next intersecting street. It was even narrower than Rue de la Bûcherie and she found herself wondering whether cars could even drive down it. On either side of the narrow lane, lined on each side with metal posts, there were sidewalks that were also so tight that they wouldn't have allowed for two people to pass one another. The entire street was like some type of threatening trap, where one would easily be hemmed in. On the other hand, maybe her paranoia was just the result of having read too many thrillers.

She turned to the right and saw number 12 about twenty or thirty meters ahead on the right side of the street. The door was equipped with a combination lock, and she punched in the code Brock had given. There was no elevator in the building, so she began to make her way up the antique wooden staircase. She guessed that the building must be at least two hundred years old, but at least the staircase had been nicely restored. The nervous tension she felt increased slightly as she realized that this staircase was likely the only means of entering and exiting the building. The apartment she was looking for was on the second floor. She rang the doorbell.

* * *

Brock extended his hand and smiled broadly at her.

"Welcome to a CIA safe house."

"The CIA? Well, if I'm honest, it had already crossed my mind," Sarah said, although she still felt just as confused.

"We put people up here who are working with us, but whom we'd like to keep an eye on," Brock explained.

Brock had softened his voice in an attempt to calm the obviously nervous Sarah. He led her through the small entryway and into a large living room. To Sarah's surprise, the entire living room was bare except for a large, thick rug in the center of the floor. Brock sat down on the rug with crossed legs and requested that Sarah do the same. Sarah followed instructions and assumed the same position facing Brock. She looked carefully at Brock's face, one which had seen a great deal of life, and made note of the fact that he was quite handsome. His jet black hair and broad jaw, together with the narrowness of his nose, gave him an exceptionally exotic look. The features that stood out the most, however, were his brilliant blue eyes, which radiated an inner strength.

"Tsitsalagi ale sagonige digatoli agine'a...it means I'm Cherokee and have blue eyes," Brock said upon noticing Sarah studying his eyes.

"I didn't realize that you were American Indian," Sarah said with a tinge of embarrassment.

"Only half, but my father was a full-blooded Cherokee. He also had blue eyes and in our culture, they believed he was a storm child who had the gift of sight beyond our world. I don't have any such gift, unfortunately."

When Sarah didn't respond, Brock decided to go straight to the point. "You're probably wondering why I asked you here."

"I'm afraid to hear."

Brock took an envelope from his pocket and handed it to Sarah.

"Open it."

Sarah pulled a stack of photos from the envelope and started to go through them. Her mouth dropped open.

"Is that Daniel? ...and Lisa – no, it can't be... I've seen this woman somewhere before also."

"Two female agents volunteered to serve as decoys when they saw those photos. I guess I should be jealous of that guy," Brock stated with a little laugh. Sarah looked up from the photos and understood suddenly the point of all this.

"You want me to seduce Daniel?"

"I want you to dig up information about him no matter what it requires," Brock said, his voice growing more serious.

"Daniel's my friend!" Sarah shouted and flashed Brock a disgusted look.

"I mean, he's...interesting, but I could never fake anything around him," Sarah continued, having calmed her tone slightly.

"Think about it this way, if you don't find out anything about him, the IOC will take over. Daniel means nothing to them and they are ready to sacrifice him if necessary. And you can be sure that they'll succeed if that's what they decide."

"I assume you're speaking theoretically...why on earth would the CIA want to harm Daniel?"

"There's another faction that wants to do exactly that. You don't need to know all the details, but we're talking about a trade in which Daniel would lose his life." Brock's voice had now taken on a chilling edge.

They sat for a moment in silence. Sarah stared angrily at Brock for putting her in this situation. Gradually, her thoughts shifted to Daniel and her anger began to dissipate. Brock saw that Sarah was beginning to come around, so he charged on. "I'm going to give you a substance that will generate euphoric lust and cause Daniel to ignore reason. Don't use it yourself, though; it's very addictive and can have unwanted side effects.''

Sarah couldn't believe her ears. She had already stated that she was just friends with Daniel.

"No way in hell! I'm not stooping that low and besides, who says I have to have sex in order to get information from him?"

"It's just a precaution. You have to get the information at any cost or things'll go poorly for him. You'd also lose your job and apartment in one fell swoop." Brock delivered the instructions with the hardened tone of a professional.

"Well, if I don't have a choice, then I'll do it, but I'm not using any chemicals. I trust completely in the power of pheromones; I have a good deal of experience in that territory. That's specifically the reason why I don't use birth control pills that might prevent the secretion of copulins. I also happen to be ovulating, so the amount of copulins is right now at its highest level. Apparently, that's why I also feel quite sexually inclined at the moment, but then again, the idea of misusing sex turns me off completely," Sarah said, assuming a note of confidence in her voice.

Brock considered Sarah's theory, which was news to him, but before he could comment, she went on to ask, "Is the bookstore involved in this somehow?"

"Of course not. Officially, I represent an American literary foundation and it would be best for the actual truth to remain just between us."

* * *

I sat drinking coffee with Pekka and Anneli around a small table in the small kitchen of a small apartment. To my surprise, their coffee was Finnish and the taste of it brought back a flood of memories.

"I figured you must miss proper coffee," Pekka stated, obviously reading my expression.

"I have a long list of questions for you," I said, getting straight to the point.

"That's why we're here. Ask away."

"Well, first off, who are you?"

"How can I explain? We're with a secret Finnish organization that has no name and doesn't really exist," Pekka answered carefully.

"What? I didn't know that Finland even had a secret service, but that sounds pretty sketchy."

"Secret, by definition, means that no one knows about it, even though we know about the intelligence services of practically every other country. For us, confidentiality is essential. We are a completely independent organization, not operated or funded by the Finnish Government. We provide our own financing and enjoy complete autonomy. Our objective is simply to organize matters to benefit Finland and to pass on information as necessary. And if you're having a hard time believing what I'm telling you, just think of it from a historical perspective. Finland was carrying out unusually successful intelligence and espionage activities already before the Winter War, and it flourished during the war as well as after. Our scouting operations within the borders of the Soviet Union were unbelievably efficient, the results brilliant and the losses minimal. MI6 tried the same by dropping agents by parachute into the Soviet Union after the wars, but not one of them ever returned. Thus, Finnish scouts were still being hired for the same purpose by the CIA in the 50s. The recordings from Finnish wiretaps in Hitler's Eagle's Nest and Peenemünde are unparalleled. The material gained about the

Soviet Union from our signal intelligence and code breaking continued to help the Americans long after the actual wars, during the Cold War period. Do you think that Nokia's cell phone and network business would have come about without the traditions born during war time? And do you suppose that intelligence operations would have ended on the demand of the Soviet Union just when the risk was at its greatest? It is precisely thanks to the Soviet Union that our organization came into being, and developed into the effective and covert entity it is today," Pekka explained.

"So you're an illegal organization?" I asked foolishly.

"Morally, we are as illegal as any espionage organization, but in terms of legality, we can only be judged based on our actions. We aren't breaking the laws of any countries, so we manage to fly under the radar. But things could still always be done more efficiently and that's where you come in," Pekka answered.

"That's what interests me the most…how I fit into all this."

"Raymond Durand, as you well know, sold the Russians intel that was damaging to Finland and he's ready to sell more. We need to stop him, but, naturally, we can't eliminate him physically. Raymond also has a hold on several Finns in key positions, and that would also hurt Finland. You have suddenly provided us with a link to Raymond and even though we don't quite have a plan in place yet, we are closing in on a solution," Pekka continued.

"And you assume I'm just ready to risk myself for all this?"

"I haven't told you everything about Raymond yet. He used to work at a high level within the French intelligence organization, and then he became a double, or actually triple, agent working with the CIA and MI6. He abused his position within the different agencies and accumulated his own storehouse of, shall we say, intel bombs. By the time everyone found out he was a traitor, he had created his own life insurance policy. If something were to happen to him, all the files in his possession would leak to the public. So, as a result, the Yanks, the Brits and the French have done everything possible to protect this guy they despise, a guy who truly needs protection from a slew of real enemies."

His thoroughness was starting to grate on my nerves, since, despite all the details, he hadn't answered my questions.

"I still don't understand what all this has to do with me!"

"Let me finish. As long as Raymond is allowed to work freely, your life will be in danger. Raymond is nuts and he doesn't give up. If he can't find you, he'll go after your loved ones. Raymond, himself, is a threat, but the information he's sitting on is gold and he has the CIA's resources at his disposal. Then again, the information he has on the Yanks, themselves, is explosive. Just seeing it would be a death sentence. When you've been pegged as the object for trade for that kind of information, what do you think your chances of survival are? And then there's Marie," Pekka said, suddenly interrupting his own explanation.

"Marie! How is Marie involved in this?" I snapped at him.

"Marie and her partner slipped out from under the CIA's radar and are, for the moment, safe, but they will have to live on the run for the rest of their lives unless something is done about Raymond. The CIA stopped following you too, for some reason, but I believe it's only temporary," Pekka answered. He looked straight at me to see whether I was finally starting to understand.

"Can I ask whether Lisa is involved too?" As I asked, I could feel my stomach tighten with fear.

"Lisa's not involved at all. Her father is the head of MI6's operations in Paris and, naturally, he co-operates with the CIA. The apartment you stayed in was one of the CIA's safe houses, which Lisa oversees, albeit blissfully unaware of its purpose."

"That's a relief. But I mean, Marie isn't really guilty of anything, is she?" I just needed to know, even though I was so sure she wasn't that I would have staked my own life on it.

After a long silence, Anneli looked at Pekka, as if asking permission to speak, and then she answered. "I totally understand your concern and I can assure you that Marie is as innocent as Lisa. But I think you should know that the CIA intends to make contact with Sarah."

"Sarah?"

"Sarah's too young to be an agent, but she might be a trainee who is being acclimated to a new culture. Unbeknownst to her, she might also be a candidate they are testing, or maybe they are trying to get to you through her, because they know she's American. I'd put my money on that last option," she added.

"The bitterness of the Yanks is obvious, since they've changed Raymond's pseudonym from Nightingale to Azael, in other words, from a warbler to a dark angel. I doubt they would have anything against us solving the problem for them. But how?" asked Pekka.

"Did you say Azael?" I asked. I suddenly got an idea for the solution. It was still a bit vague, but I had a strong feeling about it.

"Yes, Azael," Pekka confirmed with a quizzical look on his face.

"Does Raymond have anything on the Russians?" I asked, feeling my excitement grow.

"There's no blackmailing the Russians and you know Russia... Whatever anyone discloses makes no difference,"

Pekka responded, his face revealing his inability to grasp what I was suggesting. I charged on with my questions.

"Are there any Georgian agents in Paris?"

"What? Exactly what do you have in mind? Of course, Paris has a very active Georgian organization, same as the Russians. In fact, the Russians have a mole among the Georgians," Pekka explained.

"Perfect! One more thing… Does the CIA have someone specific tracking me and Marie? Someone who is physically here in Paris?"

At this phase, I was positive that I had an effective solution, albeit frightening and dangerous, for me in particular.

"Yes and you couldn't have a more difficult opponent. It's Bruce Brock, who's like the greatest hero from a spy novel," Pekka responded. The moment Brock's name came out of his mouth, Pekka realized that, no matter what the plan, Daniel wouldn't stand a chance. He didn't have time to dwell on it though, because Daniel suddenly added, "He wouldn't be my opponent, he would be a collaborator. First, I need to get in touch with Sarah and try to make contact with Brock through her."

Pekka was quiet for a moment before continuing with his own questioning.

"Could you explain a bit… How did the name Azael help you come up with a plan?"

"How deliberate a choice do you think the name Azael was for the CIA? Azael is, indeed, the name of a fallen angel, and they might be referring to that. I remember also that, somewhere, Azael was a chief of the fallen angels and guarded hidden treasure. They might mean that. Azael has other connections too. He is said to be a prisoner trapped between Heaven and Earth until Judgment Day," I explained as vaguely as Pekka had.

Pekka became impatient. "You're gonna have to give me more than that to go on."

"I'm still working on the plan. Do you have any idea what those files look like?" I asked.

"Yeah, I do. We also happen to have a copy. We managed to get our hands on a file about Finnish matters that was intended for the Russians. Well, actually it isn't a file, but rather a metal case that's smaller than a cell phone. We opened it and noticed that it was equipped with a digital seal. The recipient with the right code would be able to see from the seal whether the case had been compromised. There was nothing we could do to cover our tracks. It was good, though, that we realized the seal even existed. In the end, we allowed the case to pass to the Russians, who, of course, noticed that we opened the file, thus suspecting we had manipulated the contents as well."

"You said first that you have a copy," I stated, looking for confirmation.

"We made an exact duplicate, but the designer of the case would notice the difference in the sealing mechanism."

"That's good enough for me. Do you think all the files and cases are the same?" I asked.

"We're talking about a sophisticated piece of equipment. I doubt that a unique model is made for every case," Pekka answered.

"Then this just might work…," I claimed.

"Don't you think you might let us in on your plan now?" Anneli asked. Her indignation wasn't only in her voice, it also showed in her sharp expression.

"I'll write a letter to Lisa. She needs to know the essentials about what's happening and why I can't contact her in person. I'll ask her to send Sarah to talk to me under the guise of my needing a new hideout. Your job would be to find me an external but reliable courier to make sure the letter reaches Lisa." I chose to think out loud rather than directly answer her question.

"And?" Pekka said with escalating impatience.

For some reason, I was afraid to state my plan outright. My intuition about the plan was solid and I believed I had the ability to improvise if needed, but I just couldn't find the words to lay out a concrete and detailed plan for them.

"The more detailed a plan is, the more likely it is to fail. I'm only willing to tell you what I'm attempting to do and what I will need from you. My primary intention is not to attack Raymond, but to attack his plans."

16 THE NICE AND THE GOOD
Iris Murdoch 1968

I found myself sitting, once again, in Square René Viviani, and I couldn't avoid the feeling that I was spinning at an accelerating rate. I remembered telling Lisa, some three days earlier, that if I were ever spinning out of control, I could always spread my arms to increase my rotational inertia and slow myself down. If only it were that easy. My mind kept returning to Marie, but instead of dwelling on the longing I felt, I tried to view my time with her as just a happy memory. I replayed the image of her leaving Place des Vosges park on the arm of another man in order to get my feelings back in check.

This time I sat on the western edge of the semicircle stone fence in the shade created by the overhanging trees. The fence and shade hid me nearly completely from sight, but I had an unobstructed view of the entire park. During the days prior, I had developed a near neurotic need to observe my surroundings from a safe vantage point in the shadows. I had requested that Sarah meet me at the southwest gate of the park. That would ensure that she wouldn't be forced to walk straight through the center of the park to get around the stone fence, thus exposing her unnecessarily to any curious eyes. I knew I was being paranoid and downright ridiculous, but when I saw Sarah step through the gate of the park, I knew my instincts had been correct. Every head near the gate of the park turned to look at her. As a picture-perfect woman with her long, nearly white hair, she appeared like a bright light, illuminating her surroundings. I couldn't believe my eyes, even though I had always known she was beautiful. I wondered why I hadn't paid more attention to her looks at the bookstore, even though I'd sensed the sexual tension between us. Perhaps it was our age difference that had kept me at arm's length. She was wearing tight jeans with the hems rolled just above her ankles. With her high-heeled shoes, they made her legs look exceptionally long. She wore an anklet that emphasized her slender ankle. Already from a distance, I could see her breasts moving freely underneath her gray t-shirt, which was fortunately partially covered by an open-necked, light pink sweater. She was still several dozen meters from me when I was suddenly overcome by a feeling of defenselessness. I couldn't understand what had gotten into me. Was it so that I hadn't been satiated or was I just looking for a way to forget about Marie? What I felt came from deep within and I didn't feel like I had any control over it. I was determined to focus only on Sarah's eyes and my intended plan.

* * *

The whole way back to the bookstore from Brock's

apartment, Sarah tried desperately to figure out how she would establish contact with Daniel. Lisa seemed like her best bet, but how could she approach the issue without rousing Lisa's curiosity? When she reached the bookstore, fate stepped in and Lisa immediately took her aside to talk about Daniel. Lisa filled her in about the violent, insanely jealous Raymond Durand, who had threatened Daniel's life. She told Sarah that Daniel needed a new hiding place. Brock had told her the same things and much more, but Sarah acted surprised, which was a useful means of concealing her feelings of triumph. Sarah played her part well. She thought for a moment and then stated that she knew of an empty apartment not far from the bookstore. The apartment Brock introduced to her had transformed into her friend's apartment, which just happened to be empty and available for Daniel.

Lisa arranged for Sarah to have the rest of the day off and Daniel was waiting in Square René Viviani. Could things have worked out any better? Sarah had always felt a strong attraction toward masculine men - the more manly and different from a woman, the better. Tall, muscular men had always turned her on. She never revealed this to anyone, however, since she was sure it would simply affirm the stereotype of the simple blonde. Correspondingly, masculine men seemed also to be attracted to her feminine features, but her sharp wit and tongue scared off any candidates who were dimwitted or had low self-esteem. She had only ever seen Daniel with a winter jacket on, and so she had never considered him as anything other than a large man. Daniel also hadn't shown the level of interest that she usually received from men. Despite that, she'd always felt a natural, but secretly erotic tension between them. The photos of Daniel that Brock had shown her had further stoked the fires of interest.

Sarah sped up as she walked toward the park gate. Once she entered, she slowed her pace to try to spot Daniel as well as to disguise her eagerness. She was surprised by the complete change in her own attitude; what was once absolute disapproval had transformed into fervent expectation. Once she had accepted the idea that she was saving Daniel rather than betraying him, she allowed her true feelings to rise to the surface. Now, there was no controlling them.

Daniel sat in the agreed place in the shade of the trees and she saw him stand up when he noticed her approaching. She was startled. It was almost as if she were looking at a stranger. Daniel had on a black, fitted shirt with the sleeves rolled up and black pants, which accentuated his muscular form and made him appear unbelievably masculine. Then she remembered her mission and it made her feel ashamed and anxious. It was amazing how effectively it deflated her passionate feelings. She felt a frigid calm take over her mind.

* * *

I thought I detected a glimmer of joy in Sarah's face when she saw me. Something happened, however, as she got closer and by the time we were exchanging French cheek kisses, a strange distance was forming between us. We sat on the park bench at a safe distance from one another.

"So you got my message from Lisa?"

"Yes, and I have just the place in mind for you near here. It belongs to a friend of mine, but it's standing empty at the moment," Sarah responded in a reserved voice.

I struggled with what to say in response. She seemed oddly

reluctant, and it was difficult since I didn't really need the apartment. I knew, however, that I couldn't just tell her that.

"I don't want to be a bother or cause you any difficulties."

"Oh, my face must be giving the wrong message. I do have issues on my mind, but they have nothing to do with the apartment," Sarah laughed, a bit uncomfortably.

"How is Lisa doing?" I asked to change the subject and calm us both.

"Lisa sent her greetings. She was sorry that she couldn't offer you somewhere to stay. She's just moved in with a friend, who doesn't want any men in their apartment. Lisa said that you've met her," Sarah answered. It was obvious from her voice that she was clearly relaxing.

It was silent for a moment, but not, surprisingly, in a way that felt uncomfortable. I kept my gaze fixed on her face, particularly on her crystal blue eyes. She was barely wearing any make-up. Her naturally light eyebrows had been slightly darkened and she was wearing a lipstick that matched the tone of her sweater. I found myself wondering what about her face made her so extremely beautiful. Perhaps it was the symmetry and remarkable intensity. Her lips, as well as her eyes, had a warmth to them. I could have sworn that her lips had swollen since the moment she initially sat down on the park bench.

"Kiss me," she blurted out suddenly.

I went speechless and my heart skipped a beat or two. The situation had turned on its head in an instant. This wasn't how my plan was supposed to proceed.

"Kiss me for my sake," she repeated upon noting my hesitation.

I grabbed her shoulders gently and pulled her closer. She kept her eyes locked on mine the whole time and waited to see what I would do. I moved my hands to the sides of her face and looked deep into her eyes, as if to ask her if she really meant what she said. At first, I touched my lips ever so gently against hers and felt their softness. She didn't rush in, she just waited. I pressed my lips more firmly against hers and was overtaken by a sudden surge, followed by a humming in my ears. She grabbed the sides of my face and pushed it gently but resolutely away so that she could look at me. We were both breathing faster.

"I have to tell you something," Sarah said.

"I need to say something to you too, but let's leave it for later," I implored.

"Even though you might not like what you hear?" Sarah continued.

I responded by planting my lips against hers.

* * *

Sarah wondered why Daniel hadn't even glanced at her breasts, even though her flimsy and deeply cut t-shirt were extremely revealing. She was disappointed that she had given in and worn the clothes Brock picked for her, since they made her feel like a prostitute. Usually with men, she was irritated that they seemed to pay way more attention to her breasts than to her as a person. But Daniel was only concentrating on her face and eyes. His gaze was somehow reassuring and slowly seemed to be eliminating the anxiety that Brock's mission had generated. Her passion was returning. She was also afraid, because if Brock's information was accurate, she had no choice but to succeed in her mission. Reason told her to focus, but her emotions had her confused. As her growing passion messed with her resolve, the fear of failure grew. At the point at which the fear began to grow into panic, she heard herself asking Daniel to kiss her. The situation got out of hand quickly.

* * *

Sarah gave the address of the apartment and they headed off, closely glued to one another with their arms wrapped around each other's backs. Suddenly, Sarah was overwhelmed with a need for Daniel and she turned and threw herself into his arms, wrapping her leg around his waist while kissing him passionately. Daniel continued to move forward with Sarah in his arms. He staggered a bit, but he didn't want to waste a second. On Rue de la Bûcherie, Daniel pressed Sarah against the wall of a building recess and firmly cupped her breasts as he kissed her.

"Finally. I was afraid you weren't interested in them," Sarah said and grabbed Daniel between his legs, inspired by the photos Brock had shown her. Neither of them seemed to be able to get enough and they attacked each other as if they were afraid the pleasure could be taken away from them at any moment.

"I can tell that you're skilled in pleasuring women," Sarah said, surprising herself with this train of thought.

"How can you tell?"

"Your tongue is very strong," Sarah answered with passion in her eyes.

* * *

It was as if Sarah had put a spell on me and I could no longer access my sense of reason. If I'd had full command of my senses, I would have viewed my actions as being completely inappropriate for many reasons, but in that moment, I was totally controlled by my emotions. I had simply allowed the situation to get to the point that I was no longer even able to feel regret. I was consumed by her, and the Parisian life swirling around us was nothing but a distant distraction. My sense of feeling seemed to have vanished and I didn't react as she sunk her teeth and nails into my shoulder. We stumbled forward like two drunk people as we attempted to press tighter against one another. We travelled from one narrow lane to another even narrower lane, finally reaching a door where she stopped to let us in. I realized that once we passed through the door, there was no going back.

"I wasn't prepared for this at all," I said in a sudden burst of reason.

"If you're referring to condoms, I never do anything without them. But I'm prepared; I even have different sizes. I believe you might need the Trojan Magnum XL."

My temporary burst of reason was still in effect and I sensed something wasn't quite right.

"Don't get me wrong, I'm not loose! I've been out with countless men, but few have ever gotten farther than my front door," Sarah quickly explained, with slight desperation in her voice, since she clearly feared I would back out at the last minute.

"I'm not one to judge! This was just the last chance to make sure about this and you've already answered my question. Now, open the door before I explode."

Once inside, Sarah leapt into my arms, facing me. She was so slim and light, that it didn't even slow my ascent up the stairs. She removed her sweater and before I even had time to realize, he had removed her t-shirt as well. Her breasts swung loosely close to my face and encouraged me to pick up the pace. When we reached the second floor, she jumped down and opened the apartment door for us. She pushed me into the apartment at the same time she ripped off her jeans. We entered a large, empty living room and in the center, she turned me by the shoulders to face her. She stood before me in nothing but her high heels, her breathing more accelerated than mine, although I had just carried her up the stairs. The buttons of my shirt nearly popped off as she tore it open. She noticed the bullet wound in my side, which was well on its way to being healed. She kissed the spot gently, but didn't ask anything. Then she squatted down lower.

"I'd like to get acquainted with him before the condom goes on," she whispered as she laid tender kisses on my stomach. The lust in her eyes nearly drove me mad. No woman had ever displayed such a lack of inhibition, and I was more aware of my masculinity than ever before, as testosterone flooded my veins. She guided me to lie on my back on the soft rug and pulled off my pants and socks.

"Don't move a muscle. I'm in charge now," she commanded as she turned to retrieve the condom. She put the condom on as if she were simply caressing my cock and then she straddled me and guided me inside her.

* * *

Sarah didn't hold back and pleasured herself using a variety of positions, gyrating her hips and taking turns exciting only the outer labia or pushing me in all the way to the base of her vagina. I followed her movements, entranced and burning with desire for her swelling breasts and their expanding areolas. Finally, my self-control gave way and I cupped her breasts, gently squeezing her rock-hard nipples between my fingertips.

Now and then, Sarah turned her back to me and carried on with the same movements until she finally leaned back onto my stomach and chest and I felt her body tremble.

"Just let me rest for a moment and then it's your turn," she whispered softly.

After a few seconds, she rolled onto her side beside me and once again guided me inside her from the back as a sign that the roles were now reversed. In the end, I turned her around and entered from the front, giving her a turn to relish my enjoyment. All the while, I could feel her hands gently running over my buttocks, stomach and chest. I secretly watched Sarah's face become overwhelmed with pleasure when her eyes were closed. Suddenly, her eyes sprung open.

"You are so deep in me!" she exclaimed in ecstasy.

To that point, I hadn't had to hold back, but her words forced my pelvic floor muscles to tighten abruptly. There was a buzzing in my head as I came, and I could feel Sarah's hands gently cradling my face. Her eyes were flooded with tears.

* * *

We laid, sweaty and spent, on the floor with Sarah's back spooned tight against me. I caressed the curve of her hip and side and enjoyed the steady pace of her breathing. Suddenly I sensed an odd shift in the atmosphere, as if she had tensed with nervousness.

"What's wrong?" I asked.

She didn't answer right away, but rather, rocked her body slightly, which I recognized as an expression of anxiety. Finally, she asked if I wanted to hear what she had wanted to tell me in Square René Viviani. When she asked the question, it sounded as if she were about to burst into tears.

"Don't be afraid. Just tell me," I encouraged.

"Don't doubt for a moment that any of this was genuine, but from the start, my intention was to hit on you to get information and to switch your cell phone with an identical phone," she blurted out. She was speaking faster than normal, as if in a hurry to rid herself of all her anxiety.

"I'm guessing you were put up to this by the CIA. How on earth did they get you to go along?" I asked calmly.

"So you knew! They were the ones who arranged my stay here in Paris, even though I thought I was here on a grant from a literary foundation. That's why I agreed to listen to them, but the real reason was to save you. If I fail at my mission, your life may be at risk."

"Oh Sarah! First, I have to say that my intentions were nothing like this, but the situation just got completely out of hand. My reason for wanting to connect with you had nothing to do with needing an apartment. It'll relieve you to know that you don't need to ferret information out of me. I need you to put me in contact with Bruce Brock. I assume he's the person who's been in touch with you."

Sarah unfurled herself from my arms and turned to look at me with wide eyes. She opened her mouth to say something, but the words caught in her throat. I didn't want our closeness to end, so I decided to comfort her before she had a chance to shift gears to the cold reality that was soon facing us both.

"Can you put all that aside for a moment still and just lie with me some more? You have no reason to feel guilty, or then we both do."

She snuggled back into my arms with a deep sigh.

"I want to fondle you," I whispered in her ear.

She was quiet at first, but then she responded.

"Believe it or not, I've never been able to get an orgasm

other than during masturbation, and even then only occasionally. I get aroused too easily, but I'm never able to reach climax."

I raised up slightly and turned her onto her back.

"You don't need to. Just enjoy it," I assured her.

I got between her legs and laid my cheek against her stomach. I kissed her navel and then moved slowly downward, kissing each centimeter along the way. Her scent affected me immediately and I felt myself getting excited. Fortunately I had already ejaculated, since I wanted to keep focused. I was like a physician at work, only my job was to give pleasure.

I kissed and sucked gently on her slowly enlarging labia while I waited for her to relax into it. Gradually, it was as if they opened to the side and slightly upward. I carefully pressed my tongue against the major and minor labia on the left side and felt the smooth surface of the skin. If you do it very gently, it's almost as if you can imagine detecting each nerve ending along the surface of the skin. She moaned quietly and I had to struggle to make sure that the same feeling didn't grab hold of me and distract me from my task. I ran my tongue clockwise over her vaginal lips, passing over the clitoris and down the right side to the perineum and then upward to the opening of the vagina and urethra and back to her clitoris. I continued to take the same journey without rushing, thus enabling her to trust in the continuity of my actions. She grew further aroused and her inner labia grew so engorged that the clitoris disappeared completely. I realized that this may be the core of her problem with reaching climax, so I stopped to seek it out with my tongue – very cautiously at first. She didn't seem to react, so I pushed my tongue in deeper, until it met with the tiny, hard clitoral glans. From the hardness of my own erection, I knew I was on the right track. The more pressure I applied with my tongue and played with the glans, the more violently she moaned and the harder it was for me to focus my thoughts on her clitoris. I continued at the same rate, because I didn't want to awaken a fear in her that I might suddenly stop. About 30 seconds before her orgasm, when I was sure it was coming, I increased the movement and strength of my tongue as much as was possible. Suddenly she jolted and screamed out. Her back arched and she uttered noises that were a mix of pleasure and confusion. At the same time, she moved back from me and pressed her thighs together to force me away. She fell onto her side and pulled her knees into a fetal position and wept freely. I laid my head against her side without needing to say a word.

We remained in the same position for a long time in silence. Suddenly, without moving an inch, Sarah began to speak.

"Let's run away together and leave all this behind. We'll make sure we leave no traces beyond this apartment."

I didn't know what to say, but she continued.

"Can we even continue with this relationship after everything that's happened?"

We both knew, all too well, that neither option was possible.

17 CATCH-22
Joseph Heller 1961

Sarah called Brock and reported what I'd told her about my
intentions to try and use her to reach him. Sarah promised that
I'd explain everything if we could just meet up. Brock agreed
immediately. After hanging up the phone, she turned to look at
me. The relief was clearly written on her face.

"Brock is on his way. You were right that he wouldn't ask
for any details."

"Excellent! Now you can unburden your heart of that
concern. I don't know what you should do about your job
though, I can't help you there. I can say, however, that without
the truth, you'll always live in a state of fear."

In all likelihood, Sarah would quit her job and return to the
US, which means we would never see one another again. That
thought horrified me.

"I won't let myself be blackmailed for the sake of my job or apartment. I'm good at what I do, but if they try to blackmail me again, I'll give it all up voluntarily. I'm sure we'll still see each other in the bookstore from time to time," she said.

"If everything goes smoothly," I emphasized. I tried desperately to push away the thought that my plan could just as easily end in disaster, but Sarah saw through my denial.

"You're not suggesting that something might happen to you?" she asked, frightened. I didn't dare to respond.

"You're beginning to scare me," she stated.

"There is no good solution here. Running would be the worst option, so I chose to face my problems. It might not turn out well, but I'd rather try than live in constant fear," I explained. My solution had been chosen more on the basis of emotion than reason. The more I reflected on it, however, the more it felt like the best approach. At the same time, my fear seemed to vanish, once I noticed that my aversion to fear was stronger than the fear itself.

"Let me help you, since I'm already involved," she suggested, largely out of a similar desire to transform her fear into action.

"I don't doubt your abilities, but I already have a plan in place. You've already given me all the help I needed and I think it would be wise for you to leave before Brock gets here," I said. I nudged her gently toward the door. Before walking out, she turned around and I saw that her eyes were glistening.

"If you ever feel the need for some company, you can always call me," she whispered as she pressed her finger against my lips. "Don't say anything," she added and leaned in to plant a light kiss on my lips. She also slipped something into my pocket, but all my attention was on her departure. As I watch the door close between us, my eyes welled up as well.

* * *

The duty officer at the IOC excitedly called to the Operations Director.

"Brock's plan seems to be working. The blonde just exited the apartment, but the signal from the tracking device is still coming from the apartment. So she managed to replace the device."

"Excellent. Have we heard anything new from Brock?" the Operations Director inquired.

"No, but we know that he's meeting up with the Finn soon."

"Brock is as qualified as he is problematic. Without his skills, he would have been out of the picture long ago," the Operations Director mumbled to himself, then he turned his attention back to the contact on the line. "Keep me up to speed."

* * *

I shoved my hand in my pocket to see what Sarah had slipped in there. When I couldn't find anything right away, I removed my phone from my pocket so that I could feel around more effectively, but again, I came up empty-handed. Just to be sure, I checked my other pocket, but it was also empty. A gnawing feeling began to creep into my mind and I began to examine my phone. I unlocked the phone and checked my address book. It was empty! There should have been one number, so I realized that Sarah had, indeed, switched my phone with another at some point. Pekka had made me swear that I wouldn't let any outsiders get their hands on my phone or the Finns would lose a significant technological advantage. Now it had happened anyway and in the same instant, I had lost my support network. My plan was quickly breaking down, even before it had properly gotten underway. I would, perhaps, have been able to pull myself together if it weren't for the fact that it all came down to the realization that Sarah had betrayed me after all. I needed to sit down, but the room had nowhere to sit other than the rug on the floor.

I was suddenly startled by the feeling that someone was in the apartment with me. I hadn't heard or seen anything, but I felt an unmistakable presence. Then I heard a noise coming from behind me.

"I'm not sure how unusual it is to have that ability. It's the instinct of a wild animal."

I turned around and saw a black-haired, muscular man standing in the rear corner of the room.

"Brock, I assume," I said, masking my astonishment.

"Bruce Brock," he said as he approached me with his hand extended.

We shook hands in a surprisingly warm fashion and I felt an odd sympathy towards this guy that I had envisioned as a predator.

"Daniel Bremer, although you know who I am already. I expected you to come to the door, but it seems you have the ability to pass through walls," I said with a grin.

"I always come through the door and that, unbelievable but true, is even more surprising," Brock retorted.

"How long have you been here?"

"Longer than you think."

I didn't dare to push the matter any further and since I couldn't think of anything else to do, I indicated with my hand that we should sit on the rug.

"There's nowhere else to sit," I stated.

"This is fine," he responded curtly.

I suddenly noticed my cell phone lying on the floor next to him. Countless thoughts began charging through my brain. I must have dropped my own by accident at some point, but why had Sarah slipped another one into my pocket? Why had she been so discreet and hidden it from me? Maybe Sarah hadn't betrayed me. Perhaps my plan was still on track...

I bent forward and picked the device up off the floor as if I had left it there intentionally. I noted that Brock paid especially close attention to my actions and followed the movement of the device from the floor all the way to my right pocket.

"How did you know that we were involved?" Brock asked, consciously making the choice not to mention the CIA by name.

"I don't want to answer that."

Under no circumstances could I reveal my Finnish accomplices and I tried quickly to come up with some lie to give if he continued to press me on the matter.

"Was it Sarah?" he asked. His assumption was one that hadn't even occurred to me.

I didn't want to cause Sarah any problems, even if it would have been a convenient means of concealing my true source.

"I assume you know Marie," I continued with my hints and stalling.

"She told you?"

"Marie knows about Raymond's background."

"You're not answering my question," he insisted.

"I already told you that I don't want to answer that question." I responded with anger, ending our discussion on the matter.

He looked at me as if trying to read my mind. Then his phone rang. He glanced at the screen, excused himself and went into the bedroom, closing the door behind him. I hadn't even noticed that there was a bedroom. The door was disguised to look like a wall panel. The door appeared to be surprisingly thick, as if it had been soundproofed. I couldn't hear any of the phone conversation.

The phone call reminded me of the device Sarah had slipped into my pocket. What had Sarah been trying to do? Was it a tracking device? When the future is unsure, one has no choice but to improvise. On impulse, I decided to move the phone I'd picked up from the floor from my right pocket to my left, where I also had the device Sarah had given me.

* * *

"OK, go ahead," Brock said after he had closed the door on the soundproof room.

"The blonde lost the defective device the Finn had. If the Finn now notices two identical devices, he will definitely suspect something. We saw from the camera, same as you, that he retrieved the device that the blonde lost from the floor. What do you think? Is he starting to catch on?" asked the duty officer.

"He didn't react oddly when he found the device. He seemed to think it was his own, but it could also be the replacement device that the blonde carried in," Brock clarified.

"It wasn't. We checked it based on sound. The device's microphones didn't pick up the sounds of being handled or shoved in a pocket."

"OK, well, the device is in the Finn's right pocket," Brock

stated.

"Not anymore. He just looked at the clock on the device and put it into his left pocket," the officer corrected.

"Roger that. I'll retrieve the device without him knowing," Brock stated assuredly.

"That's not gonna be easy. When the Finn put the device into his left pocket, we could clearly hear another sound. The device that the blonde left must also be in his left pocket."

"What are you saying?"

"If he has both devices in the same pocket, then we can't keep him from figuring something out. The next time he reaches for the phone, he will surely notice that he has both devices," the officer explained.

"How about if I pretend to search for my own phone and say that it's missing. Then he'll remember the phone he found on the floor and he'll check it, at the same time realizing that he has two phones in his pocket. Then I'll make some statement about us having identical phones and I'll get back the device we want," Brock suggested.

"Except for the fact that you're talking on your phone right now. So that won't work."

"Well, I'll take this out and say that I'm missing my personal cell phone. If he doesn't understand at that point to check his own pocket, I'll ask him to show me the one he found on the floor," said Brock.

"But how will you know which device is which?" the officer asked, doubtful that Brock's plan would work.

"Have the blonde call him at precisely that moment on the device she left behind. She can pretend that she was trying to reach the Finn at his own phone. Come up with some good cover story and an explanation for how she got his number. That device will then stay with the Finn," Brock explained.

* * *

Brock came out of the bedroom and sat in front of me.

"Sarah told me that you have the solution to our problems," he said, cutting straight to the point.

"True, but I need your help."

"I'm interested to know how you know about our problems." This was the exact line of questioning I didn't want to hear.

"Did Sarah know about them?" I asked, skirting around the answer.

"So Marie knew about them?" he retorted, obviously confused.

"How about we discuss my plan rather than focusing on unessential matters," I suggested as a means of shutting down that line of questioning.

"Why do I get the feeling you're hiding something?"

We both sat there silently, measuring each other up as if preparing for battle.

"You need to contact the Georgians," I stated, attempting to direct the conversation.

"What? Sorry, you've lost me." He was taken aback with my statement.

"This may sound strange, but it will all make sense. I promise that if my plan works out, you will have your file and you'll be rid of Raymond," I said confidently.

"Raymond must absolutely not be harmed! You'll be eliminated if you even threaten to make a move in that direction," he claimed, clearly shaken.

"There's no danger of that. I know why you need him alive, so that's the foundation of my plan."

He was totally confused and studied my eyes for some explanation.

"Apparently we have handled our end of things very poorly, since you're able to take me so off guard," he acquiesced.

* * *

Brock had guessed that the solution would somehow be found with the help of the Finn. The situation seemed to be developing in the right direction, but it was the exact opposite direction he had assumed it would go. He had imagined that he would be steering the mission and using the Finn as a source or bait. As it turned out, the Finn seemed to hold the reins and the entire CIA organization was simply an accomplice to his plan. Could the Finn be carrying out a mission for another party, and if so, for whom?

"You need to rapidly contact Georgia's intelligence organization in Paris and get a couple of their agents to assist you. Make sure that at least one of them speaks English with an American accent. If that's not possible, we'll just have to adapt," Daniel said to get his plan underway.

"I'm sure that's no problem. I know one personally who was raised in the US," Brock responded. He was excited to see how this plan would proceed.

"You'll tell them that Raymond has a file that they would be interested in and of which you also would like a copy."

"Wait a minute! No one can see that file!" Brock shouted.

"I know. The Georgians are not going to get their hands on your file," Daniel reassured him and continued to explain further. "Raymond will assume he's meeting with the CIA. That's why the Georgians will need to play the role of

Americans."

"Why would Raymond believe they are CIA?" Brock pondered out loud.

"Because they will give Raymond my location and tell him to bring the file with him so that the exchange can be done in person. Why would Raymond have any reason to doubt them?"

"We can't deceive Raymond, since it isn't likely he'd hand over the file and, in retaliation, he may even leak important information if you aren't there," Brock stated.

"How are we deceiving him? I will be there!" Daniel confirmed.

"You're ready to sacrifice yourself? Why?"

"I'm not planning on sacrificing myself, unless things turn ugly. Your deal doesn't require that I remain onsite after the initial meeting," Daniel clarified.

"There's one small problem with your plan," Brock stated when he remembered Raymond's primary motivation.

"What's that?" Daniel asked, fearing that there was a fatal flaw in his plan.

"We promised to give up Marie's location after we receive the file, but we don't know where she is. You are only the starter, Marie is Raymond's primary target," Brock answered with a ring of disappointment in his voice.

"I've taken that into consideration," Daniel laughed.

"Do you think you could tell me the whole plan?" Brock began to sound as if he was starting to have faith in Daniel's plan.

* * *

Brock studied my eyes as if he were looking for clues of

deception. It seemed, however, that he was coming around and trusting in me more every minute.

"Here's the plan. The Georgians will meet with Raymond's crew at the restaurant on the corner of Rue de l'Hôtel Colbert and Rue Lagrange. The Georgians will give Raymond the address for this apartment, the door code and the key. I will wait here in the apartment. The only condition will be that Raymond has to come to the apartment alone and unarmed. Do you think he'll go along with that?"

"For Raymond, this is a question of honor, particularly in front of his men. He won't be worried that you're armed, because we've guaranteed his safety," he answered. He was beginning to see the logic of the plan, but he continued, clearly fearing there might still be holes. "Have you taken into consideration the fact that Raymond cannot be harmed in any other way either? I just don't see how you plan to survive this scenario."

"Once I leave the apartment and step out into the street, the Georgians will enter using the door code and their own key. They will get the file from Raymond as agreed, but don't worry, there is no danger involved yet at this stage," I said, avoiding his questioning expression and explaining my plan as convincingly as possible. He stared at me and, miraculously, didn't ask for any further details.

"You do realize that I have to protect Raymond? I'll stay in the bedroom in case I need to step in. If something happens to you, though, you're on your own. In that case, I'll come out and take my file back," he stated with conviction.

"That's already part of my plan. You'll wait in the bedroom until I'm gone and until the Georgians have the file in their possession. Then, when Raymond asks for information about Marie's whereabouts, you will step out and allow the Georgians to leave," I explained.

* * *

Brock was interested in Daniel's plan, but he was apprehensive about the fate of the file. It simply couldn't end up in the hands of the Georgians. Fortunately, he would be able to watch the events unfold from the bedroom, without Daniel knowing, and would be able to step in at any time.

"I have to warn you about one thing," Brock said, taking Daniel by surprise.

"Have you ever seen Raymond?" Brock continued.

"No, but I've heard that he's a sizable guy," Daniel answered.

"Sizable is an understatement in this case. He's a giant, well over two meters. And he's not just big, he's dangerous in all ways. He has expert level Krav Maga training and was a top-ranking kick boxer in his youth. He's maintained his condition and he enjoys assaulting people. The most dangerous thing about him, however, is that he unscrupulously uses methods that wouldn't even cross the mind of a normal person. He's nuts. You need to remember that there will be no rules or judges in this situation."

Daniel heard what Brock was telling him, but didn't waste any time trying to form a mental image. Fear, at this stage, when it was already too late to back out, would have been his worst enemy. He shoved his hand into his left pocket and grabbed the device that Sarah had left for him. He knew it was the device that lay closest to his thigh in his pocket. He checked the time from it and set it down, while Brock subtly followed his every movement. Brock was about to pat his own pockets as if looking for something when the whole scenario suddenly became clear to him. Daniel couldn't miss the fact that he had two phones in his pocket twice. If he took one of the devices out without any further reaction, he must be hiding the other intentionally. That would mean, also, that there was something special about the first device. Daniel appeared to be using it all the time, so perhaps it wasn't broken. Maybe it wasn't even the same device. Maybe he had received it from another player in the game and it intentionally looked identical. Most likely, he had disposed of the original. And if his assumption about the device were true, it was something so unique that the signal intelligence hadn't even been able to get any signal from it. Who had that kind of technology? Guests from outer space? But which device had he just removed from his pocket?

* * *

I noted that Brock didn't seem especially interested in the device I removed from my left pocket, not, at least, in the way he had been interested in the Finnish device I retrieved from the floor earlier and stashed in my right pocket. He must, therefore, assume that the latter was still in my right pocket. Then I came to the realization that he knew I had two devices and that the one he wanted was still in my pocket. He just wasn't aware that I had moved the device into my left pocket. Was it possible that he knew more about the significance of the Finnish device? I had a feeling that I would inevitably face more problems where the device was concerned.

We were starting to be in a hurry and Brock still had to hear the entire plan, because without his cooperation and approval, it couldn't work.

"I think you should hear what I'm planning for the file, so that you'll allow me to carry my plan to the end. Before that, however, I need to tell you what to say to Raymond once the Georgians have left," I said, carrying on with my strategy.

18 CHOKE
Chuck Palahniuk 2001

Brock listened closely to Daniel as he laid out his plan. In all its simplicity, it was both surprising and feasible. He agreed with Daniel that Raymond's new pseudonym, Azael, referred to the legend about giants. He recalled being frightened in his childhood and seeing nightmares when he had read the tales of the giants described in his mother's Old Testament as the offspring of Fallen Angels, i.e. Watchers, and daughters of men. His father had also told him a Cherokee legend in which a slanted-eyed giant married a Cherokee woman. Raymond was like the manifestation of his childhood nightmares, and if all went well, Daniel's plan would seal Azael's fate.

"I absolutely support your plan, but can I ask one more thing?" Brock asked. It was the first time he spoke out since Daniel began to explain his plan.

"Ask away," Daniel said, but he already figured he knew

what the question would be.

"It's obvious you aren't working alone. Who do you work for?"

"I don't work for anyone, but I have gotten help. I'm doing this because it has to be done and I want Marie and I to be able to live in peace," Daniel answered.

Brock looked at Daniel for a moment without moving and then said, "Let's do it!"

Both men set about getting ready. Brock contacted the IOC and received confirmation that Daniel's plan had been approved and that the Georgians were being contacted. Daniel stepped out of the apartment for a moment and called to Pekka to ask him to send a courier with the necessary items.

* * *

Fear is an unpleasant emotion. It tastes bitter in your mouth and feels like your diaphragm is being strangulated. Your breathing accelerates and your heart pounds as if you were running uphill. Beads of perspiration form on your forehead and your armpits moisten. The worst part is, however, the intensifying abdominal pains and growing nausea. In the end, your chest tightens like you're having a sudden heart attack.

Fear is a powerful emotion, and therein lies its greatest danger. A powerful emotion seizes your thoughts and transforms them into clear images. These clarifying thoughts have a habit of becoming realized both for good and evil, the former for hope and the latter as a consequence of fear. I struggled to focus on success rather than my fear, but it was in vain. I also tried to generate a feeling of anger, but instead of fury, I only felt overwhelmed by a sense of powerlessness. I was losing my self-control. Suddenly, a memory of Marie drifted into my mind and it calmed me. I also saw, in my mind's eye, Sarah's determined expression as she offered her help. It restored my composure and focus.

I recalled the advice of an old friend, who'd had a restless youth. He told me about the rules of the street. He said that the one who always wins is the one who strikes first, as long as the strike comes within the safety zone determined by reaction time, and the one doing the striking passes close enough using betrayal. He had wanted to warn me, since my large size supposedly attracted challengers. His theory proved wrong, however, since, despite his small size, he found himself tangled up in trouble often, whereas I never experienced anything of the like. Fear is many things. The process of preparing for conflict is also a type of fear, a fear that wants to realize itself. In this respect, I had been fearless.

There I was, however, with my fears, facing an inevitable and dangerous conflict. In this moment, if ever, my friend's advice would come in handy. Raymond was used to playing dirty and would undoubtedly use some form of deceit to get close to me. He would smile, speak in a friendly voice and extend his hand as he approached. Any decent person would want to believe in his good intentions and would reach out to shake his hand. I decided to draw an imaginary line in front of me on the rug. Once he crossed that line, I would attack.

* * *

Raymond had begun to get nervous when he'd heard

nothing from the CIA. When the call finally came, he didn't ask anything other than where the meeting place would be. The rendezvous was near the café where he'd seen Marie for the last time and the memory made him tense up.

The Hippopotamus restaurant on Rue Lagrange had a roadside terrace. Posing as CIA agents, the ominous Georgians had occupied the corner seats, from which they also had a view of Rue de l'Hôtel Colbert. Raymond sat with his entourage in the only available seats at the opposite end of the terrace. No one spoke. After a moment, a youngish Georgian man, who appeared to be more French than American, rose and walked over to Raymond.

"Our deal is only valid if you go alone and unarmed," the man said in French with an American accent.

"Who are you to impose conditions?" Raymond asked coldly.

"If you're afraid, we can call this off right away," the agent responded calmly.

There was a moment of silence as Raymond's men looked at their boss with slight embarrassment.

"Okay, how do we proceed?" Raymond asked as the agent was beginning to turn away.

"Come alone and join us at our table," the agent said.

* * *

Raymond smiled with satisfaction as he gripped the key and the code in his fist. If they thought he was afraid, they were sorely mistaken. The Finn might be dangerous, but Raymond had gone up against many opponents who were considerably more dangerous and he had always come out the victor. He trusted in his own dimensions and the surprise it generated. He was able to kick a man in the head from such a distance and so rapidly that it couldn't be anticipated. Furthermore, his kick could come like a bolt of lightning straight from a walking gait without even the smallest indication of forewarning. The aspect of surprise involved in his honed tactics had been taught by a trainer of the US Army's special forces. The technique involved walking toward your victim with your focus on their entire body, to assess the range of motion necessary for the kick and, only at the very last minute, to shift your eyes to focus intently on the victim's eyes. The sudden eye contact would freeze the victim for a split second. When eye contact had been established, the attacker knows that the victim's eyes are on his own and, therefore, not on the possible movements of his leg. Correspondingly, the attacker's eyes are already focused on the target for the kick, the victim's eyes, and his leg strikes the victim's temple before the victim ever sees it coming. The key is the attacker's relaxed presence, friendly expression and kind words expressed with a soft voice; it takes the victim off guard and makes him underestimate the threat for a moment.

Raymond walked up the stairs calmly so as not to wear himself out. He allowed his breathing to normalize before trying the key in the lock. The door opened, nearly on its own, and, to avoid any surprises, he stood back for a second. When nothing happened, he pushed the door open all the way and looked in from a safe distance. There was a narrow entryway that led to a large living room, where the Finn stood with his arms hanging relaxed at his sides. Raymond smiled and stepped in. He removed his jacket, hung it on the coat rack and proceeded at a natural pace toward the Finn, all the while assessing the right timing for a kick.

"Good evening. There's been a complete misunderstanding. I haven't been seeking you out to bring you any harm," Raymond said quietly. He extended his hand to shake and took a step forward with his left foot. At that precise moment, he raised his eyes to meet the Finn's eyes and instead of taking another step, his right leg rose for the kick. His extended arm swung backward for balance and to give the kick further strength.

* * *

I was alone in the living room and although Brock was hidden behind the closed door of the bedroom, I knew I was literally on my own in this situation. He wouldn't step in and get involved other than to prevent Raymond from being killed, so essentially, he was on Raymond's side. I had no desire to hurt anyone. Making sure that Raymond remained unharmed was, in fact, a necessary requirement for my plan.

The waiting time seemed to last forever. The slow passing of each minute was painful, since I didn't know when Raymond would be arriving. There was a growing paranoia in my head and I began to interpret every little noise as Raymond creeping up on me. I considered the ideas that he might try to surprise me by coming through the window or might shoot at me from another building. I told myself to relax, but I moved into the shadows beside the window to play it safe.

Even the smallest sound had begun to seem like a racket in my ears, until, finally, I heard the door to the building open downstairs. My hearing was now so attuned that even noises which one normally wouldn't hear were clearer than clear. After the door closed, I heard heavy footfalls coming up the stairs and I knew that Raymond had arrived. I moved to the rear of the living room, the furthest point from the entryway, so that I would have room to attack without any risk of Raymond crashing headlong into a wall. I heard the footsteps stop outside the door and my nerves were on edge. Finally, the key turned in the lock and the door opened.

Adrenaline rushed through my veins and the last shreds of fear took a backseat. I was in complete focus. The door opened only a crack at first, and I still couldn't see anyone. When the doorway finally filled with an enormous figure, which had to bend slightly to get in, I knew I was ready. Raymond's hair was white and it accentuated his weathered skin. There was something odd, even frightening, about his eyes and so I made the decision to avoid looking at them. He hung up his jacket and began to walk toward me. I focused all my attention on his chest, from where I assumed I would be able to notice instantly any possible surprise movements he was planning to make. He said something, but all I heard was a distant humming. The distance between him and the line I'd drawn narrowed quickly and that was my last clear thought.

* * *

Raymond exuded self-confidence as he approached Daniel, who seemed completely at ease, as if he had no idea what was coming. He'd decided to make Daniel pay for all the trouble he'd caused and wipe all the bad memories related to Daniel from his mind once and for all. The CIA could clean up after him, since they wouldn't want to draw the attention of the French authorities. He thought that Daniel's punishment was mild, since he wouldn't even have time to realize he'd reached the end of his rope. Marie, on the other hand, wouldn't be getting off that easily.

Daniel sprung unexpectedly into action as soon as Raymond stepped, with his left foot, over Daniel's imaginary line. Raymond's right leg had already been set into motion for the kick when he understood that Daniel was half a meter closer in the process of lunging in his direction. He tried to stop the motion of the kick, but the action had been set in motion, like a reflex. Instead of his shoe connecting with Daniel's temple, the upper part of his shin harmlessly grazed Daniel's upper arm. When Daniel felt Raymond's leg hit him, he instinctively grabbed Raymond under the thigh and lifted his lower body into the air. At the same time, Daniel used his right hand to reach over Raymond's left shoulder and around the back of his neck. This maneuver enabled Daniel to ram Raymond onto the rug crosswise underneath his own weight. Raymond was stunned for a split second when he crashed onto his back and Daniel dropped on top of him. During that split second, Daniel removed his left hand from Raymond's thigh and locked it together with the right hand around Raymond's back and behind his right shoulder. Then Daniel shoved his head into Raymond's right armpit. With his hands locked tightly around Raymond, Daniel pressed his right shoulder against Raymond's chin, preventing Raymond from being able to bite him.

Raymond growled like an injured tiger without any idea what was happening. Daniel lifted his own hips slightly and pulled his left knee across Raymond's stomach to the other side. Once his left knee touched the rug, he shifted his weight onto it and straightened the lower part of his leg to line up with his body so that he could press down Raymond's bent knee. In the same swift motion, he rolled onto his left side on the right side of Raymond's body. His head passed over Raymond's armpit to rest beyond his shoulder. He kept a firm grip behind Raymond's back as he switched sides, forcing the biceps of his right arm to press with increasing pressure against Raymond's neck. He began to twist his body, like the hand of a clock, away from Raymond. His shoulder tightened further against Raymond's neck like an anaconda, forcing Raymond's right arm up between the two of them. For a moment, Daniel laid there at a 90 degree angle in relation to Raymond's body. The extreme pressure on Raymond's neck cut off the blood flow to his brain. He lost consciousness instantly. At this point, only ten seconds had passed since Raymond had stepped over Daniel's imaginary line.

* * *

I suddenly became aware of someone tapping three times on my right shoulder. I looked up and saw my father bending down beside me as if he were refereeing a match. Then I understood that I was lying on my stomach, crosswise over Raymond, who was lying on his back, completely limp, in my chokehold. I had no idea what had happened or how long I'd been choking him. I had experienced similar blackouts a couple times in my youth. In my first track and field competition, I had broken the discus record with my first throw by over five meters, but I didn't remember anything about the actual execution. The second time was during the army, when I had fallen through the ice with all my gear, cross-country skis on my feet and a 10-kilo radio strapped to my back. When the blackout ended, I found myself lying on the shore, unharmed, and having received no help from any outsiders.

I immediately released my hold and looked around the room for my father. There was no one in the room other than me and Raymond, and I understood that I had likely just been seeing things. I checked Raymond's pulse and was relieved to find that he was still alive. I turned him onto his stomach and checked with my finger that he hadn't swallowed his tongue. He would regain consciousness quickly and I didn't want to be around when he did. I put on my jacket quickly and walked to the entryway. To my great relief, I found a small metal case in Raymond's jacket pocket. I traded his case with an identical one from my own pocket. Raymond began to stir and so I fled the apartment before he had a chance to see me. The Georgians needed to make it to the apartment before Raymond exited with his tail between his legs. I flew down the stairs, but slowed my pace to normal as I stepped out into the street. There were two dark-haired and sinister-looking men standing beside the door to the building. They glanced at me but didn't say a word. I held the door for them and they nodded appreciatively as they stepped past me into the building.

19 CRIME AND PUNISHMENT
Fyodor Dostoevsky 1866

Raymond had conflicting emotions. When he first came to, he didn't have any idea what had transpired. Slowly, he began to get a picture in his mind of lying on his back helpless in the chokehold of the Finn. The Finn had choked him, but hadn't taken his life, and he'd even turned Raymond over to ensure that he'd be able to breathe unobstructed. What a sign of weakness! He never would have shown the Finn that kind of mercy. Something was wrong, however. He didn't feel any of the rage or drive for revenge that had always given him strength in moments of defeat.

He had just managed to collect himself when the door opened and in walked two of the CIA agents who'd been seated on the terrace of Hippopotamus. One stayed by the door as a lookout and the other stepped in quickly to survey the apartment.

"You got what you wanted and now it's your turn to do your share," the younger agent said. It was the same agent that had spoken to Raymond at the restaurant.

"I suppose it is," Raymond answered.

He wanted the agents out of his sight as quickly as possible, since he didn't want to be forced to reveal his moment of weakness, and he really didn't want to answer any questions about his meeting with the Finn. He walked to the entryway and reached into the breast pocket of his jacket to retrieve the small metal case, which he then handed over to the agents.

"Now, where do I find Marie?" Raymond asked, feeling a sudden need to forget about her too. Suddenly a look of confusion crossed the faces of both agents as they directed their gaze past Raymond to the living room.

"Brock! Where did you come from?" the younger agent shouted.

* * *

Raymond turned around and saw a weathered man standing at the other end of the room like an apparition.

"I'll take it from here," Brock stated in a confident voice. Raymond heard the door open behind him and turned just in time to see the second agent's back before the door closed.

"Where should we begin?" Brock asked as a means of opening the conversation.

"We begin by you telling me where Marie is," Raymond answered, trying hard to match Brock's confidence.

"You got the Finn, but we didn't get the file," Brock responded calmly.

"What do you mean? Your agents just walked out with it!"

Raymond shouted, obviously confused.

"Those weren't our guys," Brock said, faking his own confusion.

Raymond's thoughts were all in a tangle and he felt dizzy.

"Why didn't you do something? Don't you understand what kind of catastrophe this is?" Raymond cried out and rushed toward the door to go after the agents. His hands were shaking so much that he struggled to open the lock, but Brock placed a reassuring hand on his shoulder.

"They didn't get the file we were after," Brock whispered close to Raymond's ear.

Raymond felt powerless. He turned toward Brock and looked at him as if begging for mercy. Because of their height difference, he had to lower his head in order to look closely into Brock's face and although the size difference normally would have demanded authority, in this instance it only accentuated his feeling of complete resignation.

"I...I just don't understand," Raymond stuttered.

Brock guided him by the shoulder back into the living room and sat him down on the rug. Then he sat down himself, a safe distance away, with his legs crossed in front of him.

"You've been operating based on assumptions. For example, the file you just handed over looked like your file, but the contents were quite different," Brock explained.

Raymond felt his chest tighten and he couldn't get a word out, which didn't much matter, because in his confusion, he couldn't think of a single thing to ask.

"You just handed over critical intel about the Russians, and that's going to make certain parties furious, to put it mildly," Brock continued, all the while checking Raymond's reaction.

"No way in hell! I'd never give up anything on the Russians, anyone else, but not the Russians or the Chinese," Raymond stated with a shaky voice. He was starting to believe that Brock was telling the truth, despite the inconceivability of it all.

"If you don't believe me, we can contact the Georgians and ask."

"Information about the Russians is in the hands of the Georgians now? That's suicide!" Raymond shouted.

"I believe you're right," Brock responded. He tried to avoid letting any of his statements sound as if he were mocking Raymond.

"Did the Finn switch the files?" Raymond asked and then continued immediately before Brock responded. "So the Finns were behind everything and this is their revenge."

"That, I don't know. Do you have any other information on the Finns? Why would they be interested in revenge?" Brock asked.

Brock was starting to wonder if it could all be so simple; that the Finns were behind Daniel's involvement. He had never heard of any active Finnish intelligence organization. Raymond didn't even hear his questions, but blurted out in panic, "You have to do something to stop the Russians from finding out! Contact the Georgians! I swear I'll compensate you many times over!"

"I'm afraid it's too late," Brock stated. "One of those agents was a Russian mole in the local Georgian organization."

The blood drained from Raymond's face and Brock feared he would faint.

"You do understand that even more damning information concerning you will get out if I die, even if it's at the hands of the Russians?" Raymond asked. Having played this card, he finally calmed down.

"That's what this whole plan was about," Brock stated evasively.

* * *

"Are you sure we're the only ones watching this?" the DCI asked the DDO as they both stood staring at the monitor image from the Parisian safe house.

"We're in a completely enclosed space that was built for these types of situations. I took the command from the supervising officer claiming clearance classifications, which is a rare but completely normal procedure. I also switched off all recording devices so that even files that are thought to be destroyed won't come back to haunt us," said the DDO reassuringly.

"It's about time to burst this boil. The pain it's causing has become more than problematic," the DCI said feeling hopeful.

"Yeah, it's not easy to get rid of a dark angel like this, who seems immortal. The Finn's solution is brilliant in its simplicity, however," stated the DDO.

"Who is this mysterious Finn anyway?" the DCI asked. He'd been so focused on Raymond Durand that he'd nearly forgotten about the Finn.

"According to our information, it appears he's just an innocent victim of the situation that some unknown party is either helping or using. Our background check did show, however, that he was a star linebacker for UCLA in the early 80s," the DDO answered.

"What party?" the DCI asked.

"We're looking into that. We have their communication device in our possession, but it's a technology we aren't familiar with," said the DDO.

"Are we sure it was safe to allow the Finn to leave with the file?"

"We had to get the file out of Raymond's clutches. The Finn is still carrying our tracking device in place of his own cell phone, so we can track his movements. The entire EDT team has been assigned to monitor him and that file. The Finn is also aware that he can't open the file if he wants to remain among the living," the DDO said confidently.

"Don't you think it's possible that the Finn knows his phone's been switched and that he's carrying a tracking device?"

"That's just it! We're sure he does know! That's why Brock placed a traditional transmitter in the Finn's clothes. So when he disposes of the cell phone tracker, he'll think he's on his own," the DDO explained with a grin, then he turned serious once again as he said "Just make sure you get that file from him as soon as possible."

* * *

"Do you know what or who is Azael?" Brock asked Raymond.

"Sounds like something with 7 snakeheads, 14 faces and 12 wings," Raymond responded in a voice that made the hair on Brock's neck stand upright.

"So you know the story?"

"What story?"

"Azael was a fallen angel, a dark angel that, according to the story, was chained in the desert until judgment day," Brock said, repeating the story he'd been told by Daniel. "On the other hand, the desert may have just been symbolic, since another version states that he was waiting for judgment between Heaven and Earth," Brock continued.

"What's this gotta do with me?" Raymond asked, but he

had a hunch he already knew the answer.

"We can't physically chain you anywhere, but we can only guarantee your safety by taking you into the witness protection program, or actually, a similar program," Brock stated the plan flat out without wasting any words.

"In the USA, you mean?" Raymond asked.

"Exactly. You will need to drop everything here and we'll fly you by military plane to our closest airfield," Brock answered.

"What about everything I own?"

"Everything you own was acquired through deception, so there's no use pining after that stuff. We can, however, guarantee you a comfortable life, albeit under full surveillance. You won't be allowed to contact anyone from your former life," Brock explained.

"And if I refuse?"

"Then we're all fucked," Brock answered honestly.

* * *

After exiting the building, I headed to the left toward the Seine, away from the terrace at Hippopotamus, where Raymond's men and the rest of the Georgian team were still seated. My nerves gradually began to calm, but at the same rate, there was a pain increasing in my left side. I gently touched the spot under my jacket and found that my side was warm and wet. In the struggle, my wound must have reopened! I could feel the blood now starting to make its way down my thigh and onto my pants. Luckily, I was wearing black, so the red color wouldn't attract too much attention yet. I looked for my phone from my left pants pocket, where I'd placed it, but the pocket was empty. Finally, I found it from my jacket pocket and knew that something was wrong. I checked the address book in the phone and that's when I understood that Brock had, indeed, stolen my device. Now I had no support network, but my biggest concern was that the device had fallen into the hands of the CIA.

My first thought was to walk to Maurice's restaurant, but for some reason, that idea didn't appeal to me. Then I remembered that I had asked Pekka and Anneli to drop off the clothes I'd purchased with Marie at Shakespeare and Company. After I got my wound dealt with, I could change into clean clothes there. It was starting to be late, but, fortunately, the bookstore was open late. I was sure that either Lisa or Sarah would be there and I would need their help.

I arrived at the Quai de Montebello at the end of Rue de l'Hôtel Colbert. The second story of the corner building on the left side extended up and out over the sidewalk. The extended section was supported by a row of angular stone pillars. I walked between the building and pillars toward Shakespeare and Company. Suddenly, an American-looking man stepped partially out from behind one of the pillars.

"Hello Daniel," he said like we were acquaintances.

I instinctively took some distance and kept my back to the wall so no one could come up behind me.

"I didn't mean to scare you. My name is John and I'm part of Brock's team. You can give me the file now," he said reassuringly.

"I won't be giving the file to anyone but Brock himself," I stated.

"Don't force me to take it from you." His tone became more threatening.

A deep calm filled my mind and I looked directly at him.

"I'm sure you don't want to attract the attention of the French authorities. I guarantee that I will deliver this file to Brock untouched, but I also plan to protect it from all other outsiders, by any means necessary, until that time," I explained, trying not to provoke any aggression.

He seemed to be thinking about what I'd said, so I decided to simply continue on my way to Shakespeare and Company. He didn't try to stop me. At that moment, I realized that using the CIA's phone obviously couldn't weaken my situation, since they appeared to be tracking me anyway. It might even be wise to show my cards, since my only intention was to return the file to Brock. I dialed Maurice's number.

"Maurice," said a familiar voice on the other end.

"Salutations, my butterfingered old quarterback!" I greeted him happily.

"Daniel! Where are you? Is everything okay?"

"It's all starting to come together. You don't need to worry anymore. I'll fill you in at some point, but right now I still need some help from you," I explained quickly.

"Whatever you need, my friend."

"My wound opened again and I need new stitches. Do you think your friend would be willing to fix me up again?"

"Of course! Where should I ask her to meet you? Are you sure everything's okay?" Maurice asked, an aspect of doubt and concern coming back to his voice.

"I'll be waiting for her at Shakespeare and Company. Call this number if she can't make it. Like I said, you can relax. I just have one little thing still to take care of and then I can get back to my normal life. I'll call you then," I told him.

"I'll tell her to hurry. Goodbye." Maurice hung up.

Somehow I felt sure, however, that neither of us believed it would only be one last little thing.

* * *

Raymond studied Brock's face closely.

"Who is that Finn? Is he a Finnish agent?" Raymond suddenly asked.

"He's actually just a nobody that you handpicked to be your victim. Some organization is using him, but whether or not it's a Finnish organization, we don't know. Do you think the Finns are planning something?" Brock asked, repeating the question he'd asked earlier.

"That's hard to say, since I've never run across any Finnish intelligence operations. They'd have cause for retaliation, sure, but...," Raymond considered.

"Well, that's our hypothesis at the moment. I think this whole chain of events has a specific purpose and that the Finns play an important role in it," Brock stated.

"You know, for years, I've been practicing my ability to project fear onto my adversaries and it's worked surprisingly well. I find that fear is crippling and makes opponents almost long for defeat. The Finn, however, didn't react to it at all, and it wasn't just a matter of courage. He appeared to have mental abilities that exceeded those of normal people," Raymond said, genuinely puzzled by what had gone down in the apartment earlier.

"I noticed that myself. Even though you set out to affect him with fear, it seems he managed to turn the tables and have an impact of a different sort on you," Brock stated.

Raymond had felt the shift. The fury that had been raging inside him was dissipating; oddly enough, so was his strength. He had to do something. He had to focus, invade Brock's thoughts and interrupt his train of thought.

"Let's shake on our agreement then," Raymond said, extending his hand.

When Brock held out his own hand, he noticed, surprisingly, that it was shaking. He felt unbelievably weak. He knew something was wrong, but he couldn't back away. Raymond looked intensely into Brock's eyes and imagined himself as a monster. It took Brock's brain a split second to understand what was happening to him, but by then, he was already in Raymond's control. Their hands met.

Brock felt a sudden pain in his chest. It became difficult to breathe and his stomach started to churn. In that same instant, he saw before him his childhood nightmare: a giant, evil-looking man whose eyes appeared to be glowing in the darkened apartment. Raymond was trying to get into his head and he struggled to maintain control. This must be thought projection, which he'd heard talk about in the CIA. Brock hadn't believed it would work or, at least, not on him.

"Now you'll see for yourself how fear works," Raymond said, feeling his strength slowly returning. "I'll agree to your proposal, but before that, I want to tell you something."

Raymond began his tale in a soft voice and Brock could do nothing but listen at first, even though he had no idea why Raymond was telling him this story. Gradually, the incredible tale began to develop a clear plot, but Brock still couldn't figure out how it was relevant for their current situation. Suddenly, Raymond mentioned a few names and Brock snapped to attention. Raymond pushed forward and then Brock heard a sentence that caused him to see a sudden bright flash before his eyes. The sentence was the glue that brought the tale together. Now he understood the whole picture and he wanted no part of it. He realized he'd allowed himself to be led into a trap.

"And now you know the background of the file," Raymond said with full understanding of how cruel and wise his move in the game had been.

* * *

"It looks like the Finn's plan worked. Raymond seems to be falling in line and will likely agree to our offer, which I think, in all honesty, is too lenient," the DDO stated. He kept his eyes squarely on the monitor tracking the events taking place in the Parisian safe house.

"What if he doesn't agree?" asked the DCI.

"I don't know yet. We'll try, perhaps, to reach an agreement with the Russians that allows them to punish Raymond but not kill him. Then, we'll have to update our proposal. There are just too many risk factors, so this plan has got to work."

Just then, his cell phone rang.

"Yes?" he answered with an irritated voice.

"The Finn is literally following the plan and refuses to hand the file over to anyone but Brock. He doesn't seem, however, to have noticed that the device has been switched, so we're still able to track all his communications. Everything seems to be under control for the moment," the duty officer explained.

"Don't take any risks; hold back and let him operate freely. Just make sure that no outsiders get involved," the DDO instructed, before hanging up and turning his attention to their options with the Finn.

"Everything okay?" the DCI asked.

"Everything as concerns the Finn and the file," replied the DDO. All of a sudden, both men heard something that alarmed them. Raymond was beginning to tell a tale that drew their attention, but also threw the DCI into a sudden panic.

"Why isn't Brock cutting him off?" the DCI asked, his voice shaking.

"Why would he? What he's saying makes no sense," the DDO answered, clearly confused.

"God damn it! Call Brock immediately and tell him to get out of there!" the DCI yelled, finally catching wind of Raymond's plot. But a second later, it was all over.

"You shouldn't have heard that," the DCI stated ominously. He was silent for a moment and then said, "We've gotta get rid of Brock now".

The DDO stared at his boss astounded.

"The EDT team would never agree to that and it would be too risky in this day and age," the DDO replied sharply.

"Then I'll do it myself," the DCI said in a chilling voice.

* * *

There are things that, because of a possible investigation, few need ever know about. The DDO was definitely not one of the few, and the existence of Arrowhead was certainly not something that he should have known about. The DCI had said too much when he'd stated that he'd take care of the matter, but the information that the DDO had heard coming through the monitor had been even more sensitive in nature and had already sealed his fate as a marked man. Normally, even the DCI wasn't privy to information about Arrowhead operations, but this time, he had personally reached out for their help. He couldn't, of course, reveal how he'd known to send Arrowhead to Paris already four days earlier. If the DDO found out that the DCI had ordered that Raymond be monitored by clairvoyants in order to stay on top of the developing situation, he would have thought the DCI had gone mad. But the DDO wasn't part of the inner circle that had witnessed the abilities of true clairvoyants. Rather, he believed the official report that stated that the CIA had cancelled its psychic espionage program in 1995. The DCI didn't bother to mention that his French colleague had called and congratulated him on dealing with Raymond in a way that had best served all parties concerned. The French never got involved in anything as long as French citizens weren't in danger. The CIA was, therefore, left to its own devices to make sure it stayed below the radar of the French police. If they were caught, it would lead to a political conflict, which the French intelligence service would do nothing to prevent. Officially, the whole phone conversation had never taken place. So, Arrowhead had also received the unofficial approval of the French.

20 UNDER FIRE
Henri Barbusse 1916

Arrowhead 5 was an ultrasecret task force that didn't officially exist. If, by some chance, it were to become exposed, it would be classified as a secret tactical reconnaissance team. In reality, the task force had anti-terrorist training and was utilized not to rescue hostages but to eliminate harmful targets. Arrowhead 5 was just one of many such groups and its area of focus was European targets. Every member of the group spoke English and at least one European language as a native language or as well as a native language. They were all ex-Delta or ex-SEAL soldiers, but they were no longer working in the service of the Government. They participated in each mission as a private person on commission without any legal protection. If they were caught at any point, they were on their own with no knowledge of the true identity of the individual who had assigned the mission or even the intelligence community for whom they were working. They had only to believe that they were working on behalf of their country. According to the contract they'd signed, however, they were not to be caught alive. For that reason, each member carried a small syrette of poison with them at all times. They were comforted by the knowledge that, should anything happen to them, the person each of them named, in advance, would receive, as beneficiary, the right to a secret life insurance account in Switzerland.

The leader of Arrowhead 5, John Grace, sat eating a late breakfast in Montana when his secured phone rang. It would come to be the only normal aspect of the upcoming mission.

"Grace, this is Patterson. How would your group like to earn double for an ordinary assignment?"

"It reeks of something that's not on the up and up... Why would you be willing to pay extra for an ordinary job?" Grace didn't even try to disguise his distrust.

"Well, you won't have any time to plan or run through any drills before you're on your way to the destination," Patterson replied to the anticipated question.

"Do you have any idea how we've managed to stay alive all this time? It's because we plan carefully and thoroughly and we drill, drill, drill and drill some more," Grace stated. He was ready to dismiss the job flat out.

"Don't worry. Time is limited, but you'll have time to run drills onsite in the actual location where the operation will take place. The mission involves storming into a normal apartment, but without attracting any unwanted outside attention, naturally. We'll deliver the target to you later to that same location," Patterson reassured Grace.

"Where will this take place and when?"

"In Paris, within the next five days, but not before Sunday,"

Patterson said.

"Ok, who's the target?" Grace asked despite knowing that the target generally wasn't revealed until the crucial moment.

"I could answer that if I knew. We have a list of possible targets and an information packet ready on each one. All our intel data will be handed to you at your holding site in Paris," Patterson answered. His enthusiasm grew when he noticed that Grace seemed to be leaning toward taking the assignment.

"Equipment?" Grace asked as he began, already, to formulate a plan.

"Sterile standard equipment will be waiting for you at the holding site."

"Transportation?" Grace continued with his standard line of questioning.

"You'll be transported by military plane to England where you will each be joined by a spouse, who will accompany you by train over the canal to Paris. Your passports and credit cards are ready for use."

"Understood. I'll contact my group. The decision has to be unanimous or we're out. I'll call you back soon," stated Grace in a neutral voice.

Patterson had no choice but to sit tight and wait, but Grace's call came within 30 minutes.

"We're on. We'll be ready within the hour. Where should we meet? I also need to give you our list of required specialized gear."

* * *

I noticed from my cell phone clock that it was nearing 11 at night. Shakespeare and Company closes at 11, so I was starting to be in a hurry. I quickened my pace and charged into the bookstore in such a hurry that Sarah, who was standing in front of the cash register, assumed I was running from something. The situation wasn't improved by the fact that I rebuffed her attempt at a hug by showing her my blood-stained shirt.

"Have you been shot?" she asked horrified. Before I had a chance to reply, Lisa also rushed up, having heard Sarah's question.

"I'll lock the front door," Lisa said in a frightened tone and ran past us.

"No, no! That's not it," I exclaimed. "My old wound reopened and it's bleeding. No one's following me," I added, trying to calm everyone down.

I looked around for possible outside listeners and when I didn't see any nearby, I continued to explain in a low voice.

"Actually, the CIA is tracking my movements." All it took was for the women to glance at one another for them to know that they were both equally up-to-speed on the situation.

"What do we do now?" asked Sarah.

"I've asked an acquaintance to send a doctor here to stitch me up. A couple bags of my clothes should have arrived here. Can I stay upstairs to take care of my wound after closing?" I asked even though I knew the answer in advance.

"Lisa, if you'll take care of closing the store, I'll walk Daniel upstairs. Remember to watch for the doctor to arrive," Sarah said in a commanding voice that left Lisa no room to argue.

Sarah told the two customers wandering around upstairs that the store was closing, and once they'd left, she helped me to lie down on the bed.

"I'm not injured," I reassured her and rebuffed her attempts to coddle me.

"You know, I've prayed for your safety and I swore that if

you ever walked back in here, I would take your advice to heart. There was no way I could just go home, so I came back here to wait on the off chance that you would show up again," Sarah said with tears welling in her eyes.

"What advice are you referring to?" I asked.

"This job was just a bribe, even though I didn't know it. Shakespeare and Company is innocent in all this. I wanted to tell the owner the truth and let her decide, but I couldn't get her involved. Dangerous or not, this is my responsibility to bear on my own. This is my dream job, but I know I have to quit or I'll be vulnerable to being blackmailed again. After all, the most important thing is to know you're doing something you've truly earned."

* * *

Brock wanted to be rid of Raymond as quickly as possible, since he was clearly unpredictable. More than anything, he was concerned about his own level of fear, which he was sure would dissipate after Raymond left. He called a car to pick up Raymond and Raymond contacted his own men to tell them they could take off.

"For safety reasons, I'm going abroad. That's all you need to know," Raymond stated into the phone.

The car arrived soon and two security men came to escort Raymond from the apartment. Neither of them bothered to shake hands.

"Heart attack, car accident, drowning, suicide... that's how these things usually end up," Raymond stated as his final words.

Brock had been thinking the same thing, but it didn't concern him. This was his final assignment. He had already decided to disappear into the northern mountains of the state of Georgia. If anyone wanted him, they'd have to come find him – and he would be ready.

Brock knew that he had to meet with the Finn in person and take back the file untouched. They agreed to meet at the same apartment, but the timeframe remained unsettled. Brock had asked for the Finn's phone number so that he could notify him when Raymond left the apartment, but the Finn had refused. Instead, the Finn had asked for Brock's number and promised to call. In the end, it was all the same, because he knew the number to the phone the Finn was carrying. Now it was time to take the final step, so he went ahead and dialed the number.

"Hel-lo," Daniel answered, jumping suddenly as the doctor stitched his wound.

"Is something wrong?" Brock inquired.

"Hey there, Bruce...my wound opened while I was wrestling about with Raymond, so the doctor is stitching me up as we speak. That's why I sound funny. How'd it go after I left?"

"All went according to plan! How quickly can you get back here so we can finish this thing? Is the file still secure?" Brock asked impatiently.

"The file's fine. Hang on, I'll ask the doctor how long this will take." Upon hearing the doctor's estimate, Daniel told Brock he would be there at half past midnight.

* * *

Arrowhead 5 arrived on Friday afternoon at the Gare du Nord station in Paris, having taken different trains to avoid attracting any unwanted attention. They continued from there on the RER-D line to Malesherbes in the south of Paris. From the station, the group drove by car to a lone house in the middle of the forest that had been carefully chosen to serve as the holding site. After arrival, all connections with the outside world were cut off until such time as the mission had been completed, and the women who had accompanied the team were ordered to remain at the holding site. The group was given 2-3 days for planning and drilling. The only problem was that they still had no idea what the actual mission was, so that made the operation quite unique. They had only been given a list of likely targets and the assignment was to either eliminate or kidnap one or more of the targets.

"Gentlemen, I'll give you the good news first," John Grace said, once all the men had gathered in the living room.

John Grace was not actually the real name of the group leader, it was a name assigned to him because of his attractive appearance. It was misleading, however, which was often helpful in deceiving targets. In reality, the beautiful exterior concealed a cold and manipulative person. The group's other seven members included Wayne, Scrag, Nebula, JJ, Speedy, Boz and Argus – all named to reflect some personal attribute of the person in question.

"The assault will take place in a CIA safe house that we will visit prior to the attack," Grace began.

"The same building has an apartment that is available to rent on a weekly basis. This is one reason why the CIA chose this building as a safe house; the building residents are used to seeing different faces in the hallways and stairwell. This works to our advantage, but the biggest plus is the fact that we were able to rent that space to use as our 'landing site', and it's located directly above the strike zone."

No one raised any questions yet, so Grace continued to list

the positive aspects of the job.

"Our target is not at all expecting our attack. Oh yeah, and the best part, we have both visual and audio connections to the apartment."

"If everything is supposed to take place without making a sound, how are we expected to surprise our target?" JJ asked.

"We will use gas cartridges that can be installed in advance and discharged remotely, as well as subliminal audio frequencies. Unfortunately we can't install anything ourselves in the apartment, but the CIA will do it for us. We also won't have visual or audio connections until right before the actual assault, since whatever is going on before we enter that apartment is none of our business," Grace replied.

"Suits me fine. I don't want to know anything about what they're doing," Boz commented.

"Won't the gas spread via the air vents to the rest of the building and set off an alarm?" Argus asked skeptically.

"I demanded special equipment for exactly that reason. The gas we're using is odorless, knocks you unconscious immediately and can be absorbed dermally, but it neutralizes within twenty seconds after coming in contact with oxygen. So we will have to install cartridges all over the apartment to ensure that the target would be exposed. And if one of you has a question about subliminal frequencies, I can't answer it," Grace explained.

"And our equipment?" asked Wayne.

"The less equipment we have, the more inconspicuously we can exit the building. The targets won't be geared up and, at the most, they'll have a small handgun," Grace said as a means of explaining his choices. "Each of you will have a Browning HP, equipped with a silencer, and the actual assault team will have H&K MP5SDs. Those of us who are entering the apartment will only be using plastic bullets to ensure that no neighbors are injured by stray shots through the walls. Any target standing in front of a window must be hit, because I don't want any broken windows. Plastic bullets are lethal up close, but just to play it safe, those on backup will be armed with standard bullets as well."

"I'm sure I don't need to mention that all the equipment is sterile. There is nothing that can point in any direction, even for the purpose of redirection. We will likely be linked with ex-SAS mercenaries, but they won't find any evidence of that. No one, by the way, is allowed to speak English anywhere in the vicinity of the target building. You'll all just speak your second language, since each of you understands enough of all these languages. If we end up having any dealings with the French, we'll just use whatever is our strongest second language and pretend that's all we know how to speak. Only the group's 'French representatives' can speak French," Grace explained.

"What about our assault gear?" Wayne asked his question again more specifically.

"The entryway of the apartment is narrow, so two people already block the route. They will be fully outfitted, anyway, just to be safe. The whole group will be wearing Kevlar vests and those storming the apartment will also be equipped with ceramic composite body armor. They'll also have ballistic helmets and CT-12 respirators. For extra protection, the set also includes a fireproof Arvex suit, Pantotex pads for knees and elbows, as well as fireproof gloves and undergarments. Everyone else will have to make do with the Kevlar vests."

"For communication purposes, a secured short-range network has been established, which works via bone conduction headsets and throat microphones," Grace added.

"How can we even formulate a proper plan without a

specified mission?" Nebula asked, having sat patiently and listening to this point.

"We make sure all the basics are in order. First, we make a plan that's as simple and flexible as possible. We consider everything that could go wrong and find solutions. Secrecy is essential. We must ensure that neither the target nor the neighbors have any reason to suspect anything. Then we'll go in and familiarize ourselves with the place, photograph everything and construct as identical a simulation course as possible back here. Then, we'll just run drill after drill using different scenarios." Grace's answer could have come directly out of a textbook for special forces.

"Remember the advantages of surprise and speed. Our window of action is very short: the door opens, the group enters, the assault begins and the door must be shut immediately to muffle any sounds. All that takes place in less than 30 seconds and then our withdrawal with the target or targets in body bags must happen one minute later," Grace said, stressing the essential objective of the plan.

As a means of compensating for expressing his doubt, Nebula stated, "In terms of surprise, having the key to the door is definitely an enormous advantage."

* * *

There was still nearly an hour until the Finn was scheduled to arrive, so that gave Brock a chance to think of his survival plan in peace. It was clear that his career as an agent was over. That thought was a relief, since he'd been considering that option for a while already. Now there was no longer a choice to be made. Europe was a good place to disappear, since he knew it like the back of his own hand and he had contacts that could be trusted in every country. No one in the CIA had even close to the skills he had in terms of making himself disappear. There were enough agency money caches in Europe to support even a large family for their entire lives, and he didn't have any qualms about using them. No one else knew about the money and if he turned the money back in, it would put him at risk. Besides, the money would then likely end up in the pockets of dishonest clerks or being used for illicit operations. He planned to spend a couple years in Europe letting the dust settle and then move back to his own home ground under another identity.

In order to successfully disappear, he would need to handle this final meeting with the Finn without the watchful eye of the surveillance cameras in the apartment. He would exit the building through the attic, which he had already checked out, and would walk along the roofs past his own EDT team which was busy surveying the street below. Even if the cameras stopped working, the surveillance team probably wouldn't dare to send anyone in, but would wait for the Finn to reemerge. So, he would bind the Finn at gunpoint and exit the building first. He calculated that his plan would afford him enough of a head start.

The fact that the cameras were off had to appear to be a malfunction in order to avoid drawing suspicion from the surveillance team. Therefore, the cameras couldn't be broken one at a time, but rather, Brock would need to damage the control unit. But how could he manage to do it while also standing innocently in the center of the living room? He went into the bedroom to check from the monitor which areas of the apartment were outside of the cameras' range. Fortunately, the control unit was attached to the bedroom wall, close to the floor, and lay outside of the visual image, so one could crawl to it without being spotted by the camera. He measured the metal cover of the unit with his eye and went to the kitchen. From one cabinet, he found a wide candle of suitable height and a lighter. While keeping his back toward the camera, he slipped the candle under his shirt. He walked back over to the bedroom door, from which the shallow dead zone began. He bent down, as if to tie his shoelace, but continued lower until he was pressed against the floor. Then he crawled quickly toward the control unit. The candle was perfectly dimensioned to fit under the unit. It left room for the flame, but wasn't close enough for the flame to lick the surface of the unit. He lit the candle and crawled with lightning speed back to his original position and stood up as if nothing had happened. Just then, his phone rang. Did someone see what he did after all?

"Spook," he answered, covering his insecurity with irritation.

"It's been awhile," the DCI greeted him with an overly friendly tone.

"What's the update?" Brock inquired. He immediately recognized the voice of his old enemy.

"We just heard that the Finn is coming at 0030. It's important that you find out what organization is helping him. Try to make friends with him and hopefully he'll give you something," the DCI instructed.

"Understood. Bye," Brock responded.

"Wait, hang on! The cameras just shut off. Try to find out what's wrong with them," the DCI said, his voice exposing his alarm.

"Got it. I'll look into it," Brock stated and hung up with a broad smile across his face.

Brock had a feeling that something wasn't adding up. The DCI was too high a position to be calling a field agent, even though the mission concerned something as serious as the file in question. Then he realized that the mission he had just been given wasn't actually directly related to the file. It appeared that they wanted to prolong the Finn's visit and that would mean they needed time for something. This raised many questions for Brock: What were they planning? Why wasn't he being told the reason? Why did they have to hide the real reason from him? Why had the DCI personally assigned him the task?

* * *

On Saturday, Arrowhead visited the operation site. By Monday afternoon, four members of the group had moved permanently into the upstairs apartment. The plan was simple. The four members would occupy the upstairs apartment and carry out the assault. The two fully-outfitted members would enter first while the other two hung back momentarily on the stairs to ensure that no outsiders happened on the scene at the critical moment. When they were sure the coast was clear, they would also enter the apartment and close the door. All of this should happen within a matter of seconds. The subliminal frequencies would begin before the assault and the gas cartridges would be set off exactly 30 seconds before entry. The other four members of the team would be standing by in the vicinity, but far enough away to avoid raising any suspicions. The getaway car was parked close enough so that it could reach the front of the building at precisely the right moment. When the assault was imminent, one of the men would move in to stand guard at the outer door to the building, one would get behind the wheel of the car and the other two would guard both ends of the street.

The first surprise came at 10 p.m. The contact phone for the closed network rang.

"The target has changed," the contact told Grace.

"I hate last minute changes! Who's the new target?" Grace asked angrily.

"Brock."

There was a moment of silence, which was broken by Grace's icy voice. "You do understand that Brock is one of our own and a colleague? What do want done with him?"

"That's the problem. That's why this is not a kidnapping, you're eliminating him." The contact waited cautiously to see what reaction this statement would generate.

"If you're fucking with me, you'll realize your error some night when my knife is entering your throat," Grace threatened with an icy tone.

"We could never have predicted this and it was confirmed for us just a moment ago. It comes from the highest level that Brock is a traitor. He's also a huge threat to US security. Just think of him as a soldier whose mission is to be a victim for the benefit of the homeland."

"Cut the bullshit. When is the H-hour?" Grace asked, seething with rage.

"No more than a few hours from now. We'll notify you of the exact time as soon as we know. Everything else is the same. The original target, the Finn, will also be in the apartment and he should also be eliminated as per the original plan. He'll be unarmed. Neither of them will see this coming," the contact explained.

"I hope you understand that you just raised the degree of difficulty by a thousand? Brock is well-versed in these types of operations," Grace stated before hanging up, his anger continuing unabated.

After 30 minutes, the contact called again.

"The operation will begin at 0015, whereby your men in the street will move into surveillance positions. The H-hour is +05 from the moment when you observe the Finn entering the building. According to our information, that will be at 0030. We'll make sure that he doesn't try to leave too soon."

* * *

Sarah seemed concerned when I told her I was returning to the apartment to hand Brock the file. She offered to deliver it for me, but I couldn't let her do that, of course. It would anyway have caused the guy trailing me to get nervous. They were likely already thrown off enough by the fact that I was wearing completely different clothes.

The guy who had talked with me earlier was standing in front of the bookstore, not even trying to disguise his presence. I walked directly over to him and asked him to cover my back for potential pickpockets; after all, we did share common interests. All the way from Shakespeare & Company to Rue de l'Hôtel Colbert I was shadowed by several people, of which I only caught a glimpse. When I finally turned onto Rue de l'Hôtel Colbert, I realized that they had all suddenly disappeared as if on command. It was oddly quiet.

Brock opened the apartment door with a strange look on his face, as if he had something on his mind. I greeted him and he showed me in without responding. At that moment, his phone began to ring in his pocket. The ring tone was familiar and by the way we looked at each other, I knew he'd taken my device and he knew that I knew. He shrugged his shoulders and handed me the device.

"Daniel," I said into the phone.

"You need to keep track of your device! We couldn't warn you, because you didn't have the device and you were surrounded by CIA. Now it's too late!" said a panicked woman's voice on the other end.

"Warn me about what?" I asked.

"In two minutes, a SWAT team will be storming into the apartment to kill you!" the woman replied, her voice shaking uncontrollably.

The woman's statement was so shocking that my brain couldn't make sense of it. I just stared straight ahead.

"Throw the phone far away from you. The self-destruction mechanism is about to go off, but in the end, it will make no difference for you," the woman stated flat out and hung up. The phone began to heat in my hand and I tossed it into the corner of the room. It didn't smoke, but there were sparks erupting from it. Suddenly, I woke up to what the woman had said.

"In roughly a minute and a half, a SWAT team will supposedly be storming into this apartment," I reported in a chillingly calm voice.

"That's what it was – a stalling tactic!" Brock exclaimed with sudden clarity about the purpose of the earlier phone call he'd received. He grabbed his gun and looked around frantically for protection.

"That's completely unnecessary," I continued calmly, which made him stop and listen.

"What if we prayed and then simply walked back out the door?" I asked.

"You're crazy!" Brock shouted.

There was a moment of silence, when a sense of calm came over Brock's face.

"It was as if those were my father's words. He was a great warrior. Let me teach you the way my ancestors prayed," Brock said as if he'd been reborn.

"One minute and 15," I stated.

"Visualize yourself walking out the door, stepping out into the street and disappearing off into the city. Be grateful for that and believe that it has already happened," Brock advised while taking me by the hand and falling into prayer. I was suddenly assured that we would make it out of there alive.

"15 seconds," I stated and led the way toward the door.

* * *

Grace shifted about restlessly in his chair. It wasn't usually like him to be restless, but this time he sensed the pressure of gathering misfortune in his frontal lobe. A half hour after the previous phone call, he was hit with a second surprise.

"Be prepared for the camera system to be down. There's some malfunction throughout the whole system," the contact explained, unable to mask his embarrassment.

"Next you're gonna tell me that this was the wrong building!" Grace stated sarcastically.

"Just be ready," the contact stated and quickly hung up.

Grace glanced at his watch and leaned back in his chair. Two soldiers fully outfitted in assault gear with helmets on their knees sat beside him and he cursed the fact that the group leader couldn't be in their position. The rush of the battle was addictive. Perhaps that was the reason they were all in this particular profession, even though, at this moment, the whole operation and, as a result, the whole profession was beginning to sour.

"Base 1, do you read me?" Grace asked the question that was intended only for the getaway driver.

"Loud and clear," the driver answered.

"Base 2, do you read me?" Grace continued like this to ensure the connection with each team member. Everything seemed to be in order.

* * *

I opened the apartment door and stepped out unhindered into the hallway. It was dead silent. The silence forced us to tiptoe as we began to descend the stairs. Brock passed me just before the door and opened it without a sound. I stepped out first and he closed the door behind us as soundlessly as he had opened it.

"Oh shit!" Brock hissed.

"What?" I asked, shaken.

"You're carrying a CIA bug," he said, stopping in his tracks.

"No, I left it in the apartment, of course," I replied with relief.

"I also planted an additional bug in your clothes," he continued nervously.

"What? When?"

"When you were exiting the apartment," he answered.

I couldn't believe what I was hearing.

"Why on earth did you do that?"

"So we wouldn't lose the file," he replied.

"In our moment of panic upstairs, you were thinking about the file?" I asked, but then it hit me that he was referring to my earlier exit from the apartment.

"Didn't you notice that I've changed my clothes?" I said, once again settling into a feeling of relief.

"You're a true warrior! Why haven't you ever thought of a career in intelligence, or have you succeeded in that deception as well?"

This surprising thought somehow felt completely logical. It was possible that I could be an actual spy.

"That's all I would need," I said as I took the file from my pocket and handed it to him. "The little amount I've been involved here was sufficient and now I just want out as quickly as possible," I said. After all I'd experienced, even the thought sent shivers up my spine.

The street was as quiet as it was when I arrived. We walked toward the Hippopotamus, all the while expecting someone to jump out in front of us. No one did.

"Do you have any idea what just happened?" Brock asked suddenly.

"Maybe it was a false alarm," I stated as the most likely explanation.

"Whoever has been helping you up to this point has been extremely competent. How could they be so totally wrong all of a sudden?"

"I admit, I think it's strange. The woman who called with the warning sounded genuinely alarmed."

"I also received an odd phone call from my boss ordering me, in practice, to stall you. I thought it was very weird, but if there was an assault planned on the apartment, that would certainly explain it."

"If you were supposed to stall me, perhaps our rushed exit saved our lives after all," I said, picking up the pace of my steps.

"Say what you will, but I believe that it was the prayer that saved us," Brock stated decisively.

"How about a cold beer?" I asked, although it made me smile, because it felt like a corny question after everything that had happened.

"I pegged you for a wine person."

"Why's that?"

"Do you remember the wine bottle you drank on Friday night?" he asked.

I was puzzled by his question.

"How could I forget?"

"It was one-of-a-kind. It was being held to give as a gift to my boss. The fact that you drank it rubbed a lot of people the wrong way, particularly because the bottle should have aged for many more years. I think you earned yourself a good many enemies with that one," he explained with a twinkle of humor in his eyes.

"Was it expensive?"

"Only 10,000 euro a bottle."

I thought he was joking at first, but his face remained serious.

"Well, it was good. I guess we can chalk it up to the Finnish boy's revenge for all this. Right now, however, beer is more suitable than wine," I said with a laugh.

"As long as you're buying."

* * *

Grace's contact phone rang again and this time, a bit too close to the H-hour. If there were any more changes, he was prepared to call off the whole operation.

"How'd it go?" the contact asked eagerly.

"What do you mean, how'd it go?"

"Are you in the car already?"

"What the fuck are you talking about?" Grace asked with growing impatience.

There was a moment of silence before the contact was overcome with panic.

"The Finn arrived 30 minutes ago. Didn't you see him?" he asked.

"You said we should move into position at 0015. It's only 0000," Grace responded, already beginning to fear the worst.

"You're an hour behind, idiots!" the contact screamed into the phone. "Oh, for fuck's sake! You guys didn't remember to turn your watches ahead to summer time on Sunday night!" he added.

"We shifted to summer time already two weeks ago!" Grace shouted in response.

"Not in Europe! You were isolated without any phones, so you don't know anything about the outside world. Let's use that as your excuse. Begin the assault now! Brock was told to stall the Finn, so they are likely still in the apartment."

21 A GHOST AT NOON

Alberto Moravia 1954

I awoke to the sharp sound a coffee cup makes when it bangs too hard against its saucer. For a moment, I didn't know where I was, but slowly my memory began to filter back in, piece by piece. We had walked for more than an hour, since Brock claimed to know of a place that was open all night, where I thought we were headed for a beer. I wasn't bothered by the length of the journey, because every step was carrying us further away from the CIA agents. He asked me questions along the way about different aspects of the previous days' events and my earlier life, until he finally stated that he was convinced of my innocence. Our destination turned out not to be a bar or nightclub, but a brothel. He asked me to watch the outside door while he stepped inside. When he came out, he was accompanied by a classy-looking French woman, who drove us in her little Peugeot to her home.

"Did you manage to sleep on that sofa, even though it's a tad small for you?" Brock called out from where he was seated beside a small table in the corner of the living room.

"I actually slept like I was comatose. I don't think I slept the previous night at all and yesterday took a lot out of me," I answered, pulling myself up into a sitting position.

"Good morning!" said the bathrobed French woman seated beside Brock.

"Go take a cold shower and then join us for breakfast," Brock suggested.

The bathroom appeared to have recently been remodeled. There was a toilet with a wooden lid to the left, in front of me a marble countertop with a small sunken sink and to the right, a shower with a sliding door. The shelf under the marble counter was piled neatly with white towels. On top of the counter, an open shelf system displayed an enormous perfume collection that made clear the gender of the apartment's owner.

Someone had recently taken a shower, since the air in the bathroom was still humid, and the mirrored cabinet above the sink was still fogged up. I wiped the side of my right hand along the mirror in order to see something and was startled at the strange face peering back at me. My eyes looked lifeless and my face seemed to have aged overnight. I felt frighteningly empty; void of any feeling. All my fears had evaporated and I didn't think I would ever feel fear again. It hadn't been replaced with courage, however, but anxiety. It was as if I'd fallen into an abyss and lost touch with everything. I had never felt so lonely. A confusing calmness shrouded my anxiety, but everything felt insignificant and vapid. It had all slipped out of my reach. I removed my underwear, stepped into the shower and turned on the cold water faucet.

"Looks like you've seen a ghost," Brock said when I arrived at the breakfast table. I said nothing in response, so he plowed on.

"I guess you've gotten a glimpse of the emptiness you're facing. I know how that feels."

I looked at him questioningly, as if asking for help.

"Emptiness isn't bad, it's an opportunity for growth and development. Emptiness always fills up, and now you get to choose what it fills with. I was never very good at that, but now I have a whole new life ahead. I'm actually looking forward to the empty feeling, even though it can be a bit oppressive," he explained like an experienced psychologist.

"It's hard to think about anything right now," I managed to say.

"In that case, how about coffee and a croissant?" the French woman offered.

Breakfast was unusually quiet. Finally, Brock couldn't take it anymore.

"I'm eternally grateful to you for saving my life."

"Isn't that a slight exaggeration?" I asked.

"I'm indebted to you for other reasons too. Because of you, I rediscovered the values my father taught me," he stated earnestly.

"What can I say to that?"

"Don't say anything. You're in a good spot; you don't have the file and you don't know its content. Furthermore, they are grateful to you for taking care of their Raymond dilemma. Just to be on the safe side, I've taken a few security precautions. Through my own channels, I've notified my boss that I'm pulling myself out of the game and hanging on to the file as life insurance. I also stated that the same goes for you and that I would be monitoring your goings-on. I plan to tell my contact in the Finnish Security Intelligence Service to turn their attention to the CIA if anything happens to you. I informed my boss of this as well, so I doubt they'd risk political suicide only to retaliate against you."

"Will we meet again at some point?" I asked, although it felt in vain to ask.

"If you're ever in need of even the most minor degree of assistance, I will always be there to help. When I get settled, I'll let you know how to contact me," he said, leaving me surprised at his response.

"Are you saying that I can really walk free from this whole experience?"

"I'm sure of it. They'll likely contact you, but you don't have to tell them anything. You probably didn't even note this address, and that's a good thing. It would be best if you left here without any knowledge of the exact location, even though there's really no danger in what you know. I'll be disappearing from here immediately after you," he explained.

"I think I'll roam around the streets for a bit and then take a cab," I stated as I made ready to leave.

It had rained during the night and so I found myself stepping around the large puddles to avoid getting my dress shoes wet. The damp, cool air forced its way beneath my jacket and pasted my shirt to my skin. I pulled the collar up and drew my shoulders forward in an effort to shut the jacket tighter to the cold, but by that point, it would have taken a winter coat to warm my already chilled body. In the end, I stopped caring and forced my stiff muscles to relax. I didn't feel good, but at least

I was no longer freezing. The emptiness I'd experienced in the bathroom was still with me and I felt like I didn't belong in Paris at all. The street smelled of roasted chestnuts, and it was a taste of which I had never had the pleasure.

I didn't know where to go. My apartment was safe again, but the loneliness that awaited there weighed heavily on me. I desperately needed company, but Brock's words about the opportunity to fill the void made me insecure. If I sought out comfort, it might steal away the opportunity before me. I knew I needed a permanent foundation, but I also realized that it may have been missing already before the events of the previous days. I had tried for many months to write a book about the nature of truth, but all I had to show for it were pages of random thoughts. Life in Paris had awakened all my senses, but my innermost being had been burning on a low flame. I had exhausted all my fuel at once over the past few days and my flame had now gone out.

Far ahead of me, I saw a cab pull over to the side of the street to let a group of Japanese-looking businessmen step out. I instinctively picked up my pace and when the cab seemed to be waiting, I broke into a run toward it. The cab driver appeared to have noticed me, because he was already turned around when I opened the back door. Before I even stopped to think, I heard myself giving him the address for Shakespeare and Company.

The cashier was a young man whom I had met many times. "Is either Sarah or Lisa here?" I asked with some concern.

"They're both off today. Sarah asked you to call, though, if you happened to show up," he said, recognizing me immediately.

"Unfortunately, I don't have a phone. Is there any way I

could call from here?" I felt a bit embarrassed to ask, but I had no choice.

"You can borrow my cell phone. Sarah's number is in there already," he offered kindly and found Sarah's number for me.

"That's very nice of you. Do you mind if I step outside to make the call?"

"No problem. Sarah was pretty determined to make sure I would ask you to call." He smiled.

I stepped outside the store, but didn't dare to press the call button right away. I took a moment to consider what I was doing. Sarah awakened feelings in me that I hadn't wanted and I knew she felt the same way. I had to call to let her know I was okay. Was this fear I was feeling?

"Sarah," A soft voice said on the end of the line.

"This public agent is notifying that the mission is complete," I said with exaggerated formality.

"Daniel, you're okay!" she shouted into the phone.

"Everything is fine and over," I stated happily.

"Do you want to tell me what happened?" she asked tentatively.

"Not really. I just want to forget it all and I'm feeling pretty drained at the moment," I said. I hoped that she wouldn't press me on the matter any further.

"I completely understand. I'd also like to forget the whole episode. I am sticking by the decision I made yesterday and have decided to follow my true dream."

"What's that?"

"I've decided to study journalism alongside literature."

"That's fantastic! I'm proud of you," I replied with sincerity.

"Yeah, but there's only one downside; I have to leave for the States already tomorrow to get things organized. I won't be coming back to Paris." She sounded sad as she uttered the last sentence.

"I don't know what to say."

She surprised me by asking if I wanted to meet up before she left. I remained silent for a moment and allowed each alternative future to play out like a film in my mind.

"I think that might be too painful," I finally said, allowing reason to take over.

"I don't know if I should say this, but I was hoping you'd say that," she responded and I could hear her choking back the tears.

"Then it's settled."

"Thank you, Daniel, for everything – you saved me."

Tears began to well in my eyes and I was losing grip on my self-control, the one thing I had done everything to safeguard.

"One of us will have to hang up," I said quietly trying to mask my emotions. I heard her breathing and then it was suddenly silent. She had hung up the phone.

I wiped my eyes, but apparently, I wasn't able to hide the fact that I'd been crying, since the salesman looked at me with empathy when I returned his phone.

"T.S. Eliot wrote that April is the cruelest month," he said as a means of comfort. I sensed, however, that he wanted to tell me something else as well.

"Oh yeah! Lisa asked me to let you know that she's washing the clothes you left here and you can pick them up from here in a couple days," he stated as I was already turning toward the door to leave.

"Thanks," I replied, relieved as my thoughts shifted to Lisa. I opened the bookstore door and felt the cool air on my face. At precisely that instant, I began to feel the void beginning to fill. I thought of an aphorism that I had written when I was young and in love:

"I want to live and experience freedom, but freedom is found in loneliness and I don't want to be alone. If you can't grant me freedom, take away my longing for freedom as well."

I didn't know what was going to happen, but I knew it would all work out. The clouds seemed to be hanging low and the darkness was gathering, even though it was only the afternoon. The rain had taken me by surprise in the same place five days earlier, and I didn't want a repeat performance. I began to run and crossed, once again, through Place Viviani. My mind leapt around like a wild stallion; my mind, which had suddenly become so light.

I had just stepped into the café when I heard the roar of a million raindrops colliding simultaneously with the pavement. I felt no need to sigh with relief, since my brain was already overwhelmed with a feeling of elation, not from having escaped the rain, but from pure joy. My regular spot with its armchair and its view of Square René Viviani was fortunately unoccupied and I sat down and looked around for the waiter. When he came over, I ordered my coffee and Armagnac. I was suddenly struck with an inspiration: I should write a novel about the past five days. No one would believe that any of it had actually happened, but it would give me a chance to grieve and open a new chapter in my life.

"A woman left you a letter," the waiter said as he laid a white envelope on the table next to my coffee.

I looked at him questioningly, but didn't ask anything.

"She was here with you a few days ago…an unbelievably beautiful woman," he explained when he noticed how confused I must look.

"Is she still here? Did I just miss her?" I asked hurriedly.

"No, no! She was here late yesterday evening," he replied apologetically. As he walked away, he simply added, "Happy reading."

My hands shook as I handled the letter. The name 'Daniel' was written on the front in graceful handwriting. I took a sip of my Armagnac and stared at the curls and lines that formed my name. I figured that I no longer had anything to lose, so I opened the letter with the stem of my coffee spoon.

"Mon chéri,

You said that one must suffer in order to be able to write and you complained about your own happiness. Now, I stand amidst the shattered remains of my dreams and in my pain, the only thing I can do is turn to writing. This is my message for you:

The traces you leave are like your life, which you can only see by looking back. The future is a mystery waiting to be discovered, but behind you, all there seems to be are arbitrary events and thoughts bouncing around from one page of your journal to the next. It's just the remains of dried ink, deep imprints and traces on scrap paper.

Your footsteps are traces of yourself that you leave behind. You know you can't take them with you, and yet, you find yourself turning around to make sure they are still following you. You wander about – from trace to trace. No matter where you step, your footfall finds your traces. The traces grab on to the soles of your boots, leaving only the outline of your footsteps. You may pause and try to lift your boot carefully away without disturbing the impression you've created. No matter what you do, people will see the traces you've left behind.

You exist in your traces and I have become part of those traces. You leave traces behind and I follow them. One thousand persistent scent hounds search for traces of you along the trampled path, seek your scent on the trail, but, for them, the traces don't continue on further than the first. Your path deviates from the trail and your time has been led astray. Your direction relies on a compass and your shadow gets lost in the darkness. I know for sure that you exist in your traces and that's why I'm following them.

You may have heard something about me from the traces I left behind, but look ahead, before you know it, I'll be standing before you once again.

Marie"

As I put the letter down, I felt myself filling with conflicting feelings of love and guilt. We had imagined that we could forget about one another, we swore to try. This letter violated that agreement and I would be forever grateful for it.

* * *

I folded the letter carefully and slid it into my breast pocket. I signaled to the waiter for my check, but at that moment, a youngish woman sat down next to me without asking permission.

"Allow me to buy the next round," she said in English.

I stared at her, amazed.

"Actually, I was just on my way out."

"Believe me, you'll want to hear what I have to say," she

said, staring directly into my eyes.

I wanted to refuse, but I just shrugged my shoulders instead. The waiter appeared by our side.

"Beer?" the woman asked as if she had read my mind. I simply nodded as I surrendered to the situation.

"One large glass of beer and Campari with juice, please," the woman ordered in fluent French.

When the waiter had walked away, she turned to face me and smiled warmly.

"You appeared to be very much in love while you were reading that letter," she stated.

"How could you see that?" I participated in the discussion without a great deal of interest or enthusiasm.

"Do you believe that'll last?" she asked suddenly.

"You came over here to talk about my letter?" I asked. I felt myself starting to get angry.

"Forgive me, I didn't mean anything by it."

We both fell silent for a moment and I stared past the woman at the hustle and bustle outside the window.

"You were interested in this book," she claimed as she removed Heidegger's 'Basic Writings' from her handbag.

My heart froze.

"Who are you and what do you want from me?" I was completely confused.

"You're interested in the truth? I had to read that section of the book many times before I begin, intuitively, to understand what Heidegger was saying. Do you want to hear my conclusion?"

"Is that why you asked me to stay?"

"It serves nicely as an introduction and it interests me professionally."

I had no idea what was going on, but I had an ominous

feeling. The woman continued to smile as if she were proud of her own achievement. She made me wait as she took her sweet time. Finally, she began to explain.

"Traditionally, when we think of the truth, we think about what's real or pure and true. But when we claim something to be the truth, we force the truth into the mould that we have created for it. We can study the truth as science does, but then we shut out the possibility of discovering that there is something behind the truth of which we are unaware. Heidegger talks about mystery, not about any particular mystery, but about the 'concealing of what is concealed'. An essential aspect of the truth is allowing things to be as they are and viewing them with an open mind. The core of truth is freedom! Heidegger, himself, admitted that it may sound like a strange claim, but in his definition, freedom did not refer to human whims and impulses. The truth is only retained if we accept the mystery; we admit we don't know the truth and not as a sign of apathy. We understand we can grasp something, but that we'll never know the whole truth."

She looked at me and waited for my reaction, but I simply stared back at her, trying to figure out what was really going on here.

"So, what did you think of my analysis?" She was like a little child waiting for her parents' approval.

"I'm not really in a philosophical mood at the moment," I answered, wondering whether she might be a bit off her rocker.

I was, however, very concerned that she had picked this particular book as the topic of our discussion.

"The truth isn't always pleasant, is it?" she asked.

Her eyes suddenly took on a frighteningly cold appearance and her face lost its friendly glow as well.

"We may need your help in the future and we would appreciate your cooperation. We were impressed by your competence and we're ready to pay for your service accordingly" she stated without warning.

"Who's we?" I asked, although I already knew the answer.

"The CIA and entire intelligence community," she replied, lowering her voice.

"Forget it."

"We wouldn't require you to do anything that would jeopardize Finland or its position," she argued.

"There is no way I'm getting involved in the intelligence business," I stated angrily.

"You brought this on yourself," the woman retorted and dug in her handbag to find a thick envelope, which she pushed into my hand.

"What is this?" I was afraid that it contained money.

"It contains professional photographs of you and three different women. We also have quality films from the same situations. It certainly would be unfortunate if they ended up in the wrong hands," she said arrogantly.

I handed the envelope back without even glancing at its contents.

"If I were you, I'd make a decision quickly after considering all the possible consequences."

"I had already decided to tell my wife about everything, no matter what the outcome."

"The material could always end up on the Internet or who knows where," she said, her voice retaining its new monotone quality.

"I've also decided to write a book about my experiences. Any material you share would surely boost my book sales and it would enable me to tell the story as the truth, with all its tales of extortion."

I could feel the woman losing her grip and she tried to keep it together by relying on aggression. She was about to snap back at me, when she suddenly became calm and her eyes revealed that she'd had a flash of inspiration. She smiled to herself and then became serious once again before beginning her narrative. I had no idea what a crushing blow it would prove to be.

"Just think how all your adventures would sound to your children in light of what's happened. Before you say anything, let me fill you in on what's been going on while you've been out having your adventures."

An overwhelming fear gripped me and began to grow until I felt trapped in a huge, black bubble. Deep inside, I could feel myself being crushed by desperation.

"Your family tried to get in contact with you for many days. You should have been home, because your wife was diagnosed with an unusually aggressive case of leukemia three days ago and on the third day she died; that was early this morning."

EPILOGUE

Shakespeare and Company was packed with invited guests. My book had been published in Finland and had been picked up almost immediately for translation into English. When I went to present my translation to Shakespeare and Company, they had suggested that I hold the publishing event for the English translation in their own premises. Undoubtedly, they deserved it. I was nervous, even though I felt Sanna's presence supporting me. That's at least what I wanted to believe, even though I didn't deserve it.

The interviewer was the young and attractive Sylvia Whitman, daughter of the famous George Whitman, the American man who reopened Shakespeare and Company after the war in 1951. As per my wishes, Sylvia focused on the themes in the book and their background without directly asking what role I played in the events of the book. The floor was opened to audience questions, which covered a wide range of issues until finally, someone dared to ask how much truth there was behind the story.

"Does Amy still work here?" a young French reporter asked.

I took a deep breath.

"The book is a work of fiction. There was never anyone named Amy working here, nor anyone who even resembled that character," I responded calmly.

"All of our regular customers have known our employees for years and know that there has never been a French-English Amy or American Joyce working here, nor anyone who served as the basis for these characters," Sylvia Whitman chimed in.

A French journalist wrote something in her notepad and raised her hand again to ask another question.

"Yes?"

"I quote from your book, where you said that all books leave a trace. Were you aware that a French physicist, by the name of Marie Allègre has just published her collection of short stories in French? Its name is 'Discontinuity'," the journalist asked in true investigative reporter style.

"No, I was not aware of that," I said with genuine surprise.

"The titles of the short stories are, for example, In the Arms of a Tiger, Time Travel for the Mind, Clothed in Passion and Obelisk."

ABOUT THE AUTHOR

Alexander Jalo, M.Sc. (Tech.), retired from a successful business career in 2008 at the age of 47 and decided to pursue his dream to be a writer. He currently lives in Finland.

Traces is the first part of a trilogy that was originally written in Finnish. The remaining two books, Moves and the Light, will also soon be published in English.